WELLINGTON WISDOM

WELLINGTON WISDOM

Nellie E. Robertson

iUniverse, Inc.
New York Lincoln Shanghai

Wellington Wisdom

iUniverse, Inc.

For information address:
iUniverse, Inc.
2021 Pine Lake Road, Suite 100
Lincoln, NE 68512
www.iuniverse.com

ISBN: 0-595-31083-4 (pbk)
ISBN: 0-595-66257-9 (cloth)

Printed in the United States of America

This fictional account of the Wellington Disaster in Washington's Stevens Pass in 1910 is dedicated to the people who lost their lives in the avalanche and to those who recorded those terrible events.

Nellie E. Robertson

CHAPTER 1

With one last look at the stately mansion in which she had been so happy, Laurie hurried down the stairs from the room she had shared with her husband, her jaw clenched with determination. The cook came out of the kitchen through the swinging door wiping her hands on a towel but Laurie didn't see her or respond to her greeting.

The young woman stopped by the bank and withdrew money from the account she shared with her father. Still furious, she bought a ticket for St. Paul at the Everett Great Northern depot. She might as well go back to Minnesota, she thought, that's where she came from.

Miserably she sat in the station waiting for the train to leave, oblivious of the people around her. Her perfect life now lay in shards around her. She thought of each event leading to her decision to leave.

She wished they'd never come to this town. Why did they move here? The answer lay in the fact that her father couldn't find a job in Minnesota during the panic of 1893, the deepest depression the country had ever suffered. Hearing about the Everett lumber mills in Washington State, he left his young family in search of work. He had the same dream as most workers; to have a steady job and own his home.

A letter to his family at the turn of the century told them of the Clough-Hartley Mill, the largest red cedar shingle mill in the world. "They hired me and I'm learning to be a shingle sawyer," he wrote. The job gave him a step up from ordinary laborers. The shingle weavers, who fashioned cut shingles into bundles, rated high on the employment ladder, too.

"The weather is wet a lot of the year with little snow," Karl Krafft wrote. "It's not like we're used to in Minnesota. You'll like it though, we won't be snow-bound."

He saved enough money for a down payment on a house in the town's Riverside district and sent for his family. His wife, Lydia, sold what little they had left and took her son and daughter on the long train trek to Everett.

The frontier town had scared young Laurie at first. The flagrant brutality made her cower; fist fights exploding out of saloon doors, irate drovers whipping horses, and labor disputes erupting with angry shouts and brawls on street corners. The young girl found it all difficult to understand.

The conductor's announcement of the train's departure brought Laurie back to the painful present in this new year of 1910. She picked up her purse with the one-way ticket. Her bag had been checked through.

She found an empty coach seat and pulled her heavy coat tighter around her. She closed her eyes, unwilling to see Everett as the train wound around the waterfront toward the Cascade Mountains. I never want to see this town again, she vowed. Her only comfort came from thinking about her mother.

What a wonderful person Lydia was. Whenever anyone needed help, she gave it. She had such a calming effect on people who suffered physical or emotional pain. One winter old Mr. Jenson next door lay dangerously ill with bronchial pneumonia. His daughter-in-law was at her wits end with children and her husband to care for besides the ailing old man. Lydia took over the nursing chores and created a calm haven until Mr. Jenson recovered. She never denied help to those who asked.

What a disappointment I must have been to her with all my judgments about other people, Laurie thought. Why couldn't I have been more like her? Father was right to call her Lady Lydia. The restlessness she felt then must have been because the world just didn't measure up to what she thought it ought to be. She wanted so much more out of life than to be just a housewife with its drudgery and dullness. And how she hated her father's drinking.

She remembered a typical Saturday afternoon and her own pronouncement.

"Father won't be home for dinner, Mother." At fifteen, Laurie felt she knew it all. With a flash of anger in her deep blue eyes she added, "It's payday and he's probably drunk up half of it already." She crossed her ankles beneath her kitchen chair and jiggled one foot impatiently as she retied the ribbon in her long, honey-blonde hair.

"I'll put his dinner in the oven to keep it warm, Laurie. You can clear the table." Lydia pursed her lips and added, "You judge him too harshly."

Laurie continually spouted ultimatums. "I won't marry a man who drinks or fights, or one who dictates to me. It's 1905. Women these days who allow men to run their lives aren't equals." She sniffed and vehemently added, "I'll be the equal of any man in my life. You have to stand up for yourself, Mother, even in Everett. Tell Father to quit drinking or get out. He's disgusting when he's drunk. How can you put up with him?"

Lydia frowned, "It could be worse. He does the best he can. You should appreciate him instead of censuring him. There are events from the past you don't know about." She straightened her neck. "You don't know what you'd do in someone else's place unless you've trod down his path a while. And I don't see what living in Everett has to do with it. It's nearly as civilized here in Washington as it was in Minnesota."

"What don't I know about the past?" Laurie asked. Curiosity smothered her anger.

"When we have lots of time and we're alone, I'll tell you, Laurie, I promise. Now's just not the right time," her mother answered in her cultured English accent.

Endearing tendrils of blond hair escaped from the bun at the back of her mother's head.

Now, as the train began to gather speed, she thought of the mother she had adored. Laurie's anger turned into an almost unbearable pain. How could she bear this? She had everything and now she had nothing.

The blowing snow matched the chill of her heart. A memory flowed through her mind about another restless weekend.

Laurie had gone to her room to read one Saturday night. Her mother had spread her needlework out on the table. She sewed for some of the millowners' wives to help supplement the family's income and to put a few coins in the sugar bowl each week for Laurie's education. She didn't intend for her daughter to be without skills to support herself.

Writing in her journal and reading were Laurie's passions. She fell asleep halfway through a chapter in her favorite book and roused when she heard her father's step on the porch. The clock next to her pillow registered two o'clock, late indeed, even for her drunken father.

She lay in her narrow bed with the quilt pulled up tightly over her ears but she could still hear her parents through the thin floor.

"Karl, you promised to come straight home from work after you picked up your pay," said her mother in a surprisingly angry voice.

"I meant to, Lyd, but I won a bet and had to buy the boys a round," her father slurred. The springs groaned as he lowered his big frame onto the bed.

"We need that money, Karl," said Lydia. "We have children and a home to care for."

Laurie could visualize her mother, flannel nightgown buttoned to the throat with her long, flowing hair released from the bondage of the bun she wore. So often the girl had been an unwilling listener to the same words. She tried to shut out what went on in her parents' bedroom with scant success.

Her mother's incriminations dwindled into soft murmurings and finally died away. The household settled down into the wet night. Laurie felt her anger drain away and snuggled into the rough muslin sheets. The downpour thrummed on the roof just above her head and finally lulled her to sleep again. She loved the rain. It washed away the filth in the world.

Laurie awoke to the sound of clanking iron as her mother started a fire in the wood cook stove. Stretching her arms above her head, she gathered the new day to her. She ran her hands over her ripening body, a little embarrassed by her curves.

She cherished her private domain, each part familiar and important to her. The mirror, propped up on the dark brown chest of drawers, reflected the morning sun shining through the room's only window above the head of her bed. A runner she had embroidered partially covered the nicks and scratches on the chest. Toilet articles awaited her hand, just where she had placed them.

The ceiling tapered down to the shelves where she had placed her books with loving care. Some she had bought with hoarded funds. Others had been given to her.

A glass of water and a lamp stood beside the clock on the dark brown night stand. Laurie's robe rested in graceful disarray on the straight wooden chair next to her bed. Small lavender flowers sprigged the white wallpaper and brightened the garret room, even on the dreariest day.

The sound of the milk wagon horses, clopping along the street, roused her from bed. It's Sunday and time for church, she thought. She listened for sounds from Will's room which shared the other half of the house's second floor. Her irrepressible younger brother had a special place in her heart which no one else suspected.

She shrugged into her camisole and settled the dark dress over her plain, white petticoat. As she reached down to button her high-topped shoes, she thought of last night and the words came unbidden into her head again with heart-wrenching pity for her mother.

A glance into the mottled mirror showed her how much she looked like her mother. Her fair hair crackled with electricity as she brushed it. Her face, long and narrow, matched her slender and delicate hands. Not really a beauty, her patrician features and reserved manner gave her an elegance unusual in one so young. She fixed a bow in the back of her hair and smoothed her long skirt.

She skipped down the narrow stairs and emerged from the hallway. Her mother leaned over the stove that dominated the outer wall of the kitchen. "Um, the bacon and eggs smell good this morning," Laurie said. "I'm starved. I can hardly swallow the oatmeal we usually have." She hid the pity she felt for her mother.

Lydia, always slim and straight, pushed a stray lock of hair toward her bun with the back of her hand. Even with a gingham apron tied around her Sunday dress she looked regal.

How dignified she is, thought Laurie. Even after her husband had swallowed most of his pay at the saloons, Lydia treated him with respect and patience although her anger flared occasionally.

In a kitchen corner, her father's work clothes huddled in a heap where he had shucked them off the night before. Aromatic cedar sawdust clung to the overalls and filled the kitchen with its scent.

Laurie crossed to the sink and drain boards that lined the corner next to the back door. After drinking a glass of water, she moved to the cabinets filling two walls of the room. She lifted out the dishes and pulled the silverware from the drawer. She set the big, gate-legged square table which split the area between the cook stove and the entry into the living room. She had already pulled out the side legs to support the table leaves on each side.

Young Will stumbled down the stairs knuckling the sleep from his eyes, his knickers still unbuckled. A big, sturdy lad of twelve, he had a thatch of black hair like his father. Although dressed in his church clothes, he displayed his reluctance to go. "Why can't I stay home with Father?" he asked.

His mother answered absently, "Wash yourself and comb your hair."

He scuffed slowly down the hall toward the bathroom still grumbling about church. An indoor bathroom had been a novelty at first but now it seemed there had always been one although the family called it a water closet because that's what it was to English-born Lydia.

As the children ate breakfast and Lydia sipped her second cup of tea, Karl opened the bedroom door.

"Come have some breakfast," Lydia called quietly.

"O.K., Lady Lydia," he answered sheepishly. He lurched out of the hallway and gently lowered himself into the chair at the end of the table as if his head were a brittle eggshell. Black stubble covered his cheeks and chin. His dark hair curled down on his forehead and his mustache cut a black swath across his lip. His huge left hand curled around the hot thick coffee mug. Laurie got up from the table nauseated by the whiff of beer that oozed from his pores.

With breakfast eaten and the meal debris cleared from the table, Lydia and her two children walked down the street to church. Laurie relished the fresh spring day taking deep breaths of the newly-washed air. The sun shone brightly and danced across the river. "Tide must be in," said Laurie. "The mud flats are covered."

Will shouted to his friends and dashed to meet them. All the neighbor kids liked the gregarious boy.

Laurie and her mother nodded to friends and neighbors as they entered the cool sanctuary. Both were reserved and had few close friends; neither had exuberant personalities.

Laurie and Will followed their mother's willowy figure down the church aisle. Lydia acknowledged the ladies who formed part of Everett society as she stepped lightly into the usual pew. She sewed for many of them and Laurie recognized dresses made from fabric that had cluttered her mother's dining room table.

The Kraffts joined in the opening hymn with Lydia's fine contralto blending with Laurie's pure soprano. After a nudge from his mother, Will joined in, his voice hearty but off key.

The Rev. John Fowles's sermon came from the Ten Commandments and he exhorted his flock to "honor thy father and thy mother." The glasses perched on his nose gave him a scholarly look although one might wonder why he wore them since he peered over their wire rims most of the time.

Laurie scarcely heard his words as she reflected about how hard it was to honor her father. He treated her well, she supposed, except when he stuck his head in a beer stein. Then his shouting frightened her and she kept out of his way. He had cuffed her around the ears a few times in bleary-eyed drunkenness then apologized afterwards. She recalled the last time. He had told her to help him off with his boots and when she refused, his anger pushed him off the kitchen chair and he slapped her. She scampered up the stairs to her room with tears of rage coursing down her cheeks. When she came down again, emotions throttled, her father said, "I'm sorry, honey, I don't know what came over me. I wouldn't hurt you for the world."

Laurie's inner ear heard the strains of the final hymn that Sunday as the train chugged its way up into the Cascade Mountains. The spectacular accumulation of snow and glimpses of huge evergreen trees meant nothing to her. Neither did the consternation of the passengers as they eyed the winter storm. Instead she recalled the home she had shared with her parents and her brother.

The two-story narrow house overlooked the Snohomish River in Everett's Riverside area. One mill hugged the bank in Riverside but Laurie's father worked at Bayside where most of the mills belched smoke into the sky.

The spotless house reflected Lydia's values; cleanliness and industriousness. Laurie learned early how to clean, wash, cook and sew. Because of their mother's English background, the children called their parents nothing except "Father" and "Mother" and the meals were lunch and dinner.

It seemed her father was the direct opposite of her mother; big, clumsy, and weak.

I should have been more compassionate, Laurie thought. Father worked six days a week, eleven hours a day. The job sapped his energy and he had little left to share with us. If she'd only known the whole story then, she would have been a better daughter.

As the day wore on, a small bird of an elderly woman saw the painful look on Laurie's face and an occasional tear that coursed down the pale face. She sat down next to the young woman and gently put her hand on the girl's arm.

Dully, Laurie opened her eyes and lifted her head.

"My dear," the lady said. "I'm Mrs. Kirby and I'm traveling alone. I thought we might chat to pass the time."

The last thing Laurie wanted to do was talk to a stranger but her upbringing made her straighten a little in her seat and respond politely, "I'm Laurie Davis," she said.

"I'm glad to meet you, my dear. I'm on my way to visit my son in St. Paul. He's stationed there with the railroad," Mrs. Kirby said in a quiet warm voice. "He's getting married in two weeks and wants me there for the wedding."

Laurie wished she could warn the bride-to-be about men and the hazards of marriage. "I'm going to St. Paul, too," she said. "I'm going to work there."

CHAPTER 2

❀

Mrs. Kirby gently probed for the cause of Laurie's anguish. "I can see you're terribly upset about something, my dear. You'd feel much better if you talked about it and I'm a willing listener."

How could she tell anyone about what happened, Laurie asked herself at first. She had always been reluctant to share her feelings. A glance at Mrs. Kirby reminded her of her mother, so gracious and caring. Laurie wouldn't have had much trouble sharing with her mother, maybe she could talk to Mrs. Kirby.

Hesitantly she began the story of her life telling about the community in which the Kraffts had lived.

"Our dear old neighbor, Mr. Jenson, told me that there were thirty people in Everett in 1891 and five thousand in 1893. We lived in Riverside at the eastern edge of town. Hewitt Avenue is the main link between Riverside and Port Gardner Bay."

"I saw part of the town from the train," Mrs. Kirby said.

"Did you see all the brick buildings?"

"No, I didn't. Are there very many?"

"Quite a few for such a young town," Laurie answered, pulled from her misery by talking. "There are a number of saloons, too, on the north side of Hewitt. They were forbidden on the south side. And of course there are women plying the oldest profession in town, too. My mother used to care for some of the girls."

Laurie remembered the night a loud pounding on the door stirred her from her deep slumber. She rubbed her eyes and crawled up to the head of her white iron bedstead to peer over the windowsill to find who caused the disturbance.

She couldn't see anyone. She heard her mother's slippers shuffle across the floor as she hurried to answer the door.

Laurie squirmed out of bed, pulled her robe around her, and settled her feet into her slippers. Her insatiable curiosity drew her down the stairs.

She inched her way along the hallway to the living room door so she could see and hear the nocturnal caller. She saw a girl a few years older than she clad in a soiled satin dress with a feather boa slung around her neck. The girl's frightened eyes stared out of a white round mask like pieces of coal in the snow.

"Please, ma'am," the girl pleaded, "Rosie's hurt real bad and she won't let us get a doctor." She wiped the back of her hand across her runny nose and smeared her lipstick. It cut a red scar across her ashen face. "Doctor wouldn't come anyway, even if we was to go to him."

Lydia put her arm across the girl's rounded shoulders and asked what had happened. Laurie strained her ears to hear the reply.

"One of Rosie's customers got real drunk and beat her up. He's a regular and he don't often drink that much," she sniffed. "Rosie's arm is broken and the bone's stickin' out. She's crying awful hard."

"Wait for me, I'll get a few things," Lydia said. Starting for the bag she kept handy, she caught a glimpse of Laurie. "I'll be gone for awhile so be sure to get your father off to work and Will ready for school. I'll get back as soon as I can."

As Lydia and the young harlot hurried toward the Hewitt Avenue cribs, Laurie trudged back upstairs to her bed. Sleep eluded her as her mind dwelt on the prostitutes' tawdry lives. Some of the books she squirreled away told of their sordid existence. She also remembered the tales her classmates had snickered about. She felt a fleeting pang of compassion for the girls. She thought none of them willingly chose their trade.

She got up on her knees in bed and leaned her elbows on the windowsill. With her head in her hands, she wondered what terrible fate had led these girls to sell their bodies. She shuddered when she considered someone touching her like that. However, she remembered the previous summer with a wistful smile. After a wild game of tag, she and a boy from her class had sat on the back steps talking. He slipped his arm around her shoulders and she melted inside. An exquisite warmth filled her again as she dreamed about it. She had recorded every vibrant feeling in her journal. She'd never forget John Stevens, she had thought at the time. Little did she know what the future would bring.

She recalled the lonely train whistle that shrilled through the night adding to her unfocused longing. Trapped by gender, an alcoholic father, and the times, she yearned to break out, be a person in her own right. She wanted her own identity.

As she speculated about the girl who had fetched her mother, she wove a story around her. She came from a proud but starving family in the south. Violated by the young son on the neighboring plantation, her family and friends cast her out. She embarked upon the only career she could pursue. As Laurie's fairy tale took shape, she watched the ring of dawn push back the night and waited for the mill whistles to blow, a signal to get up, start the fire, cook the oatmeal, and pack the lunches.

Her mother had told her about that night at the cribs. The young prostitute had ushered Lydia into the one-room wooden cubicle where the injured Rosie lay moaning, her eyes rimmed with red and salty tear tracks down her cheeks. A jagged bone pierced her arm's flesh. The wounds on her bruised face and scraped skin were superficial. Several of the other working girls crowded into the small room with concern. The air, heavy with cheap perfume and the odor of unwashed bodies, made it hard for Lydia to catch her breath.

The solemn looks the girls gave each other revealed they knew it could easily have been one of them.

"One of you get me some hot water and two narrow boards," Lydia said, and pointing to the girl who had summoned her, she added, "You stay here and help me. The rest of you go back to your rooms. You can't help and will just get in the way." Then she said in a gentler tone, "Rosie will be just fine."

With sympathetic looks and murmuring, the girls filed out of the door. Their rooms duplicated this one; cheap silk dresses trimmed with fake feathers or moth-eaten fur hung on a wire, a scratched commode holding a pitcher and bowl, faded pictures torn from magazines pinned to the walls, and sometimes a photo of a special person.

Lydia poured some water from the pitcher into a glass and added a few drops of laudanum. She carefully supported the young girl's head and said, "Drink this, Rosie, it'll make the pain go away." As she waited for the opiate to take effect, she poured another glass of water for herself.

One of the girls tapped on the door and brought what Lydia had asked for. When she saw that Rosie drifted into a drugged stupor, she showed Rosie's friend how to hold the upper arm in a tight grip. "Now, I'm going to jerk the rest of her arm so the bone goes back together in the right way. If we don't do it, she'll have a crooked arm the rest of her life," she said. "She might cry out at first but she'll go back to sleep."

With the girl anchoring Rosie's shoulder, Lydia grasped the wrist and jerked the arm rapidly, letting the bones mesh. Rosie screamed then drifted into a sedated slumber. Lydia washed the wound made by the jutting bone and covered it with disinfectant salve. She quickly placed the boards on two sides of the arm and wrapped them tightly with bandages. She couldn't help but notice the holes in the crook of Rosie's arm made by drug needles. She knew some of the girls, more conscious of their looks, shot the drug between their toes or into the veins under their tongues so the tell-tale needle holes wouldn't show.

Compassionately, Lydia murmured aloud, "Maybe that's the only way these girls can abide their lives. And drugs are so easy to get in this seaport town. They're as close as the drug store. I wish with all my heart they'd pass a law against the sale of such drugs."

"Did you say somethin', ma'am?" asked Rosie's friend.

"No, dear, just talking to myself."

After applying some salve on the facial bruises and abrasions, she settled back into a bedside chair to watch her young patient. Her eyes roamed around the room. The dim lamplight did little to hide the squalor. Rosie had attempted to brighten her hovel by nailing pictures on the wall and stringing a wisp of muslin across the one window, but a crib it remained. Round holes made by loggers' "cork" boots punctured the wooden floor.

"These poor girls," she reflected beneath her breath. "I wonder what brought them to this end, and end it will be. Once they embark on the path to prostitution, the path becomes a rut and the rut becomes a grave."

As she clenched her hands, she muttered, "I'll see that my daughter won't be reduced to this. It would break her spirit completely. Yet spirit is what will see her through the bad times."

Lydia dozed a bit and roused when Rosie turned over onto her side. The girl rested easily and breathed normally, so Lydia repacked her bag and spoke to Rosie's friend who had wakened from her cat nap. "I'll leave a little laudanum and show you how to give it to her. She should be fine except for some aching from the broken bone. If you need me, send one of the girls for me. I'll drop by in a couple of days to see how she's doing."

Wearily she walked out the door and saw that the sun had dispelled the gloom of the night. She wrinkled her nose in distaste at the stench from the open sewers as she plodded home.

"Your mother sounds like a wonderful woman, my dear," Mrs. Kirby said sympathetically. "It must be difficult to leave her."

"She's gone," Laurie said and wept quietly.

Wisely, Mrs. Kirby said nothing.

Finally with a wistful smile, Laurie said, "We even enjoyed doing the laundry together. When mother got home from the cribs that morning, she took a short nap while I heated the water."

Laurie had hauled out the old copper boiler and stoked the fire. She dumped pan after pan of kitchen tap water into the boiler. While the water heated, she trotted upstairs to get laundry from Will's room and her own. Soon the water's hissing bubbles told her to wake her mother.

She set the wash tubs out on the back porch on sawhorses—one for soapy water, one for bleach and one for rinse. She ladled out the hot water and added enough cold water so she could just barely put her hands into the tubs. Not waiting for her mother to help, she pushed the wash board into the sudsy water and scrubbed the bedding. First came the white laundry, then the colored clothes, and finally her father's stained work coveralls. Lydia awoke and helped.

Laurie had filled the boiler on top of the stove again and soon had more hot water to add to the tubs. Lydia hung the clothes on the backyard lines as soon as she rinsed them. With backs nearly breaking from bending over the tubs, the two women dished the soapy water onto the garden to rid the plants of bugs. Most everyone in the neighborhood grew what vegetables they could between the stumps left from when the trees were felled.

After the rinsed tubs hung on stout nails driven into the porch wall, mother and daughter went into the house.

A kettle of beans shared the heat from the fire that warmed the wash water, a washday ritual; no point in wasting all the heat just to heat water when you could cook dinner as well.

Though Lydia's eyes showed the lack of sleep from last night's trip to the cribs, she began to work on the sewing for a customer. Laurie perched across the table and offered to hem the blouse for the suit Lydia made.

As they sewed, they shared the affectionate, companionable feeling of two close friends. Lydia looked at her daughter quizzically. She cleared her throat, laid aside her work, and asked, "Remember when I said I'd tell you about the past?"

"Of course, Mother, I've made up all sorts of stories about the great mystery," Laurie said, her fatigue falling away.

"Being with those young prostitutes made me realize that maybe you should hear it now," Lydia began.

"What could the past have to do with prostitutes?" Laurie blurted out, more curious than ever and somewhat alarmed.

Just as her mother started to speak again, the neighbor woman pounded on the door. "Are you there, Lydia?" she hollered.

Lydia groaned gently and answered, "Yes, Sally, we're here. Come on in." To Laurie she quietly whispered, "Now we'll hear a lot of gossip and whining."

Mrs. Kirby broke into Laurie's story. "I had a neighbor like that, always interrupting me when I'd rather she stayed home. What kind of woman was she?"

"Sally Jenson rattled on about most anything switching from one subject to another. She reminded me of a flea hopping from place to place both physically and verbally in spite of her bulk. She was round; round face, round body, round piano legs and round arms. Her apron usually showed what she had fixed for breakfast and lunch, and what she cooked for dinner."

"That describes my neighbor exactly," Mrs. Kirby said.

Laurie continued with her story of that afternoon.

Sally wrapped her arms in her apron and said, "Did you hear about the big ruckus down at the cribs last night? One of those hussies got beaten up good by one of her customers. Serves her right, I say. One less of 'em would be fine by me. I heard the shingle weavers are trying to organize the other millworkers. My Henry said they were fighting down at the mill last night when it wasn't even running." Spittle gathered at the corners of her mouth as she rushed on. "Henry said if they win, the men will get big raises and not have to work such long hours. We could sure use some extra money with three little ones and another on the way, and of course having Henry's dad is an added expense. Oh, did I tell you we're going to have another baby?"

Lydia, masking her reservations about another child, said, "How nice you're expecting again."

She can't take care of the kids she already has, observed Laurie to herself.

Will bounded in the back door and grabbed a couple of cookies out of the jar as he dashed upstairs to change his clothes. He raced back down again and said, "I'll meet Father at the streetcar after I see the firemen." He flung out of the door, hopped once on the steps and set off running.

"Well, I guess that means my brood is home from school, too," said Sally and she pushed herself up out of the kitchen chair on which she'd finally alighted. "I'll come back tomorrow so we can really talk."

I hope she forgets, Laurie silently wished. She arose to stir the beans and pour a cup of tea for her mother.

"Help me clear the table, Laurie," her mother said, "and we'll get it set for dinner."

As Laurie sliced the homemade bread, she glimpsed her father and brother walking up the wooden sidewalk from the streetcar. Karl, a bundle of kindling balanced on his shoulder, slouched over in fatigue. Ten hours a day sawing shingle bolts didn't leave a man with much energy. The hour-long lunch break did little to replenish it.

Will capered alongside as he talked excitedly. "We're going to build a cabin near the tideflats and pretend we're marooned on a desert island," he babbled. "The firemen said they'd help."

Karl nodded his head absentmindedly. "That's fine," he said. He dragged up the front steps and lowered the kindling bundle to the porch floor. He shook the sawdust off his clothes, opened the door and wearily stepped over the threshold.

"Here, Karl, let me help you off with your boots," Lydia said as she led him to a kitchen chair. She saw the bloody bandage on his left hand. "What happened?" she asked with alarm.

"Oh, it's nothing," Karl mumbled. "The saw caught my glove again and nipped my hand a little before I could pull free. It's o.k., Lady Lydia, nothing for you to worry about. You can look at it after we eat."

After dinner, Lydia peeled off Karl's dirty bandage, cleaned the jagged wound, and wrapped it again in clean gauze. Relaxing in the cozy living room, Karl drifted into a doze. His gentle snoring provided a droning background for the two women who sewed. Will had been sent to bed in spite of his protests.

Lydia pulled the lamp closer and mused quietly, "I'll have to think about getting glasses soon so I can see the fine thread."

Glancing up from her hemming, Laurie saw her mother studying her with a pinched frown between her eyes. "Have I got some gravy on my nose?" she asked with a grin.

"No, Laurie, it's just hard for me to realize you're almost sixteen. I wonder what awaits you." After another sip of tea, Lydia plied her needle again. "Are you excited about entering Acme Business College in the fall?"

"I guess so. I'm a little afraid but I know you want me to learn a skill." Although she helped her mother with the dressmaking, she didn't choose to do it for a living. It gave her a tender feeling to sew with her mother but she resented filling the gaps of income caused by her father's drinking.

"With the economic ups and downs that plague Everett, I don't want you dependent on a husband who might work just part of the time," Lydia said.

"I don't want to depend on a man for any reason," Laurie replied with the voice she used for pronouncements.

"I know you're going to Acme to please me but what do you really want to do with your life?"

"Promise not to laugh?"

"Laurie, dear, have I ever made fun of you?"

"No, Mother, you'd never do that. It's just that it'll never happen and I might seem foolish."

"Go on, dear."

Laurie gulped some air and said, "I want to be a writer. I don't know what kind yet but that's my secret ambition."

"'Tis proud I am that you have such dreams. Your training at Acme should help you toward your goal, don't you think?"

"I never thought about it that way, but you're right, Mother. It could be the first step."

Karl's coughing brought a temporary end to their conversation. His work in the mill had given him cedar asthma. Even though he wore a damp sponge beneath his nose to trap the sawdust, he developed chronic bronchitis from the constant exposure to the fine dust. Many Everett millworkers' homes echoed with coughing.

Karl heaved himself off the couch and shuffled down the hallway to bed.

"What was it you were going to talk with me about before Mrs. Jenson came over?" Laurie asked with a puzzled expression. Always curious, she waited for her mother's reply.

"We'll talk about it another time when we're not so tired. Why don't you go to bed now? You didn't sleep much last night, either. I want you to deliver this suit and blouse to Mrs. Baker tomorrow morning. She needs it for Thursday."

Laurie gave her mother a kiss on the cheek. She scaled the stairs to her haven where she could read the books she loved so much or spill her innermost emotions onto paper. She opened her journal and began to write.

Mrs. Kirby asked, "Did you ever find out what your mother wanted to talk about?"

"Oh yes," Laurie replied, "But that was much later."

Mrs. Kirby patted her hand. "There goes the dinner gong. I insist you join me for dinner, my dear." Together they walked back to the dining car. An undercurrent of concern rippled through the diners about the accumulation of snow alongside the tracks but the two new friends didn't hear it. The food helped revive Laurie somewhat and after eating a leisurely meal, the two returned to the coach.

CHAPTER 3

As the train chugged up into the mountains, Mrs. Kirby encouraged Laurie to talk. "Did you enjoy delivering your mother's sewing?" she asked.

"I remember the day I delivered the suit I mentioned very well," Laurie began.

The June morning had dawned damp and misty. Fog shrouded the Cascade Mountains and Laurie could barely see the leaden river from her window. She dressed in her best skirt and blouse and topped the outfit with the matching jacket her mother had made. Today I'll see how rich people live, she decided. She'd look around when she delivered the suit to Mrs. Baker.

She knew her father and brother had already left the house. As she entered the kitchen, her mother put the final touches on the parcel Laurie was to carry. Lydia's bleary eyes told of midnight sewing to get the suit completed.

The irons on the cook stove and the ironing board nearby gave mute testimony that her mother had just finished pressing the garments before packaging them.

"I'll go now, Mother," Laurie said, hoping to forego the glob of oatmeal awaiting her on the table.

"You'll eat first, Laurie," her mother responded. "You'll not leave without eating your breakfast. You need the nourishment."

After Laurie finished the bowl of oatmeal and munched on a piece of toast, she took her dishes to the sink and rinsed them. She dried her hands on the towel and looked in the small mirror above the counter. She pinned her hat to the back of her head. Soon she would put her hair into a bun. That would happen in a couple of months when she turned sixteen. She wanted to get used to the trappings of an adult before she went to business school.

She grasped the string on the package and took the streetcar change from her mother. She quickened her steps for the next car was due very soon.

As she climbed on board the streetcar, the motorman pulled the rear connections loose and put the front connectors on the overhead lines. She dropped her coin into the slot and settled down for the ride to Grand Avenue where millowners and their families lived.

Still fairly early in the morning, the shops had just opened. Laurie could see the potted fern in Peterson's Floral Shop as the streetcar rumbled by. Mr. Peterson unlocked the door of his establishment and put out his street sign advertising funerals as one of his specialties. He cast an eye at the misty skyline before he turned to go back into his shop.

The Kraffts occasionally patronized the Fulton Meat Market on Hewitt. As the streetcar passed, Laurie could picture the hams hanging on wall hooks, buckets of lard dangling from wires, and different kinds of meat on the counter. Butchers and customers alike watched the scales suspended from the ceiling; sellers making sure every ounce was recorded and the buyers watching their pennies.

"Clam chowder a specialty" declared a sign in front of a Hewitt Avenue lunchroom. Laurie had eaten in restaurants only on the trip from Minnesota after they had consumed their packed lunches, and then they ate in small cafes next to the train depots. Some day I'll lunch at a restaurant and have some clam chowder, she mused, possibly with a young, handsome man who hangs on my every word. Maybe it would be John Stevens. She wondered why he hadn't been in school this last year. Maybe he moved away. She could feel his arm around her shoulder as she thought about him.

The horses that pulled the drays and carriages along the avenue seemed to ignore the gongs and rattle of the streetcar. A flick of an ear and a bored gaze showed their lack of interest.

At the other end of the line, Laurie alighted, package in hand, and strode toward the Baker mansion. She had never been inside before and hurried eagerly to see its grandeur.

The square house stood in white immaculate splendor with the stately colonnades marching across the front. On the side, a covered drive sheltered a carriage and pair of dapple gray horses.

Laurie didn't know which door she should approach. She decided to go to the front entrance because her parcel was for the lady of the house, not for one of the help. And she wasn't a servant.

She lifted the brass knocker and let it fall several times. A girl in her early twenties opened the door. She wore a dark high-necked dress with a white apron. The white collar and cuffs echoed the white fluff of a cap perched on her dark hair coiled neatly on the top of her head. "Whom do you wish to see," she asked haughtily.

"I'm here to see Mrs. Baker," Laurie replied pulling herself up with dignity.

The maid ushered Laurie into the foyer and told her to wait. She hurried up the stairs and a moment later came back down. "Mrs. Baker will be right with you," she said and disappeared down the hallway.

Gawking like a schoolgirl, Laurie hoped no one saw her lack of sophistication. From the large square entry hall, a gracefully curved stairway linked the second floor with the first. The dark balustrade glowed with the patina of oft-polished wood.

The parquet floor equally glowed with polish. An Oriental rug was a fitting foundation for the majestic round table in the foyer's center which bore a huge bouquet of lilacs. The heavenly scent lulled Laurie into a state of euphoria. What would it be like to live in a house like this with all the amenities money could provide? She contemplated what she would do if servants did all the work.

A deep booming voice startled her from her reverie. "Are you waiting for me?"

Laurie whirled around and beheld an older man about her height. He was almost square. A heavy gold chain looped across the expanse of his vest with a watch fob dangling from it. His full beard and drooping mustache compensated for the lack of hair on his head. A pair of glasses balanced on his mighty nose.

"I'm Mr. Baker," he said. The loud voice belied the man's stature.

Breathlessly Laurie explained she was delivering a suit her mother had made for Mrs. Baker.

"My, you're a pretty one," oozed Mr. Baker, with a leer in his beady dark eyes. He tweaked her cheek and patted her shoulder.

Laurie imperceptibly shuddered and drew away. She thought, you might be rich, old man, but nothing gives you the right to touch me.

An imperious voice sounded down the stairs, "Clarence, Mrs. Krafft's daughter is here to see me. It's time for you to get down to the office. Dinner will be promptly at six so don't be late again. We're having guests."

Mr. Baker pulled out his big, gold watch and mumbled something as he put on his bowler hat and strode importantly to the team and carriage awaiting him.

The tall, busty woman at the top of the stairs motioned for Laurie to come up. Laurie felt small and insignificant on the wide staircase as she looked up at the imposing Mrs. Baker.

The matron led the way like a parade marshal into her upstairs bedroom overlooking Port Gardner Bay. "You wait here while I try these on," Mrs. Baker commanded. As she stepped into her dressing room, Laurie could hear her telling the maid to help.

Heavy, dark dressers and clothes presses lavishly furnished the bedroom. Laurie rubbed her hand over the red flocked wall covering. She fingered the matching plush draperies, rich but overpowering. Tasseled valances spanned the space between the drapes. Laurie could envision the mighty Mrs. Baker crawling into the huge four-poster bed that took up nearly half the room's space. The light blue coverlet and bolster relieved the pervading red.

Heavy drapery drew her attention to the windows. Tall sailing ships, sails furled, were moored beside the sawmills. Activity on their decks became frenzied as slings of lumber swung from mill docks to ships. Whidbey Island across the bay emerged as the mist cleared. The sight filled her with the same longing a wailing train whistle did; a longing to live, to experience, to emerge as a person.

Mrs. Baker swished into the room wearing the new suit and whirled in front of Laurie. "It fits very well," she said with a supercilious lift of her head. "Of course my figure makes it easy to fashion clothes that compliment me."

Laurie was more than a little astounded at this woman's arrogance. The tightly-laced corset the woman wore pushed upward and provided a shelf for her glasses suspended from a fine chain. More than a gathering of material caused the expanse jutting out behind. Laurie smiled inwardly.

"Go down to the parlor and wait for me while I get the money for your mother," Mrs. Baker ordered. "I'll be down as soon as I change."

Laurie went to the head of the stairway and lost herself in a dream world. She gracefully and slowly sauntered down the stairs, a royal princess descending to her waiting minions. She held her head high as she swept into the parlor on the left of the entry gathering up her imaginary train. Her pretense forgotten, she stared in wonder at the room.

Here the same heavy-handed decorating overpowered the space although the colors were deep green and gold. The heavy sofa and overstuffed chairs sat in formal configuration against the wood paneling. Laurie moved around the room feeling the texture of the drapes, the cool of the marble mantle and the sleekness of polished tables. Her sense of touch transmitted these exquisite sensations to her.

She stepped up to the large, ornate urn trimmed in gold sitting near the fireplace. She had just reached out to touch it when Mrs. Baker's voice stopped her hand in mid-air.

"Don't touch that vase. It's very old and very valuable. You might break it." Her words arrested Laurie's awe-inspiring trip around the room.

She took the envelope from Mrs. Baker who admonished her to take it straight home to her mother. As Laurie opened the heavy, carved front door she pledged that someday she'd have a grand mansion filled with her own treasures. She didn't know how yet, but it would happen.

She climbed onto the streetcar headed in the other direction, and lost herself in fantasies about what she wanted to do with her life. She knew she presented a reserved facade but beneath she seethed with emotions. Memories of her mother warmed her and she had a deep affection for her brother. They had shared secrets, hopes, triumphs, and defeats. She had never let anyone know how much she cared for him and had treated him as her annoying little brother in front of others. Even though just a few years separated them, she felt like his second mother. Bursting with life, he glowed like a ray of rare northwest sunshine.

She mused about her father and the few times he had really been a father, like when she had dissolved in tears because a boy at school had thrown mud on her. Her father brushed off her dress when she came running in and held her in his big arms until her sobbing tapered off into a hiccup. "It's not so bad, honey, someday he'll want to be your fellow, and you'll forget he threw mud on you."

She recalled the book she had read about the perils of "demon rum." His demon is alcohol, all right, that's what changes him into someone she feared. When he started yelling, she just wanted to hide. And when he told her how snotty and lazy she was, it hurt her inside. He never had time for his family. He said he loved both Will and Laurie but when the mill closed periodically, he drank, felt sorry for himself, and then wallowed in self-pity.

She skipped lightly down from the streetcar and walked across the street. Putting her thoughts behind her, she hummed merrily as she neared her home.

A knot of neighbors milled around a dray parked on the street in front of her house. With growing concern, Laurie hurried through the cluster of people and dashed through the door. Lydia came out of the bedroom holding a basin filled with bloody water.

"What's wrong, Mother?" she asked anxiously. "Is Father hurt? Is Will all right?"

"Your father has had an accident. His hand was pulled into the saw and he's lost some fingers. Doctor Long is with him now," her mother said quietly. "When Will comes in, take him upstairs with you until the doctor leaves then we'll talk."

Rev. Fowles minced out of the front room, his hands fluttered ineffectually. He had come to comfort the family but they carried on without his succor. He finally left saying, "I have other duties to perform, dear lady. If you need me, please send Will for me."

Laurie kept busy stoking the fire, and making tea for her mother. She refused to think of what would happen now.

Mrs. Kirby said, "My goodness, that was the second accident to his hands in such a short time."

"That's true," Laurie answered. "You could tell which men were sawyers by their mutilated hands. When it happens to your father, it seems worse, though."

CHAPTER 4

The train labored up the slope between ever-deepening snow banks and went through the two-and-a-half-mile tunnel near the summit of Stevens Pass. The contrast between the white snow and the black tunnel blinded Laurie. Some of the passengers became really alarmed by the snowfall. The conductor said the snow fell at the rate of a foot an hour at Wellington, just west of the tunnel.

Laurie felt no anxiety as she continued telling her story to Mrs. Kirby about the Krafft family after her father's injury.

Up in her room, Laurie propped herself against the head of her bed while Will sat cross-legged at the foot. He dropped his shoes to the floor and unbuckled the knees of his knickers.

"Is Father going to be all right?" asked Will with tears puddled in the corners of his eyes.

"I don't know, Will," replied Laurie. "Mother just said he'd lost some fingers. It's sure he won't be able to work for awhile."

"I wonder how bad it hurts to have some fingers torn off?" he asked, curiosity momentarily masking his fright.

"The pain probably gets so intense you pass out." Laurie's voice cracked.

"Without fingers I couldn't play baseball or help the firemen with the horses." Will paused with a frown. "Are you ever afraid, Laurie? You always seem so strong."

"I'm afraid lots of times, Will, I just don't let it show. I was afraid at school when the other kids made fun of me but I didn't let them know it. Most of all I'm afraid to tell what I really feel. I keep the real me locked inside so nobody knows."

"Why did the kids tease you?"

"Sometimes because I grew taller than most of them, even the boys. And they called me a snob."

As they shared their contemplations, they heard their mother's slippers slowly coming up the stairs. She turned into Laurie's room and lowered herself wearily onto the bed.

Gathering her children to her, she said, "Three fingers on your father's left hand are gone and he's lost a lot of blood but Doctor Long said he'll be all right with lots of rest, good food and care. I'll need both of you to help me in the weeks to come. He's had some laudanum now so he'll sleep for awhile. We'd better all get some sleep, too." Pushing herself up from the bed with a sigh, she hugged each child in turn and kissed their cheeks. "I love you both very much."

Karl became more demanding as his wound healed. "Hey, Lyd, I need some coffee, and my hand hurts so bad I can't stand it," he called out in a wounded tone. Putting aside her sewing, Lydia got the coffee and headed to the bedroom.

"Here's your coffee. I'll prop your hand on another pillow and that will help ease the pain. I can't give you any more laudanum for a while. You shouldn't have it too often." Lydia moved to the other side of the bed. The solid wooden head and foot boards made the bed seem ponderous and Karl's bulk amplified the feeling of great size.

"I want to go back to work," Karl said plaintively. "A man should earn a living for his family and I've lain here for more than a week already."

"What will you do, Karl, with just part of your left hand?" Lydia asked with measured calm.

"Oh, they'll find something for me to do. I won't be able to handle the cedar bolts. There're other jobs to do though I won't earn as much. At least I'll be doing something."

"It's too soon, Karl. You lost a lot of blood and haven't moved around much yet. It takes time. We'll get you up tomorrow and into the front room."

"Have Will come in to talk to me," the cantankerous man ordered.

"He's working over at the firehouse grooming the horses. He's fortunate to have the job," Lydia told her husband as she looked into the full-length mirror on the left of the dresser. She saw Karl's clenched jaw reflected in the glass.

His son's job diminished him even more. Karl said, "I just have to get up and go back to work."

A knock on the door interrupted his complaining and Lydia hastened to see who waited on the porch. One of the men from the mill had come to see Karl and Lydia ushered him into the sick room. She left them alone glad to get back to her sewing. Karl demanded so much of her time she fell behind in her orders.

"I'm so grateful you're home to do the cleaning and most of the cooking," she told her daughter as Laurie passed on her way upstairs, broom in hand.

But peace and quiet were not for Lydia. Sally Jenson came bursting through the back door with just a token knocking. Lydia put on her most patient face and listened as the human flea flitted around the table, telling all the news.

"They completed the double train track to Seattle, finally, now it will be easier to get down there, my Henry said. There's a meeting of lumbermen scheduled to discuss closing all the straight shingle mills for three months during the winter. They have the same committees in Whatcom and Skagit counties, too. They're all going to get together in Seattle next month. I wonder how we'll get by if that happens. Oh, did I tell you that big, dumb-looking man who's been staying with the Olsens disappeared?" Not waiting for a reply, she continued, "He was last seen Tuesday in the saloon at the end of Hewitt next to the river. They say there's a trapdoor in the back end and they give a man a drugged drink then push him through the trapdoor into a boat and they take him out to the bay and put him on a ship. As sure as pitch is sticky that's what happened to him. He's so big, he'd make a good sailor."

She paused for a breath then asked about Karl.

"He's restless and wants to go back to work but I told him it's too soon," Lydia said. "I'm going to get him up tomorrow so he can get his strength back. Here, Sally, let me pour you some tea."

"Where's Laurie, is she around here someplace?" Sally asked between blows on the hot tea.

"She's upstairs cleaning the bedrooms," Lydia replied.

"Well, you asked me to invite the neighbors to her sixteenth birthday party. I need to tell them when, where and what to bring for the potluck. I didn't know if Karl's accident had changed anything."

"We can't let her birthday go unnoticed and it will help Karl to have people around," Lydia explained. "We'll have it on the first Saturday in August here at the house. We'll make some tables out of sawhorses in the back yard. I'll bake the cake and some beans. Oh, I'll fix the corn on the cob, too. Our corn looks good this year. It would be fun to surprise her, but that's almost impossible. I appreciate your spreading the invitation. It would be hard for me right now."

Laurie knew Saturday would hold something special. She turned sixteen then. She pretended to know nothing and went about her usual chores. She heard her mother in the kitchen Friday night putting wood into the stove's gaping firebox and rattling pans. She's making my birthday cake, Laurie concluded.

Saturday's sunshine woke Laurie early. She couldn't repress her excitement. Hopping out of bed, she put on her new white blouse and the skirt to her suit. She postured in front of the mirror and tried out her new hair style. Brushing it made it fly in all directions but she finally managed to twist it into a bun on the top of her head with a pompadour. She smoothed the loose ends with the comb she had plunged into the glass of water on her night stand.

She hummed softly to herself as she gamboled down the stairs eager for the day to begin. She started the kitchen fire and contemplated breakfast. Today she'd fix hotcakes and eggs. We can afford it this time, she decided.

Lydia heard the commotion and quietly arose from the bed where Karl still slept. As she pulled on her robe she slipped into the warm kitchen, her blonde hair falling over her shoulders.

"Why are you up so early on your birthday?" she asked.

"I was so excited I couldn't wait for the day to begin," Laurie explained.

"So you know about your birthday party," Lydia remarked with a smile. "I knew we couldn't keep it from you. People will start arriving about eleven so there's still lots of time." She suddenly noticed Laurie's new bun. "I like it, Laurie, you look very mature."

Laurie self-consciously raised a hand to smooth her hair at the compliment.

While her mother returned to her bedroom to dress and do her hair, Laurie whipped the pancake batter, brewed the coffee and steeped the tea.

Karl's strength had grown and he seemed in better humor. He came into the kitchen soon after Lydia's reappearance. "Well, honey, today you're sixteen," he said to Laurie heartily. "You're a young lady now and your whole life is ahead of you. Come here and give me a hug."

Laurie scooted over to him and squeezed him, forgetting for awhile his propensity for liquor. He handed her a small white box and told her, "Go ahead and open it."

"It's beautiful," she said breathlessly, gazing at the shiny gold locket nestled in cotton. As she carefully lifted it out, her eyes misted as she saw her initials etched into the gold. She fastened the chain around her neck.

"Your mother and I wanted to give you something special to remember this day," Karl said affectionately as he beamed at his daughter.

It's going to be a glorious day, Laurie decided.

The bustle of preparations lasted the morning and neighbors joined the family close to noon. Karl and Will set up the tables in the back yard and Lydia covered them with butcher paper. Women placed hot dishes on the back of the kitchen stove and the other food waited on the cool back porch until dinner time.

Some of the men from the mill came. One brought a keg of beer but Laurie vowed it would not spoil her day.

Kids played tag among the corn stalks and around the stumps. The Jensons brought their brood and old Mr. Jenson. In spite of the day's heat, he wore his coat and vest. His white drooping mustache glistened in the sun. He sat on a stump with hands crossed on the head of his cane, nodding benevolently to everyone who passed. To those who stopped long enough to listen, he told stories of Everett's early days.

The food in colorful bowls and on fancy plates decorated the tables. Women wore their Sunday-best clothing lending a festive air. Smells of baked beans and potato salad mingled in the warm air.

When the time came to eat, Karl and Lydia escorted Laurie to the head of the table. The girl glowed with all the added attention, her usual reserved facade shattered by her delight. The others gathered themselves around the makeshift dining accommodations and passed the food from hand to hand with a great deal of chatter. Mothers filled children's plates and sent them to sit on a blanket to eat. Judging by their exuberance, they were glad to be out from under the grownups' watchful eyes.

When guests settled back after gorging themselves, Lydia brought out the birthday cake, a work of art in a time when such extravagance was unusual. Karl lit the sixteen candles lining the edges and Laurie made a wish before she blew them out.

"What'd you wish, Laurie?" Will hollered.

"Can't tell, Will, or it won't come true," she replied with a laugh. She couldn't tell anyone else about her secret desire to write. Only her mother knew.

One of the mill men called out, "Sweet sixteen and never been kissed, eh Laurie?"

Her cheeks flamed in remembrance of the time pimply Gerald Banks had told her he'd never kissed a girl before and wanted her to show him how. Anxious to show her worldliness, Laurie demonstrated how to place his arms around her as she imagined they should be and kissed him. By the next day, the whole school knew about her kissing class. Her classmates greeted her with smirking grins for days.

As the women cleared away the traces of the meal, the men gathered around the keg. Henry Jenson kept looking Laurie's way. Baffled by the attention, she concluded maybe her new hairdo prompted the looks. The more he drank, however, the more she resented his stares. She saw his eyes crawling over her body and she shivered involuntarily. He was nearly as round as his wife and he swaggered as he headed for the beer keg again.

She avoided him as she helped clean the table and take food back into the kitchen. "Oh, Mother, it's been such a wonderful day and I love you for planning it," she said as she grabbed her mother around the waist and twirled her in a quick caper across the kitchen.

Her mother laughed with her and went back outside to supervise the dismantling of the tables. Laurie went down the hallway to the bathroom feeling mature and confident. As she looked in the mirror, she appraised the water box suspended from the ceiling with the dangling chain used to flush the toilet. Mother's water closet is really modern, she decided. It's better than an outdoor privy. The bathtub took up one whole wall and the sink hung opposite it with cabinets on both sides of the mirror. I do look older and more mature, she thought as she wiped her hands. She left the bathroom and started down the hallway studded with loaded coat hooks.

Mr. Jenson lurched into the doorway from the kitchen. His hot eyes bored into Laurie who tried to pass him. He stretched his arms to prevent it. "So now you're sweet sixteen and I bet you've never really been kissed," he drawled in a suggestive manner. He grabbed her around her shoulders and clutched her to him.

She could smell the beer on his breath and see the blue veins in his bulbous nose. Don't panic, she resolved. Drawing herself up as best she could, she said, "I don't want to be kissed by you and I'll tell your wife if you try it." She hoped her determined voice would mask the quaking she felt inside.

As Mr. Jenson tightened his grip around her, she felt instant revulsion. With his fetid breath blowing in her face he said, "You'll like it, sweetie, I know you will. I've taught lots of girls how to make a man happy."

Laurie struggled to free herself but she felt her resolve not to panic crumbling. The coat hooks poked her back as she fought to break his hold. She switched her head from side to side as she tried to avoid the blubbering lips. Bile welled up in her throat and she could barely move. Dizziness engulfed her.

She gathered her strength and in one big lunge, she brought up her knee and slammed her foot down as hard as she could on Mr. Jenson's instep.

Startled, he loosened his hold. Laurie broke free from his grasp with a mighty surge of power and scrambled up the stairs as her mother came into the kitchen.

"Laurie," called her mother. "Some of the neighbors are leaving and want to wish you happy birthday again." She came into the hallway and saw Henry Jenson adjusting his shirt with a guilty look.

Standing severely silent, she waited to see what he would do. What he had attempted in the deserted hallway shown in his eyes. He turned and went back to the bathroom. Lydia hurried upstairs to her daughter.

Laurie sobbed in a collapsed heap on the bed while she scrubbed at her lips. Lydia cradled her across her lap and patted her back. "It's all right, Laurie, dear, you're safe now. Don't let this spoil your birthday."

The sobbing quieted. Laurie sat up and hugged her mother. "How could he do such a thing? He has a wife and children, and he knew all those people were out in the yard. He makes my flesh crawl," she moaned. "I don't ever want to see him again."

"He's a good husband when he's not drinking but I know how you feel. Don't let it hurt you inside. Kissing from the right man can be a wonderful thing. You might not believe it now, but it's true."

Laurie decided she never wanted to be kissed again, by anyone.

Lydia gave her daughter one last clasp and said as she turned to go downstairs, "I'll tell everyone you're a little under the weather from such an exciting day. You don't have to come down until you're ready."

Laurie wiped her eyes, took the hairpins out that held her bun, and brushed the shining hair that fell well below her shoulders. I will not let that man spoil my memories of this day, she pledged.

She heard Will on the stairs and pasted a smile on her face. He held his hands behind his back and looked shyly at her.

"I got you a present, Laurie, from me to you, and I earned the money for it myself." He held the package out to her, excited and apprehensive.

Carefully, she unwrapped the paper and saw the new leather journal Will had bought just for her. She hugged him, kissed his cheek and said, "Thank you, Will, this is a very special present, especially since you thought of it and earned the money for it." She turned to the first page. "I'll start it today and keep it with me always."

"And did you? Keep it with you always, I mean?" Mrs. Kirby asked.

Laurie reached inside her heavy coat and produced the journal. "Does that answer your question?" she asked with a glimmer of a smile.

Mrs. Kirby nodded. "That was a terrible experience you had in the hallway. Some men," she said in disgust.

CHAPTER 5

✿

Mrs. Kirby patted Laurie's hand and asked, "Did you get your chance to write?"

"That's really a long story, Mrs. Kirby." Laurie fidgeted. "Are you sure you want to hear it?"

"Of course I do, dear. It will take my mind off this terrible storm and all that snow."

"I entered Acme Business College in Everett that fall. That first day of classes filled me with something approaching fear. I had little self-confidence, I guess."

The school seemed different from when her mother had brought her in to register for the fall term. Then there were just office people and her mother. Now a raft of other people eddied about.

The students ranged in age from young people like Laurie to middle-aged folks. The number of boys enrolled surprised her. Evidently some courses attracted men as well as women.

The sugar bowl her mother kept had paid the tuition for typing, shorthand and bookkeeping. It also yielded enough for two outfits including new shoes.

Laurie chose to walk to the school on Hewitt Avenue, a good hike from Riverside. The jaunt invigorated her and saved car fare besides. She hung her coat in the cloakroom and went to her first typing class. She left her sandwich in her coat pocket.

She had been shown the room when she registered. The black Underwood typewriters sat squarely on their tables with the chairs tucked neatly underneath. The blank keys gave no clue to the letters they represented but a chart on the wall showed their designations.

A white blouse and black skirt adorned the prim instructor. Mrs. Prine stood tall and rigidly straight, her shoulders braced. Her forbidding manner daunted Laurie who thought the teacher's dark hair twisted into a tight bun might describe her mind. The dim shading of fine hair on the teacher's upper lip added to her grim aspect. She told the students to pick out their desks and sit down. "Open your books to page three," she commanded.

Fifteen students filled the room including a few boys lined up in the back as if they gathered strength from being together. Lights hung from the high ceiling and cast a bright glow reflected in the windows that looked out upon the weeping sky.

Mrs. Prine showed her students how to do finger exercises in the air to limber their hands. In their first lesson, they learned the home position and what fingers pushed what keys. "You'll learn it all in good time," Mrs. Prine said, her lips compressed in permanent censure.

They slowly went through the keys as they looked at the chart in front of the room. The clock chimed ten and some of the students started to arise from their chairs. "You will not leave until I dismiss you," Mrs. Prine said loudly as she exerted her control.

From the typing class, Laurie dashed to the ladies' room then went to her shorthand class. She had looked at her text book and could make neither heads nor tails out of the curling slashes. The teacher, young and pretty, was small in stature with blonde hair. Her easy, warm manner made her seem more like a student than a teacher. Chalk lettering on the blackboard gave her name as Miss Galbraith. She smiled broadly at her new students.

Laurie, at least a head taller than the petite teacher, felt an instant kinship. She could talk to her, she decided. She'd never felt like that about a teacher before.

"Make sure your pencils are sharp and we'll begin," Miss Galbraith said. "We'll learn the short forms for words as we go along and you'll soon become familiar with them by practice."

Laurie could see there were no boys here as she twisted her head around to look.

With pencils poised, the girls began to make scratches on their papers. The foreign scrawls meant nothing to them now but as the days wore on, they'd grow more adept at making the marks and reading them.

After the shorthand class, Laurie had time to eat her sandwich before bookkeeping. As she sat in the lounge, she saw a copy of the *Everett Daily Herald* on the table. She gathered up the pages and began to read. This established a habit she followed every school day. She became knowledgeable about Everett and the world around it. She learned about labor problems from the reporters who had much more credibility than Sally Jenson. She devoured the papers, article by article. How she wished she could write some of those stories.

When she walked out of her bookkeeping class, there stood Gerald Banks, her kissing student, with a knowing grin on his face. Shame and anger at his leer filled her. She grabbed her coat, gathered her books and slammed out of the door ignoring Miss Galbraith's question about what bothered her. Must I always be reminded of shameful events, Laurie asked herself silently?

The days settled into a comfortable routine of going to school, coming home, practicing shorthand forms and doing bookkeeping homework in the evening. Laurie liked what she learned. She excelled in her classes except for bookkeeping. Word classes seemed easy to her but numbers proved more difficult. Determined to do well because of her mother's sacrifices, Laurie worked hard to learn. Fortunately, Gerald Banks was in none of her classes and she seldom saw him.

Her father had gone back to work though not as a shingle sawyer. He cleaned up cedar debris and helped with grading. His days were as long as before but he earned less. The hard physical work drained his strength.

Will was back in school, as exuberant as ever. He wasn't the best student for his mind dwelt on more physical pursuits. Always anxious for school to be over, he could scarcely wait to go play. Lydia usually snatched him as he came home from school to make sure he did his chores in the garden and around the house before he escaped to be with his friends or the firemen.

Lydia continued to sew for the town's elite. Her style sense and skilled needlework kept her in constant demand. Without Laurie to help with the everyday housework, Lydia had to sew at night. Laurie helped when she could but homework came first.

Some of the boys in typing and bookkeeping began to talk to her in a companionable way and Leroy Helgeson had asked her to go to a movie with him. He towered over her but didn't have her flowing grace of movement. Instead, he seemed clumsy and self-conscious. When she looked past his blemishes, she could see his earnest countenance. His strong, supple hands made typing class a cinch for him.

"I know we've just met," Leroy said as he stumbled over his words shyly and turned red. He looked at his feet and acted like a sixth grader. "I'd like to know you better. Will you go to the movies with me Saturday?"

Although he didn't evoke the feelings that the mention of John Stevens' name did, she thought him nice. She answered, "I'd like to go, Leroy, if my mother doesn't need me. I'll let you know Friday at school." She ardently hoped Gerald Banks hadn't told him about her foolishness.

When Laurie asked her mother, Lydia replied, "'Tis fine with me, Laurie. I'm glad you're making friends. Ask him to come by to meet me before you go."

Mrs. Kirby interrupted, "How was your date with Mr. Helgeson?"

"That date never happened," Laurie choked.

"Oh, my, what happened?"

"It's almost too painful to talk about."

"It helps to share, my dear," the little woman said.

"The Saturday I had the date with Leroy, I had to clean the kitchen."

The noise of the fire engine spurred Laurie out the door on Saturday morning. She had to see why it seemed so loud. Suds from the dishwater still covered her hands. Will raced to the corner ahead of her on the rain-slicked board walk. The sound of the thundering hooves grew closer. She could see the three-horse span as the engine rounded the corner a moment after Will reached it. Black smoke billowed out of the boiler.

Laurie ran after Will to pull him out of danger. The next few seconds were frozen in her mind forever. Will slipped on the wet boards and fell into the street. The hooves and wheels rolled his young body over and over like a limp rag doll. Laurie would never forget the horrified look of the driver who couldn't stop the racing horses.

Laurie heard someone screaming over and over again, and finally realized the screams came from her. She ran to the lump of clothing lying in the street sobbing Will's name. Others held her back as they created a circle around the boy. "Run for Doc Long," shouted one of the men.

Lydia came out of the house wiping her hands on her apron to see what caused the commotion. Laurie ran to her, buried her face in her mother's shoulder and cried out what had happened. Lydia hurried to where her son lay, the neighbors parting a way for her. She knelt and pushed the black hair out of the boy's face. She stayed as still as her son. She reached out to hug him to her but her hands dropped beside her.

"We've sent for Doc Long," they told her.

She rocked back and forth as she crouched in anguish, whimpering all the while.

Laurie dropped to her knees by her mother and without words offered comfort. She put her arm around Lydia's shoulders as she suppressed her own grief. Although she had seen the accident, she couldn't believe it had actually happened. The pain numbed her.

Doctor Long's horse and buggy came careening down the street. He threw a line to one of the men. He bounced down with his black bag and shook his head at what he saw, his dark beard jutting out from under his brimmed hat.

The neighborhood women attempted to lead Lydia and Laurie into the house but neither would leave. The doctor lifted Will's limp wrist to take his pulse, and he bent to listen for the beating of the young heart. His deft hands felt along Will's legs and arms. He took off his coat and covered Will's body very gently. "I'm sorry, Lydia," he said as he arose and put his arm around the shocked mother. "He's gone to his Maker. He's a mass of broken bones. At least he's not in pain."

The men lifted the broken body into a wagon that had been pulled up and took Will to the mortuary. Only then would Laurie and Lydia allow themselves to be led into the house, too grief-stricken to cry. The neighbors told a shocked Leroy Helgeson what had happened when he arrived for his date with Laurie.

When Karl came home from the mill, he shook himself off on the porch as usual and called for Will to come help with the kindling. He pushed open the door when he received no reply. He saw his wife and daughter sitting mutely at the table, hands clutched. "Where's Will?" he asked, "What's wrong, is he hurt?"

Lydia heaved a great sigh, rose and leaned against him. "Will was running toward the corner to see where the fire was when the engine came around it. He slipped and fell and the horses hit him and killed him. He's at the funeral home now."

"How do you know he's dead?" Karl wailed in disbelief. "Did you see for yourself? Did you see if he was breathing?"

"Doctor Long came and tried to help but it was too late. Yes, I saw for myself," and she finally started to cry. Karl put his big arms around her and began to sob, too. They clung to each other for a long time.

Laurie held herself rigid. If she didn't acknowledge the tragedy, it wasn't real. She wouldn't cry, she told herself. If she didn't cry, it didn't happen. Will would come in the house in just a minute and prove it was all a bad dream. She got up from her chair and heated water for tea, her movements automatic. Always in times of stress, tea helped. She had forgotten her movie date with Leroy Helgeson.

Laurie roused from her story to find Mrs. Kirby's arm around her shoulder, her tears reflecting those coursing down Laurie's cheeks.

"How terrible for you and your parents. I think it'd be the worst possible loss to lose a child."

With a shake of her head, Laurie tried to put the memory of Will's death behind her again. "This snow's getting very deep," she said, apprehensive at the heavy snow blanket.

"I don't think there's anything to worry about," said Mrs. Kirby. "If there were, they'd tell us, I'm sure."

CHAPTER 6

The train crested the summit and started down the other side to Leavenworth and Spokane beyond. It gathered speed as it descended from the Cascades just as Laurie's thoughts accelerated. Mrs. Kirby had settled into a catnap beside her.

She couldn't shake the thought of Will. She remembered the difficult time she had had after the accident, even in her sleep.

Laurie raced down the street after Will. He remained just beyond her reach. She ran faster, afraid she wouldn't catch him in time. She lifted her skirt so she could run freer. Just as she got close enough to grab her brother, her skirt dropped and she tripped, falling, falling, falling…

She sat up in bed wiping the sheen of clammy sweat away with the corner of the sheet. Why do I keep having the same nightmare, she asked herself? Why am I trying to catch Will? Her throat ached with unshed tears.

Will's accident in mid-December still obsessed Laurie in February. The nightmare kept recurring. She read late into the night to avoid sleep and buried herself in her schoolwork to block out the memory of Will's death. She had not wept for the loss of her brother, her feelings kept rigidly inside her. Even when she went with her mother to the mortuary, the florist and the church to make arrangements for Will's funeral, she hadn't shed any tears. Her grief was too great to pour out and her penchant for protecting her innermost feelings refused to let her mourn in public or share her pain.

When friends and neighbors came to the house Laurie moved as if in a trance. She functioned automatically. She helped with the food, took coats, escorted callers to the door when they left. Rev. Fowles visited the house on a number of occasions but his comforting remarks did little to assuage her grief. She barely remembered Rosie from the cribs coming by to see her mother and offer condolences.

Christmas had been nearly non-existent in the Krafft home. It had been Will's favorite time of the year. Without him to incite others with his excitement, it became a bleak holiday. Laurie would rather have continued going to classes instead of facing long hours of Christmas vacation in the home Will had made so merry.

Money was scarce, too. The funeral expenses put a big hole in the budget and Karl's drinking had escalated to drown out the memory of his lost son.

Lydia kept her needle moving. She couldn't afford to remain idle and besides, Laurie knew as long as her mother kept busy, she could cope with her loss. Lydia comforted the remaining two in her family and dealt with her own sorrow by herself. Once in awhile, Laurie could see tears slip down her mother's cheeks and knew Lydia mourned.

Laurie had kept up with her schoolwork and in a few weeks would conclude her business courses. She'd have to find a job to help out at home. The prospect of applying for work terrified her. She had no experience in asking for help. Because she needed work so badly it made her feel like a beggar seeking alms.

Leroy Helgeson had asked her to go to the movies a number of times since the accident, and she accepted a few of his invitations. He proved to be a good companion but she just went through the motions of living. He tried to put his arm around her in the dark theater but she shrugged it away. His amorous glances in typing class prompted a pathetic smile in Laurie but her emotions remained frozen.

The only times she forgot about Will's death were when she immersed herself in the newspaper at lunchtime. The larger scope of life took over then and made her little world bearable by perspective. She read it all from the first headline to the last classified ad in the back.

Miss Galbraith had complimented Laurie on how well she did at shorthand and usually paused after class to chat with her a little. She was a warm and caring woman, more like a contemporary than a teacher.

As the end of the February neared, Miss Galbraith asked Laurie to stay after class. When all of the other students had gone, she took Laurie into the teachers' lounge where they sat in a corner by themselves. Miss Galbraith broached the subject of Will's death. "You loved your brother very much, didn't you Laurie? I'm sure he loved you, too, and wouldn't want you to grieve forever. You don't show it on the outside but I know what you're feeling inside. It's all right to cry, dear, it helps the healing."

She put her arm around Laurie's shoulders and held her close. Laurie couldn't hold it inside any longer and with the warm words she heard she burst into sobs. She cried for a long time and finally felt the handkerchief Miss Galbraith pressed into her hands. She took long shuddering breaths as she wiped her eyes. She felt better, as if the pain had poured out with the tears through the breach in the dam of her grief.

When Laurie had composed herself somewhat, Miss Galbraith smoothed her skirt with a dainty hand and said, "Now that we've faced that problem, I have something else to talk with you about. There's a job opening I know you would be well suited for. You're very mature for your age and with your shorthand ability, I think you'd be perfect." She smiled broadly showing her even white teeth.

Laurie wiped her nose again and said, "I do need a job and I don't have any idea where to begin. I was going to ask you about it." Maybe looking ahead wouldn't be so terrible now.

"Well, my dear, a friend of mine works at the *Everett Daily Herald* and he asked me if I knew of anyone who could be a girl Friday in the office. You would take shorthand, type, file and answer telephones," said Miss Galbraith. "I'd be happy to write a recommendation for you if you're interested."

"Oh, yes," Laurie said earnestly. "I read the paper every day. I'd love to work there. I don't know if I'm good enough but I'd try very hard. When should I go over there to see about the job?" Her voice trembled in her excitement and apprehension.

"Your classes will be over next week. I'll make an appointment for you to see the managing editor a week from Friday. His name is Bill Hunt. He's rather gruff but he's got a heart of gold."

Both rose from their chairs and Laurie impulsively wrapped her arms around Miss Galbraith. "Thank you so much for caring. Your friendship means more than you'll ever know."

"After next week, I expect you to call me Alice because I won't be your teacher any more," Miss Galbraith said. "I'll see you in class on Monday, dear, and don't punish yourself any more for your brother's death. There's nothing you could have done to save him. It was an accident. You have to let it go and get on with your life."

As Laurie hurried home, she wondered about her nightmare. Could she have saved Will from being trampled by the fire horses? Seeing the accident again in her mind, she realized she could not have reached him in time. The knowledge cleansed her of guilt. She had gone from the depths of despair to the peak of anticipation in a matter of minutes.

When Laurie walked in the door, Lydia said, "Sit down, Laurie, and tell me what's happened to you." She wore a compassionate smile.

"Miss Galbraith asked me to stay after class so she could talk to me," Laurie said with a rush. "She told me I wasn't to blame for Will's death. I sobbed and sobbed. When I finally quit crying I felt a lot better. She said there was no way I could have prevented the accident and I believed her. Maybe now the nightmare will go away."

"What nightmare, Laurie?" her mother asked with alarm.

"The same one I've had since Will died," Laurie responded. "I run down the street after Will as fast as I can but I can't quite catch him. Just as I'm close enough to grab him I trip and fall. I keep falling until I wake up in a sweat."

Her mother got up and reached for her, folding her warm arms around her. "Oh, Laurie, if you'd only told me about it I would have told you weren't to blame," Lydia said. "I knew you were grieving inside but I didn't know about your nightmare."

"I couldn't tell you, Mother; you had your own pain to bear." They stood together, arms around each other and cried quietly. Their tears consoled them and Laurie knew the agony had disappeared.

A loud knock on the door jarred them back to the present. Mother and daughter wiped their eyes and they looked at each other as Sally Jenson hollered through the door. They smiled indulgently and Lydia said, "Come on in, Sally, we've just started to get dinner."

Sally lumbered in with her round body distorted by the child she carried within. "I wanted to talk to you about my baby's birth, Lydia," she said as she plopped into a chair with a sigh of relief. "You've delivered my last two and I hope you plan to deliver this one, too. It's due next month and I have to make sure of the arrangements. I thought maybe when the time comes, I could come over here and let Henry keep the other kids at home. It's so hard to work around them at a time like that," she said breathlessly and endlessly.

She gulped some air and went on, "I hope Karl won't mind, after all, it'll be easier for you and he could sleep in Will's bed for a couple of nights if it comes to that. Would that work out, Lydia?"

"I'll have to talk to Karl about it, Sally. I'll let you know in time for you to settle things at home," Lydia said calmly. "It might be simpler and easier at that."

"Thanks, Lydia. Did you hear that the lumbermen's manufacturing association has fixed lumber prices? My Henry says it's become a lumber trust just like the railroad trust. He says anyone with a shack and a saw can mill cedar shingles. If we had some extra money, he said he'd do it. But we have too many mouths to feed and I hope he doesn't decide to do something so doubtful." She paused and added with a faraway look in her eye, "But it would be nice to be a millowner's wife."

Laurie couldn't picture stocky Mr. Jenson as a millowner. She had never forgotten his fumbling attempt to kiss her.

"I have to get on with dinner now, Sally, and Laurie has schoolwork to do," Lydia said kindly.

"Oh, I have to go home now anyway and tend to those squalling kids. Old Mr. Jenson just goes into his room and ignores them. Let me know what Karl says about birthing here." With a mighty effort she heaved herself out of the chair and made for the back door. The flea had become an elephant.

After Sally had moved her ponderous body out the door, Laurie said, "I have some other news, too, Mother," barely hiding her excitement.

"Tell me quick, Laurie," said her mother reflecting her daughter's mood.

"Miss Galbraith is recommending me for a job at the newspaper. I can't think of another place I'd rather work and I won't have to go out knocking on doors to find a position."

Their hug now expressed joy.

That night, Laurie wrote in the journal Will had given her about breaking her emotional log jam, the chance of a job at the newspaper, and the possibility of helping her mother with Sally's delivery. The rest of her life had begun.

CHAPTER 7

Mrs. Kirby roused from her nap and noticed Laurie's reflective smile. "You did get over your grief after your brother's death, didn't you?"

"Yes, thanks to a teacher and friend at Acme. I had a terrible nightmare nearly every night and she explained I had blamed myself for his death because I didn't catch him in time to save his life."

As the train descended from the snow-shrouded Cascade peaks, Mrs. Kirby said with renewed energy, "Now, tell me how your school led to writing."

"The teacher I spoke about knew of a job at the *Everett Daily Herald* that she thought I could fill. It was for a glorified clerk but I loved the paper so much I would have done anything there and I wouldn't have to go searching for a job. The thought terrified me."

"Tell me about it, my dear."

"Well, my heart fluttered in my throat as I approached the *Herald* office. The white brick building stood at the corner of Colby and Wall. The arched windows gave it a modern look."

She entered the door in the center of the building and stood awestruck for a moment in the imposing lobby. The dark wood counter sat below iron grill work just like a bank. Bars covered some of the grill openings.

Unsure of where to go, she approached the open window in the grill. The sign above it read "Engraving and Printing" and the nameplate identified Charles Shaefer.

"What can I do for you, honey?" the tall, thin man asked distractedly. A green eyeshade shielded his eyes and black elastic garters banded his shirt sleeves.

Laurie straightened her shoulders, cleared her throat nervously and said, "I have an appointment to see Mr. Hunt."

"Oh, you must be here about the office job," he said as he pointed the way down the hall to the right of the counter. "Go down there and bang on the door but don't go in until he answers. He's particular about that."

She tried to show a confidence she didn't feel as she moved resolutely down the hall. Alice Galbraith had characterized Mr. Hunt as gruff but with a heart of gold. She hoped she'd be here long enough to find that out for herself.

Ben Davis, the *Herald*'s ace reporter, stopped in mid-stride as he watched the young girl leave Charlie's cage. She moves so regally, he thought. He'd never been so stricken by a woman's manner of moving in all of his twenty-three years. Ladies' charms were not foreign to him, though. With his boyish good looks, he'd never had a problem securing female companionship of any sort.

He'd heard the term "thunderstruck" before, brushing it aside as flowery rhetoric but now he personally knew what the word meant. He smoothed his wavy brown hair shot with red.

He pushed the feeling aside and resumed his dash out the door intent on his assignment. He determined to find out who she was when he got back.

Laurie tapped on the door Charlie had indicated with no response. She knocked louder and finally a deep voice said, "Yeah, I heard you, come on in."

Laurie pushed open the door and waited just inside as she beheld the barrel-like stature of the man at the massive roll-top desk. He continually ran his hands through his thin gray hair which stood up in all directions. He glowered at her from under his heavy brows, a cigar clenched at the corner of his mouth.

He twirled his swivel chair around and fixed her with a glaring stare.

"Well, what do you want?" he bellowed. "I don't have all day. I have a newspaper to run."

Laurie gulped and then said crisply, "I have an appointment to see you about an office job."

"Oh, yeah, Alice called me and said you'd be the right one to keep me organized. Can you take shorthand and type?"

After an affirmative answer he went on, "Do you know the alphabet well enough to file, too?"

"Of course I do," Laurie said testily. "I got the highest marks in school for transcribing my shorthand and spelling."

"Sounds as if you have a little fire, too. Well, you can see by my desk someone needs to keep track of all these things. I keep losing 'em. I'm not easy to work for, they tell me, but I'm fair," he said. The bare electric light that hung from the ceiling cast an eerie glow on top of his head. It showed the scalp underneath the sparse hair. Various kinds of papers covered his desk. All the pigeonholes spewed forth bits and pieces of notes.

Laurie wondered how he found a clear space to work. "I'm a very organized person," she said quietly. "I've read your newspaper every day for six months and I think it's wonderful. I'd like to work for you and I'm sure I can do the job." She tried to exhibit self-assurance.

"We haven't had anyone in this position before, so you'll have to start from scratch. Think you can handle that?" he asked with a piercing look from his pale gray eyes.

"I can try if you'll give me a chance," Laurie said intensely. She smoothed her skirt and braced her shoulders.

"All right, Miss Krafft, we'll try working together for awhile and see if you can handle the hustle of a newspaper office. You know, we're all a little strange in this business," he chuckled. "I'm going to call you Laurie. Is that all right?"

"Yes, that's fine," Laurie replied, as her tension eased a little.

"Well, your desk will be right outside my door in that alcove. We'll have the phones hooked up there. I don't want anyone to come into my office unless I send for 'em or unless there's an emergency," he said brusquely. "You're supposed to protect my time as well as organize things. I want you to set up a filing system for all these papers, too. I'll dictate my editorials to you and you can type them up for the typesetters. Now go out and see what kind of supplies you'll need. We'll have a filing cabinet hauled in from the press room."

In a daze, Laurie went out to her desk and sat down in disbelief. She had the job. She could have shouted for joy. She looked in all the drawers and found absolutely nothing. She took a pad of paper from her bag and made a list of the things she'd need; paper, pencils, pen and ink, file folders, calendar and a desk lamp.

Mr. Hunt came out of his office and said gruffly, "Goin' to lunch." She handed him the slip of paper. "Don't give it to me," he said. "Get some money from Charlie at the front desk and go get 'em yourself. The typewriter will be delivered this afternoon."

Laurie spent the afternoon gathering the things she needed, mostly at Hawes Stationery Store on Hewitt, and getting her desk in order. While she shopped, the typewriter had arrived and the file cabinet stood next to the desk. She laid her supplies close at hand, put on her hat and left for home.

"Oh, Mother, I got the job," bubbled Laurie when she got home. "Mr. Hunt is blunt but I think we'll get along fine. He's about fifty years old and tries to intimidate people but it's mostly bluff. Anyway, I'm thrilled to have the job."

"I'm so pleased you're looking ahead instead of back. I love to see you so excited. What sort of things will you do?"

"I'll take dictation, type, file, answer phones and organize Mr. Hunt's papers."

Laurie spent the weekend floating on a cloud of elation. She worked for the newspaper she dearly loved. She'd be where all the news was assembled. She'd know about events before they hit the printed pages. She gathered some things she wanted in her niche at work and even Karl's drunken arrival late Saturday night didn't dampen her enthusiasm.

Lydia, delighted with Laurie's triumph, asked questions about the office to keep her daughter talking as she vicariously enjoyed the thrill Laurie felt. "This is a real opportunity for you, Laurie." She added in her sedate English, "Maybe you'll have an opportunity to write."

How well she knows me, thought Laurie. Maybe I will get to write. She suppressed the thought. First things first, she decided.

Monday morning dawned cold and misty, typical for March, but it didn't lessen Laurie's anticipation. She couldn't wait to get out of bed, and get ready for work. How wonderful that sounded. She had been so afraid to look for a job. Now she had one which seemed especially designed for her.

She carefully coiled her hair into the bun she wore now and settled her skirt over the white petticoat. Her buttoned shoes, polished to a high sheen, completed her outfit, and her image in the mirror satisfied her.

As she floated down the stairs, she couldn't feel the steps beneath her feet. Her mother already had the oatmeal ready for her as she came into the kitchen. "I'm so excited I can't eat," Laurie said nervously.

Lydia replied, "You need the nourishment, Laurie, so eat, and I have your lunch packed for you."

Laurie had decided to catch the streetcar because of all she had to carry. She pulled the stop cord as the car neared Colby. She gathered her parcels, arose from the seat and made her way down the aisle. After the car jerked to a stop, she held the rail as she descended.

She felt someone fall into step beside her as she walked down Wall Street. Looking up she saw a man in his twenties, a head taller than she, with freckles sprinkled across his nose. Startled, she started to protest as he took a couple of her bundles.

"Don't worry, we're going to the same place," he said with an easy smile. "You're the boss's new secretary and I'm Ben Davis, a reporter for the *Herald*." After he had completed last Friday's assignment, he had sidled up to Charlie's cage to find out about the girl that so intrigued him.

"I'm glad to meet you, Mr. Davis. This is my first day on the job. I hope I can please Mr. Hunt," Laurie said. Her eyes sparkled with enthusiasm.

"You will, Miss Krafft, and call me Ben. No one would know who you meant if you called me Mr. Davis," Ben said with a laugh. His easy manner diminished Laurie's nervousness.

"And please, call me Laurie," she said as they entered the door of the *Herald* office.

Ben plunked her parcels on her desk, and wheeled around. He said, "I'll see you later, Laurie. Nice to know you." That'll do for a start, he thought, just a start.

Two telephones perched on Laurie's desk and for a moment she wondered why and then recalled the two telephone companies in Everett. You couldn't call from one company's line to the other which made it necessary for a lot of businesses to have both. A mound of papers covered the top of her desk and Laurie's instinct told her they came from Mr. Hunt's office. A cursory look proved her to be right. She pushed them to one side as much as she could and put some of her personal things around to make the space her own.

She hung her coat on the rack in the alcove's corner and started to sort the mess overflowing her desk. She had to decide just how to file the papers for easy recovery. She became engrossed in her task and jumped when Mr. Hunt's office door slammed open and he shouted for her to get her pad and pencil to take his editorial.

"This is going to be a lot easier for me than scratching it out myself," he said with a satisfied chuckle. "If I go too fast, just stop me. I've never given dictation before."

After he completed his editorial about the lumber trust, he told Laurie to get Ben Davis for him, then type up the editorial. "What shall I do with it when it's done?" she asked.

"Let me read it then call for the copy boy to take it to the backshop," Mr. Hunt said impatiently.

She went into the lobby looking for Ben and found him in the newsroom where several reporters had phone receivers glued to their ears. Others wrote their stories. In the back corner of the room she saw Ben hunched over his desk in earnest concentration. As she threaded her way through the desks, she took a good look at him. He probably topped six feet. His cinnamon-colored hair showed flecks of red. It curled onto his forehead above his deep brown eyes. His square jaw gave him a look of strength and maybe denoted a touch of stubbornness.

He smiled as Laurie approached showing his even, white teeth. The smile lit his whole face and she responded with a smile of her own. "Mr. Hunt wants to see you now, Ben," she said.

"I'll be right there," Ben promised, surprised at the emotion this slip of a girl stirred in him.

Back at her desk, Laurie typed from her shorthand notes and when Ben came out of Mr. Hunt's office, she went in with her transcription. She stood uneasily as he read it. He scribbled a note or two on the page then told her to give it to the copy boy.

Again on a voyage of discovery, she asked the laconic Charlie where to find the copy boy. "Oh, I just saw Johnny go into the backshop," he drawled. "Just go down that hallway and you'll hear the linotypes."

Laurie strode down the hall with purpose toward the clanking she heard. She opened the door and asked, "Where's Johnny, the copy boy?"

"He's over by the presses," one of the printers told her and as she started in the direction the man pointed, she stopped in disbelief. She stared at the copy boy unable to speak. Just then he looked at her and grinned.

"Hi, Laurie, I haven't seen you for a couple of years," he said as he headed toward her. "You must be Mr. Hunt's new secretary. Everyone's talking about you."

He was the John Stevens she had dreamed about so often, dreams that filled her with giddiness when she gathered them to her. Finally able to speak, she said, "Here's Mr. Hunt's editorial, John. He said to give it to you. I'm so surprised to see you. I thought you had left town or something. You weren't in school that last year."

"We did leave town but we're back now. Let's eat lunch together and get caught up on old times," Johnny said, "and call me Johnny, everyone else does."

In a daze Laurie made her way back to her desk and tried to concentrate on the task before her but images of Johnny crowded into her head.

Mrs. Kirby asked, "Is he the one you wrote about in your journal?"
"Yes, the very same," Laurie said with a nostalgic smile.

CHAPTER 8

Laurie sensed the relief the other passengers felt when the train chugged into Leavenworth. They had made it out of the ever-deepening snow in the mountains.

She and Mrs. Kirby bought sandwiches from a passing vendor and settled down for the trip across the frozen plains of Eastern Washington.

"Did you see much of Johnny at the paper?" the frail lady asked Laurie.

"Yes, I did, and I got to know him much better. We had lunch together that first day."

Organizing the files engrossed Laurie until hunger finally forced itself into her awareness and the wall clock registered twelve-thirty. She had expected Johnny to come by sooner and wondered where he could be. Anxiously, she wanted to renew the friendship they once had. She wondered if he'd ever considered her in the same way she'd remembered him.

As if the thought prompted his arrival, she saw him stroll down the hall toward her. "Did you bring your lunch?" he asked. She nodded and he added, "Get it then, and I'll show you where to eat. We can talk while we eat," he grinned. He carried his lunch bag in his hand. He now topped her by a few inches but remained slim. His dark brown hair still refused to lie neatly against his head. His lips remained in a perpetual pout.

He ushered her into the lunchroom where past issues of the paper, scribbled notes, crumpled lunch bags, and spilled coffee cluttered the tables.

The two young people sat at the end of the back table and cleared a space for their lunches. "What did you do when you got out of school?" he asked as he bit into his sandwich.

"I went to business school. I took typing, shorthand and bookkeeping. The figures were hard but the rest was easy," Laurie replied. "What happened to you?"

"My folks moved over to Snohomish for awhile. Dad had a chance to go into business but it didn't work out so we came back to Everett about six months ago. We live out in the Beverly addition," he said. "My dad knows Mr. Hunt which helped me get this job. I really want to be a reporter but it takes time and this is a stepping stone."

Laurie felt his arm brush hers as he reached for another sandwich with a hand whose nails were bitten to the quick. A tremor in her throat made it difficult to speak. She cleared it and asked, "Do you see any of the kids we used to go to school with?"

"I've always meant to get out to Riverside but haven't made it yet," he answered casually. "How's your family? I bet Will is really a big kid now."

Laurie answered slowly as she folded her lunch bag, "Mother and Father are fine but Will was killed in an accident last December. He fell into the path of some fire horses. He didn't have a chance."

Johnny put his hand over hers and told her earnestly, "Hey, Laurie, I'm so sorry. I didn't know." His green eyes registered his sympathy.

Just then, Ben came into the lunchroom and spotted the two in the corner. He saw Johnny's hand over Laurie's and his welcoming smile turned grim as he turned and left the room. Again he couldn't understand the emotion this tall sylph engendered in him. I'm a sophisticated man, he thought, yet I feel like a dumb school kid.

The newest edition of the paper came out in mid-afternoon. Everyone stopped work and scanned the issue. The odor of ink filled Laurie's nostrils and she hoped this smell would always be part of her life. The excitement of being among the first to read the day's news thrilled her.

After work, she put on her coat, adjusted her hat, and picked up her bag to start for home. She felt good about what she had accomplished on her first day. As she stepped out into the half-light of the March dusk, Ben waited for her.

"I'll walk you to the streetcar," he said. "A young girl shouldn't be on the streets alone when it's getting dark. It's too risky with all the labor unrest and the ruffians in town. Known Johnny long?" he asked, a frown gathered between his eyes. He had never been jealous before. He had easily gotten the women he wanted and he'd never been concerned about their other amorous adventures.

"We went to school together in Riverside. He used to come over to our house once in awhile. We played games and talked," Laurie explained. "He wasn't in school the year I graduated and I didn't know what had happened to him so I was surprised to see him."

"Were you sweethearts?" asked Ben with intensity.

"No, just friends," she answered. A flush suffused her face. She wouldn't share her mental fantasies of John with anyone. Ben seemed relieved although Laurie noticed neither his intensity nor his relief.

"How long ago was that?" Ben asked.

"I finished school last May."

"You seem older than that, Laurie."

"It must be the influence of my English mother," Laurie said with a reflective smile on her face.

"She's from England?" Ben asked. He noticed her smile and knew some special bond existed between Laurie and her mother.

"Yes, although she won't talk about it. She always tells me to wait until I'm older."

The streetcar trundled to a stop and Ben said, "See you tomorrow," as he helped her board the car. His contemplation of Laurie deepened as he walked home. Completely preoccupied, he passed his house. He realized he'd gone by it, turned back, and ran up the stairs.

Lydia waited for Laurie at the door. "How did the first day go, Laurie?" she asked with an expectant catch in her voice.

"It was confusing, wonderful, exciting, and it's exactly where I want to be," Laurie said. "There's so much to do and it's all important. I love it. I was afraid to answer the phones at first but after the first few times I wasn't so scared."

Karl was late again. The two women sat down to eat together while his dinner kept warm on the kitchen stove. They had become used to the practice since Will's death. Saloon stops often interrupted Karl's homeward trip.

"I saw John Stevens today and we ate lunch together. He's a copy boy at the paper. He said his dad had a chance to go into business in Snohomish so that's why he wasn't in school that last year," said Laurie as she held her teacup between her hands. "They moved back about six months ago and live out in Beverly." Her mother sipped her tea and turned as she heard a sound at the door. Karl stumbled in the doorway. "Sorry, Lady Lydia," he mumbled. "I was so tired I had to stop and rest on the way home." The reek of beer that emanated from him told where he had rested.

After the dinner table had been cleared and Laurie had finished the dishes, she went up to her room. Coming to terms with Will's death and getting her job had dispelled the gloom that had resided there making it the haven it used to be.

She took off her clothes and put on her flannel nightgown and robe. She brushed out her hair. Her image in the mirror showed rosy cheeks as she thought about Johnny. She took out the journal Will had given her and began to write.

She leafed back through the hand-written pages to her entries about John. Her face felt hot when she read about the sensations he precipitated and her dreams about the future. Fate, she thought, that's what brought us together again.

Laurie eagerly went to work the next day and as she got off the car, Ben waited to walk her the two blocks to the office. "Have you been in the backshop yet?" he asked. He had decided that if he introduced her to the inner workings of the paper, it would cement a relationship between them.

"I went there to find Johnny but didn't have a chance to really look around," she answered. "It was all so confusing."

"If we have time today, I'll be your personal guide and show you what it's all about," he smiled as they walked into the lobby. He went to the left, and she went to the right after she greeted dour Charlie Shaefer.

She noticed more papers mounded on the top of her desk. Mr. Hunt must have cleaned out his desk drawers as well as the pigeonholes, she thought.

Laurie hung up her coat and unpinned her hat. She started to file the heap. Each piece of paper held fascination for her. It all dealt with news. There were bits about editorial ideas, facts about business, items dealing with breaking news, and references about story assignments.

Mr. Hunt came down the hallway toward his office, growled "Good morning" and gave her the mail to open. "Just open 'em and clip the envelopes to the letters then bring 'em in to me. By that time, I'll be ready to dictate my editorial."

After she finished the transcription of Mr. Hunt's editorial and received his approval, she looked for Johnny. She found him leaning over the desk of a girl in the classified ad department. The girl looked up at him as she fluttered her eyelashes. Laurie felt a real pang of jealousy and struggled to keep her face from showing her consternation.

"Here's Mr. Hunt's editorial, Johnny, please take it to the backshop to be set," she said more haughtily than she intended.

"Sure, Laurie. Have you met Jenny yet?" he asked. When she said she had not he introduced them. "Jenny Hunt, this is Laurie Krafft, an old schoolmate of mine. And Laurie, Jenny is Mr. Hunt's daughter. She's worked at the paper for quite awhile. She even used to hand-spike type before the paper got the linotypes."

"I'm pleased to meet you," said Laurie as warmly as she could under the circumstances, seething with jealousy underneath. Jenny's dark hair was pulled back into a bun with tendrils wisping around her alabaster face. Dark lashes shaded her pale blue eyes.

Jenny replied, "I'm glad to meet you, too. Papa told me you've already got him pretty well organized and he's delighted you can take his editorials. He hated writing them out in longhand."

Laurie felt a note of insincerity in Jenny's voice. As Laurie went back to her desk, Ben caught up with her.

"Is this a good time for the tour I promised?" he asked. "I have to go out on assignment pretty soon."

"Sure, I'd love to see it now," Laurie beamed a little too vehemently, her blue eyes snapping.

Ben guided her down the hall to the backshop. Holding her elbow sent an electric shock through him even though she pulled away at first. He'd done his share of touching many different women. His search for news took him from mansions to hovels, from the best clubs to the sleaziest saloons. None of those touches had jolted him like this one.

"Those three linotypes clanking away were installed when the newspaper moved into this building a couple of years ago. Before then the type was spiked by hand," he explained.

"What does 'spiking' mean?" Laurie asked. "Johnny said Jenny used to hand-spike type."

"The type was set letter by letter, space by space, by hand. The typesetters put them into a type stick. The letters were backwards so they would print forwards. There were big type boxes with slots for each letter and space. Each font, or type style, had its own type box. It was a very tedious job and after the paper was printed, the typesetters had to distribute the type they had used for that edition back into the proper boxes so they could be used again. There were a few women who did it along with the men," he continued in his best tour guide voice.

"Sitting next to the wall are the electric presses with the big double-feed Dispatch press," Ben went on as if he were a lecturing professor. Laurie tried to lodge it in her memory. There were so many strange sights and odors to absorb.

"There's a funny smell besides the ink," she said.

"That's the melting lead in the linotype hot pots," he explained. "In the corner is the new Miehle book press. It cost three thousand dollars and it's the latest word in job printing presses," he said proudly as if he were the one who invented the machine. "We do custom printing for different clients besides printing the daily paper. Charlie's in charge of that. And we have the Associated Press telegraphic news service so we can print current news from all over the world."

As she saw his enthusiasm surface, Laurie concluded that he was a true newsman. She watched him as he talked of all the elements in the backshop. He's really pretty handsome, too, she thought.

"Well, that's enough bragging for one day," Ben said, nearly shouting to make himself heard above the linotypes. They were getting the type ready for the day's paper.

Time flew by and the events of the first two days established a routine for those that followed. The phones continually punctuated Laurie's time and Ben assumed the role of companion, biding his time while he hoped for a deeper rapport.

Her mother, always anxious to hear what had happened during the day, lived the excitement of the newspaper through Laurie's experiences. Her quiet grief ebbed away and she was once more the warm, loving mother Laurie knew. Although Laurie had always talked to her mother, she still reserved her innermost fantasies. Now that she worked, she found it a little easier to share events and how she felt about them.

She told Lydia about Ben and Johnny.

"You seem more animated when you talk about Johnny but when you mention Ben, your words are matter-of-fact," Lydia said. "I know Johnny but what does Ben look like?"

"Oh, he's about six feet tall, not too thin and not too heavy. His wavy hair has sort of a red tinge to it. He has a few freckles," Laurie said. "He's in his twenties, I think, maybe twenty-three. That's pretty young for a reporter but he has a knack for it. He knows what's really news and gets excited about what he's working on."

"You'll have to ask him over for dinner soon so I can meet him," Lydia said.

Laurie agreed reluctantly and wondered why her mother suggested Ben instead of Johnny. She really didn't want anyone to see her father drunk, but maybe if she asked Karl to come straight home from work, it'd be all right.

Laurie finally invited Ben to dinner toward the end of March. She told her father they would have company for dinner at six and asked him to be on time. She tried to show an enthusiasm she didn't feel, afraid he wouldn't comply with her request.

The Friday of the dinner invitation, Ben walked her to the streetcar as usual and verified the directions to her house. He had a story to work on so he couldn't go with her. He promised to be there at six. He had never anticipated a dinner date this much. They'd be in a different setting and maybe she'd look at him a little differently.

As Laurie helped her mother get dinner, she chatted away amiably, with a hint of nervousness in her voice.

Lydia noticed it and made an effort to assure Laurie. "Don't worry about your father, dear, he promised to be home on time."

Laurie went up to her room to comb her hair again and before she came downstairs she heard the knock on the door. That has to be Ben, she thought, and Father's not home yet. She raced down the stairs and entered the dining room as Lydia opened the door.

"Hello, Ben, you found the way, I see," Laurie said. "Come in and let me take your coat. Oh, this is my mother, Mrs. Krafft. My father isn't home yet."

Ben saw Laurie's resemblance to her mother and thought them both lovely women. He could see where Laurie got her dignity and wonderful way of moving.

He handed Lydia a bouquet of roses. She glowed like a young girl as she looked for a vase in which to put them.

To Laurie he gave a small box of chocolates. "You shouldn't have, Ben," she said, pleased with his thoughtfulness.

"I have some tobacco for your father. I didn't know if he smoked a pipe or not," Ben said.

"No, he doesn't but he'll be pleased you brought him something, too."

After waiting until six-thirty, the three had dinner. "Maybe something detained your father," Lydia said to Laurie. "I'm sure he'll be home soon."

After dinner, the three sat around the table, the two women drinking tea, and Ben on his third cup of coffee. "I drink a lot of coffee," he said half apologetically. "It helps me keep awake when I'm on a late story. It's a habit."

Just then, the door burst open and Karl stood there in all his glorious drunkenness. "Meant to be home on time, Laurie honey, but I just couldn't make it. Somethin' came up," he slurred.

Laurie, indignant and ashamed, said with tight lips, "Ben, this is my father, Mr. Krafft. Father, this is Ben Davis. He's a reporter for the paper."

Ben held out his hand and said, "I'm pleased to meet you, Mr. Krafft."

Karl took the proffered hand and said, "I'm glad to meet you, too."

"Why don't you two young people go into the front room while I feed my husband," Lydia suggested, her compressed lips failing to conceal her exasperation.

Eager to get Ben away from the spectacle of her drunken father, Laurie led the way.

"What's wrong, Laurie, you seem upset?" Ben said easily.

"I hoped Father wouldn't get drunk tonight. I didn't want you to see him like that," Laurie said dejectedly as she smoothed her skirt.

"Don't worry about it, Laurie. He's probably got his reasons, and besides whether he's drunk or not doesn't change the kind of girl you are." He took her hand in his earnestness and felt it tremble. His own trembled as well at the touch.

"Thanks, Ben," she said on the verge of tears. "I hate drinking and what it does to people."

The clock chimed ten, interrupting their conversation and Ben had to leave. "Thanks for a great dinner and a delightful evening," he said cordially to Lydia and Karl. He went out onto the porch with Laurie. As he swung down the steps, he saw her shiver. "I'd like to keep you warm, Laurie," he said with an enigmatic smile and trotted down the street.

A gentle smile played across Mrs. Kirby's face. "It sounds as if romance were in the making," she said quietly.

"That and much more, Mrs. Kirby," Laurie responded. The despair she felt had been tempered by reviewing the circumstances that led up to her presence on this train.

CHAPTER 9

Laurie peered out of the train's grimy, frosty window. She asked herself if she would have done anything differently if she'd known what the future held. She had been confused then and confusion began to fill her again.

Mrs. Kirby urged her to continue the story. Laurie remembered the night she hovered between sleep and wakefulness fantasizing first about Johnny, then Ben. Their faces got confused in mid-dream.

With a start, she realized someone stirred in the kitchen. She heard the lids of the cook stove banged down and water running.

She looked at the clock on her night stand in the half light and saw it was only four o'clock in the morning. She donned her robe and went to find out what caused the commotion.

"Oh, good, Laurie, I was about to call you. It's Sally's time and I need you to help me," Lydia said. "Fix Will's bed so your father can sleep there. He's not going to work today."

Laurie gathered the bedding she would need and hurried upstairs. She stripped off the quilt and put flannel sheets on the bed then replaced the quilt. She was too busy to think of her brother who used to fill this room. A clean pillowcase finished her job upstairs.

On her way to see what else her mother wanted her to do, she stopped by her room to get dressed.

"I'll get your father upstairs, then you can remake our bed down here for Sally," Lydia said crisply. "We'll need a number of sheets so just take them into the bedroom, then go tell Sally she can come over. Keep the fire going and heat lots of water."

When Laurie knocked on the Jensons' door, Sally called for her to come in. She hadn't seen Sally for some time and didn't realize how big she had become. "Here, let me help you up," said Laurie as she went into the kitchen.

Sally took a deep breath and clutched the huge bulge of her stomach. Sweat broke out on her face. The spasm passed and she said, "I'm ready."

Laurie took both of her hands and pulled while Sally got her feet under her and laboriously arose. Laurie put Sally's coat around her shoulders and led her slowly over to the Krafft home. It seemed like they traveled inch by inch but they finally reached the front steps. They paused on each of the stairs until they reached the door.

"Good morning, Sally," Lydia said cheerily. "How long have you been having contractions?"

As Laurie lifted the coat from Sally's shoulders, the pregnant woman replied, "A couple of hours, I guess," she said distractedly. "They seem harder this time."

Lydia led her into the downstairs bedroom and helped her into the big four-poster bed. She had tied torn sheets to the two bottom posts for Sally to pull on when she felt the pains.

Each time the contractions came, Sally groaned and pulled on the sheet ropes. Lydia talked continually to keep Sally's mind off the pain. Lydia called to Laurie and asked her to continue the conversation while she collected the rest of the things she needed. This was the first time Laurie had been involved in the birth of a child and anxiety filled her. She hid it as best she could to encourage Sally.

As Lydia came back into the bedroom, she sent Laurie to stoke the fire again to keep the water hot. Laurie poked the last stick of wood into the fire box as she heard a tapping on the front door. She found Henry Jenson standing there with a cradle in his arms. He blushed as he handed it to her without a word. She thought his blush might be caused by the memory of their encounter in the hall on her sixteenth birthday. She had avoided him since.

She took the cradle, aloofly thanked him, and closed the door. She went into the bedroom to prepare the cradle for its precious cargo. A couple of hours passed and as the pains got stronger, Sally's groans grew louder.

"This is worse than ever before, Lydia," she moaned.

Lydia wiped the perspiration from Sally's brow and the trickle of blood from the corner of her mouth where she had bitten her lip. "It won't be long now, Sally, keep bearing down," she said calmly. Laurie could see why her mother was in such demand during times of crises. She remained so calm, supportive, and capable with her precise movements.

With an animal howl, Sally pushed with all her might as she clutched on the sheet ropes. Lydia said, "This is it, Laurie, push down with your hand just below her ribs." Lydia reached between Sally's legs and held the head of the baby as it pushed from the warm, moist place. She tied the cord in two places and used her sharp scissors to cut between them. She held the baby boy by his feet and swatted him firmly on his bottom. An angry squall rewarded her. "It's small for one of Sally's babies," she told Laurie.

"Why does Sally's stomach still bulge," Laurie asked her mother.

"It's the afterbirth. We have to deliver it, too," Lydia replied. She told Sally to bear down once more and asked Laurie to push where she had before.

Again, she reached between Sally's legs and waited, but what she delivered was not the afterbirth but another baby, this time a girl. With a cry of delight, she told Sally she was the mother of twins. Sally responded with a wan smile.

Laurie wiped Sally's face then hugged her in a rare show of exuberance. "The cradle Mr. Jenson brought over won't be big enough for two," she said.

Laurie helped her mother clean the twins and change the bedding so Sally could sleep. She had never held a newborn before and the experience filled her with wonderment. The baby was so small and so dependent. She touched the tiny fingers and the tiny toes. How does such a wee thing grow into an adult person, she asked herself? There are so many obstacles to overcome, it's a miracle any of us make it.

She shared her wonder with her mother as they sat at the kitchen table. The babies and their mother slept.

"Let's wait a few minutes before we go tell the Jensons," Lydia said with a satisfied sigh. "This is the first pair of twins I've delivered," she smiled, obviously thrilled with the event. "And they both seem to be very healthy. No wonder Sally was so big."

"Does it always feel like this?" Laurie asked. "Is it always so inspiring?"

"I've delivered a lot of babies and it never ceases to be a wondrous thing for me," Lydia answered. "Why don't you go up and take a nap now and then later I'll nap while you keep watch."

Laurie headed up the stairs to her room in an incredible euphoric state. She peeled off her dress and crawled under the covers in her petticoat. What a miracle she had witnessed. Thinking of a time she would be a mother, she drifted off to sleep.

While her mother slept, Laurie watched as Sally fed first one and then the other of her twins. Henry Jenson had come bringing a hastily-made cradle with him. Laurie watched him as he bent over his wife and kissed her cheek. He then knelt by his babies and the glow that suffused his face amazed Laurie. The man really loved his family. The new image of him started to replace the repugnant one Laurie had carried since their last encounter. Her mother was right, he was a good husband and father when he didn't drink. He hurried back to supervise his other three children.

Laurie took the sleeping baby girl from her improvised bed and held her close for awhile then put her in her newly-made cradle. She brought some food for Sally with plenty of milk. The new mother needed the nourishment. As Laurie removed the tray, Sally heaved a deep sigh and turned on her side. She was asleep in minutes. The births had sapped her strength.

As Karl worked in the backyard and Lydia still napped, Laurie washed the dishes. She heard a knock on the door. She wiped her hands on a towel and answered the summons as she pushed back her long hair which she hadn't had time to twist into a bun.

There stood Johnny, a rakish grin on his face. "I decided to visit the old neighborhood and thought you could walk along with me," he began as he stepped across the threshold. His breezy manner brought back her fantasies of him.

"It's good to see you Johnny, but I can't leave right now. Sally Jenson had twins here early this morning and Mother is sleeping now," Laurie said as a faint blush colored her face. She wished now she had put her hair up and put on a clean dress. "If you want to, why don't you sit down and I'll fix us some hot chocolate."

"That'll be great," Johnny said. "How many kids do the Jensons have now, anyway?"

"This will make five for them," Laurie said. "The twins are so cute, with dark hair, so small and cuddly."

"That's a bunch of kids to take care of," Johnny said. "They're such a bother. I don't know if I ever want to be a father. There are too many things I want to do. I wouldn't want to be tied down."

As the two chatted over their chocolate, Lydia came into the kitchen. "Well, hello, John, it's nice to see you again after all this time. After I check on Sally, why don't you two take a walk down to the river? The weather's balmy for this time of year and it may rain for the next forty days."

Johnny agreed so Laurie went to get her coat. They strolled along Everett Avenue and recalled who lived in which house. Laurie updated Johnny on all the people he used to know.

"Have you seen Gerald Banks lately?" he smirked, referring to the incident when she had given Gerald a kissing lesson.

She stiffened in consternation. Her cheeks flamed as she said, "A few times at business school."

They went down the bank to the river. Johnny offered a steadying hand for Laurie. His touch reminded her of how his arm had felt around her shoulders. The incoming tide covered the mud. They found a log that wasn't too dirty or damp and looked at the Cascade range across the lowlands. The sun tinted the snow-covered tops a vibrant pink as it began to set, a truly majestic sight.

Johnny put his arm around Laurie and all the fantasies she had stored about him bubbled to the surface. She leaned into him and he turned her head toward him as he kissed her lips. It was a gentle, warm kiss like all her novels described. He got more aggressive and kissed her harder and started to fumble with her coat buttons impatiently.

She wrenched herself away and straightened her garments, reminded of her hallway encounter with Mr. Jenson. Her eyes were moist as she got up.

"Hey, I'm sorry Laurie," Johnny said as he arose. "I don't know what got into me. You're just so darn pretty and I got carried away. Maybe I wanted a kissing lesson, too. Forgive me?"

Laurie paused then said, "Of course, Johnny. You took me by surprise. I remembered a very bad incident I had last year. Let's forget it. And I'd like to forget the kissing lesson, too." But she didn't forget the warmth she felt after his first kiss.

After they reached the house, Laurie turned and asked, "Do you want to come in?"

He replied, "I have to get home. I'll see you at work Monday."

She stopped in the bedroom to see her mother and Sally with her twins. The reverence she felt at their birth had not diminished at all even when she recalled Johnny's words about not wanting children.

Up in her room, she dug out her journal and recorded the momentous events of the day. She leafed back through other entries. She found her references to Johnny and how she had felt then. She also discovered the passage written when her mother said she needed to talk to her. That talk had never taken place. Laurie made a mental note to ask about it.

Her dreams that night were all of Johnny.

Mrs. Kirby straightened her back, fumbled with her hair and said, "What a remarkable experience you had helping with the birth of twins. Not many women have done that." She patted Laurie's hand and added, "I'm surprised you dreamed of Johnny, though, the way he treated you."

"It took me awhile to see him as he really was. The years of dreaming had a strong hold on me."

CHAPTER 10

The snow continued to fall, mounding up beside the rails. It contrasted to the unusually calm weather of that April Laurie remembered so well.

She had stepped out of the house to catch the streetcar. The whole world held its breath as if it waited. It wasn't sunny, nor was it raining.

As she left the car at Colby, she wondered why Ben didn't meet her. This was the first time he hadn't waited on the corner for her and she had a vague feeling of alarm. Maybe she had taken him for granted.

As she hastened into the lobby of the *Herald*, the whole place was in an uproar. She saw Johnny run down to the backshop with papers in his hand and Ben hurried toward her. "I'm sorry I didn't meet you, Laurie, but I couldn't leave. Mr. Hunt wants to see you right away with your notebook." He turned on his heel as she hurried toward her desk. Even experiencing suppressed excitement, she felt hurt by Ben's off-hand manner.

She hung her coat and hat on the hook, grabbed her pad and pencil, and knocked briefly on Mr. Hunt's open door.

"Come on in, Laurie," he said.

She'd never seen him so keyed up before, like a bundle of energy waiting to explode. His sparse hair stood on end as he ran his fingers through it. His coat was draped across a chair and his tie hung askew. He clamped an unlit cigar in the corner of his mouth.

I wonder if he's given up smoking or if he just forgot to light it, Laurie pondered. "What's happened, Mr. Hunt?" she asked absorbing his exhilaration.

"There was a terrible earthquake in San Francisco early this morning," he answered. "The news coming across the wire gets worse with every transmission; people killed, burning buildings."

He paused to take a breath then told her, "Go find Ben and have him dictate the events coming across the telegraphic wire. Transcribe them as soon as possible for today's edition of the paper."

She found Ben in the newsroom with other reporters and staff members who could leave their work. Everyone huddled around the wire service.

"Oh, good, you're here," said Ben intensely without a hint of his usual warmth. "Mr. Hunt said I was to dictate to you from the wire so you could transcribe it. It'll be faster that way."

Those gathered around made way for her and she sat in a ladder-back chair as she readied her pad and pencil. The fragmented reports came out of Oakland across the bay from San Francisco. All other sources of information in the city itself had been cut.

Ben began, "The greatest calamity has overtaken the city of San Francisco. This morning at five-thirteen a.m., a tremendous earthquake rocked the city by the Golden Gate for forty-seven seconds. Several aftershocks occurred immediately following the initial quake and fires have broken out all over the city from overturned stoves and gas lamps, broken electric wires, and exploding gas mains."

Ben took a deep breath and asked, "Am I going too fast?"

Just as excited as he, she said "No."

He continued, "Details are meager but it's reported that hundreds have been killed and thousands injured. Fires are burning out of control. The water mains have been disrupted. There was no wind or fog when the quake shook San Francisco to its core. San Franciscans arriving in Oakland say it began with a low roar and grew in volume until it ended in a crescendo of noise."

He continued in the same earnest manner until everything they had been told was dictated. "As further details become available, they will be published in the *Everett Daily Herald*," Ben concluded. "Get that typed up as soon as possible, Laurie, so we can go to press with it."

She had never seen this side of him. His easy-going manner had given way to intense concentration. No wonder he's such a good newsman, Laurie thought. The story he's on is the most important thing to him. It's as if he's forgotten everything else in the world.

She hated to leave the press room because she didn't want to miss anything but she did as she was told. As she got to her desk, Mr. Hunt came out of his office and asked what she'd heard, still chomping on his unlit cigar. His tie had been completely removed and his sleeves rolled up. Laurie gave him a quick preview of the news release and started to type the copy. Mr. Hunt said, "I'm going to the press room to keep track of things. Bring the copy to me as soon as it's done."

After Laurie finished typing, she rushed to the press room to show the copy to Mr. Hunt. As he read it, she listened to the reporters talk. One said, "It's strange we haven't heard from the three big newspapers down there. I guess they have no electricity or wire service available." Another said, "We'll hear more and more as reporters get into the city."

"I just got off the phone," Ben said. "No one's allowed into San Francisco, not even reporters. I talked to one at the *Oakland Tribune* and he said Pier Three had crashed into the bay and that the Ferry Building tower whipped back and forth like a straw in the wind. He's talked to people who just came from there. They said the damage was worse on the fill ground. And the retaining walls didn't keep houses and yards from sliding down the hills. Whole fronts of apartment houses were pulled away."

Completely involved, Laurie had missed Alice Galbraith standing in the newsroom. Alice came up to her and said, "Laurie, I see you've become a part of the newspaper."

"Hello, Alice. Everything is so jumbled, I didn't see you," Laurie said and wondered about her presence. She saw Alice laid an affectionate hand on the arm of an older reporter, Aaron Fields. I'll have to find out about that, Laurie decided.

"Let's have lunch next week," Alice said before she left for her teaching job.

The entire staff nervously waited for more news, every report worse than the one before. Laurie took the news release from Mr. Hunt and looked for Johnny to take it to the backshop. She saw him talking to Jenny with great animation. His arms waved around as he described what he had heard in the press room. A few dark curls escaped Jenny's pompadour as she listened intently to him. Although a few years older than Johnny, she looked the same age. Even in the heat of the breaking news, Laurie felt again the pangs of jealousy. She wondered if he'd kissed her?

He turned and saw her looking at him. "Hi, Laurie, it's exciting, isn't it? I'd sure like to be down there and get the story first hand."

"Don't say that, Johnny, lots of people are dead and the fires are raging out of control," Laurie said in alarm. "Here's the story for the typesetters. Mr. Hunt wants it done right away."

After the presses started to roll, everyone gathered in the press room to talk, all semblance of a regular routine forgotten as they eagerly awaited further news of the disaster. When nothing came across the wire, they talked about the terrible events and recalled other calamities they had reported.

Laurie went back to her desk to get other work done, but found she just couldn't settle down. The phones rang incessantly. She finally escaped again to the press room with the others. After school, the newsboys added to the frantic activity. They were anxious to get their papers and spread the news of the earthquake.

Toward the end of the day Johnny came in and leaned nonchalantly against the wall next to Laurie. He asked in an undertone, "Would you like to go on a picnic this Saturday? I promise I won't try to get fresh with you again. If you hadn't looked so pretty I wouldn't have tried the last time." He grinned with a leer. "Do I need a kissing lesson like Gerald Banks?"

"No, you don't," she said as she turned red. "I'd like to go on a picnic with you, Johnny, but I'm going to work Saturday to help organize the wrap on the earthquake. What about the next Saturday? I'll pack the lunch." She was afraid if she turned him down, he'd not ask her again.

A little sulkily, Johnny said that was okay and he'd talk to her later. With his attitude, Laurie was glad she hadn't told him she'd be working with Ben. She feared he'd think she had some special attachment to the reporter.

Exhaustion filled everyone by quitting time. As Ben escorted Laurie to the streetcar, he became again the relaxed companion she knew. Recalling his forcefulness and how he commanded the attention of others stimulated her imagination and she remembered Alice in the press room.

She asked, "Why was Alice in the newsroom?"

"She's engaged to Aaron and I guess she wanted to be in on the excitement with him," he answered. "They've been going together for some time but they keep putting off the wedding date."

The next two days went by at a feverish pitch as more and more news reports came through. Ben dictated the facts to Laurie. She thought it the next best thing to being a reporter herself.

Ben's dictation continued. "San Francisco's five hundred and five firemen are scattered throughout the city beyond communication with each other. The screams of wounded horses mingle with those of trapped humans.

"Looting is unrestrained in the city and looters are being shot or hanged on the spot. Wild activity is seen as the fire approaches. Temporary hospitals have been established. Extortion is rampant. A five-cent loaf of bread now costs a dollar and a dozen eggs sells for five dollars." Ben shook his head in disgust as he dictated that information.

"It's so terrible, Ben," Laurie said. "I just can't imagine what it's like down there."

As the week wound down, Laurie felt drained. She wondered how reporters could sustain such fervor. A good night's sleep should replenish her energy for the next day's extra work with Ben.

As Laurie pushed open the newspaper's lobby door on Saturday, Ben walked down the hall toward her. His welcoming smile showed he anticipated their day together. She found she also looked forward to it. Although a few others worked in the office, the two of them seemed to be in a world of their own.

"I'm glad you agreed to work with me today, Laurie," Ben said. He hoped the day together would bind their relationship even closer.

"I wouldn't miss it for the world," she replied. She suddenly realized that being with Ben intrigued her as much as working on the story.

After they had completed their comprehensive work, Ben asked, "Would you like to walk down to the bay? The weather's mild."

"Sure, Ben. I love to sit and watch the water."

They took deep breaths of the April air as they stepped out of the door. From the crest of the hill on Hewitt, they stood and looked at the sun lowering across Port Gardner Bay. The snow-capped Olympic Mountains pierced the pale blue sky and dollops of white clouds hovered above them. The sight of the lumber ships at the mill wharfs sparked again the feeling of expectation in Laurie, the hint of something to come but she no longer felt the restlessness that had plagued her so often.

Ben saw her wrap her arms around herself. "What's the matter, Laurie?"

"I always feel like something special is going to happen to me when I see the horizon and the ships loading for other ports. I don't know when or what, but it'll be special," she said dreamily.

The two linked arms after Laurie had pulled away at first. They strolled on down the hill and drank in the salty breeze that lifted from the water. A fight broke out in front of the Marion Building and they quickly crossed the street to avoid it. Men poured out of the saloon to watch and encourage the fighters. It scared and disgusted Laurie. Ben felt her quiver. "What's wrong, Laurie?" he asked with concern.

"I hate fighting almost as much as I hate drinking. It terrifies me," she said in a choked voice. Ben held her arm a little tighter.

As they reached the docks, they found a place to sit and relax. Ben put his arm around Laurie's shoulders and she was startled to realize it evoked an exciting tingle in her. She had thought Johnny the only one capable of making her feel that way.

Laurie removed her hat and shook her hair loose. She wanted to feel free. The gentle wind stirred her long, honey tresses. She turned to look at Ben and found him gazing at her with yearning. It had replaced his easy manner. She wondered if she imagined what she saw.

Ben had tried to hide his feelings afraid he would scare her away but after the intimacy they had shared all week, his resolve shattered like a fragile teacup dropped on the floor.

He towered over her even while they sat. He leaned down, cupped her chin in his hand, and said, "You're beautiful, Laurie. Don't ever change that young breathless feeling you try to hide with your dignity." He kissed her lightly on the lips and released her chin.

She could feel his constraint and experienced slight disappointment. What's happening to me, she wondered? Johnny had always been her secret love.

Ben got up from the wooden beam where they had lounged and stretched his long frame. The April breeze tousled his cinnamon hair as he pulled Laurie to her feet. She fell into his arms and he held her tightly for a moment before he released her. "I'll walk you to the streetcar," he said quietly.

Silently, hand in hand, they strolled up Hewitt, both filled with emotions they couldn't share although each knew the other approached a new depth of feeling.

As she went up to her room that night, Laurie felt too tired to sort out her feelings. What she had felt didn't seem to be valid any longer. She wrote down her confused thoughts. Later while she brushed her hair, she looked to see if she were truly beautiful or if Ben looked at her with different eyes.

Mrs. Kirby noticed the glint of tears in Laurie's eyes. "For some reason, it pains you to think of Ben, doesn't it, dear?" she asked gently.

"Yes, it does," Laurie answered with a sign. "There's a lot more to the story, though, some of it very painful." She settled into her seat, closed her eyes, and remembered.

CHAPTER 11

As Laurie sat with pencil poised above her pad, Mr. Hunt shuffled through some of his notes. It was that time of a February morning which hovered between darkness and daylight. The rain clouds shrouded the sky and filtered what little light came through the big window in the editor's office.

Mr. Hunt, who had stopped smoking but still clutched a cigar between his teeth, removed the brown shaft from his mouth and started to dictate his editorial.

"The role of a woman in our society has always been one of nurturing her husband and her children. In turn, she is protected and cherished by him. He makes the decisions that are best for her so it's really not in the public good for women to have the vote. They are neither worldly nor informed about national and state issues.

"The current movement for women's suffrage began in the latter half of the last century...."

As his words continued, Laurie got angrier and angrier. How dare he assume that women were not qualified to vote. Laurie's pencil scratched across her pad and the sound got louder as she pressed harder and harder.

Feeling her agitation, Mr. Hunt looked back at her from the window where he stood. "What's wrong, Laurie? Am I going too fast for you?" he asked solicitously.

He saw her clenched jaw and the color that rose into her cheeks. "Oh, I see. You don't agree with me," he said. With a calculated gleam in his pale gray eyes, he asked, "How do you feel?"

She exploded. The words tripped over themselves as they fell from her lips. "Women are perfectly able to make their own decisions about national issues and state issues too," she said vehemently. "By 1870, four states already recognized the value of women and had given them the right to determine their own destinies. I'm surprised a well-informed man like you would say such things, and in print, too. You men are afraid if women get the vote, they'll vote to prohibit the sale of alcohol, and that really wouldn't be a bad idea."

"Write it," directed Mr. Hunt when she stopped to take a breath.

"What do you mean?" asked Laurie, afraid to believe what he said.

"I said 'write it'," replied Mr. Hunt. "You write what you think. If it's good enough, I'll put it on the editorial page next to my column, and I'll give you a byline."

"Oh, I can't do that. The only things I've ever written are in my journal at home," said Laurie. She wished she dared be brave enough to write for others to read.

"Try," Mr. Hunt told her and turned his back. "It won't be so different from putting your thoughts into a journal. Just tell how you feel about the right of women to vote. If you really believe what you say, you can do it. If you don't, forget it," he said tersely as he turned his back to her.

She angrily typed Mr. Hunt's editorial and called for Johnny to take it to the backshop. She shut out the office turmoil and began her article.

She wrote, "Equality is what women's suffrage is all about. Women have worked alongside men from the very beginning of our nation. They've suffered the same deprivations, the same heartaches, the same challenges as men who have always had the right to self-determination. In this year of 1907 it's time for women to be granted the same privilege."

The words poured out onto the typed page and the more involved with her subject she became, the more eloquent she grew. Her caged emotions, released from the tightly-laced corset of her gender, grew into a fierce zeal which possessed her thoughts and hands. Never before had she laid open her private feelings to anyone other than her mother with such vehemence.

When she read her piece, she signed it with a flourish and took it in for Mr. Hunt to read. Even though only in her late teens, her insatiable appetite for reading all sorts of books, papers and magazines had given her the background she drew upon for her article.

Mr. Hunt ran his fingers through his hair and seemed engrossed in what she had written. When he finished, he looked up at her with a speculative glance, and said, "You really do feel strongly about this, don't you?" He didn't wait for an answer to his rhetorical question. He signed the paper with the direction to the typesetters to set it as a sidebar to his editorial and to give Laurie Krafft a byline on it.

With her passion spent, Laurie relaxed, and as she carried the column to the backshop herself, she strode with assurance and pride.

Johnny tried to talk to her but she kept walking. "What's happening, Laurie?" he asked with a puzzled look on his face. His dark hair added a question mark on his forehead.

She didn't reply but elevated her head a notch.

Ben looked out of the newsroom as Laurie went by. He saw the carriage of her head, her purposeful movement and the paper in her hand. He knew the look of someone who has written something special. "Is it going to be published?" he asked with a grin on his face and a twinkle in the deep brown pools of his eyes.

Without a word, Laurie turned and smiled at him. Dispassionately she had told him often during the past six months how she felt about the role of women today. He shared her feeling and even without a reply from her, Ben knew what the article concerned. Mr. Hunt had told them in their editorial meeting what his subject would be for the day's paper.

After she had given the column to one of the linotype operators, she went back to her desk to carry on with her regular work. She felt drained, actually very tired. She really didn't want to eat her lunch with Johnny. She went out to tell him she'd have to eat at her desk.

The desire to be alone was not unusual for Laurie, but there seemed so little time these days to find enough moments together for that. Her job took most of every weekday and she saw Johnny and Ben intermittently on weekends. She spent the rest of her hours at home helping her mother and when she could, she'd go over to Sally Jenson's to cuddle the twins. She loved watching the precious babies grow and learn.

Her mind arched back through the last several months as she dawdled at her desk. Sally seemed grateful for her visits because they relieved her for a while so she could sit and rest. With five children her flea-hopping became a necessity instead of a character trait. With a fuller understanding of Henry Jenson, Laurie came to terms with the dreadful memories he used to evoke.

Her father didn't talk much about the mills but Henry did. Right after the earthquake, the shingle and lumber mills flourished. Added shifts produced more lumber to help San Francisco rebuild. The mills paid no duty on reconstruction materials going into the city and the stock exchange had pledged eighty-five thousand dollars in twenty minutes on that fateful day in April, to help San Francisco rise again. The national government poured funds into the rebuilding, too.

He told her as the new year began that the market would probably be glutted because every lumber mill on the west coast did what Everett did. His deep depression showed when he talked about it. Laurie sensed his concern for his family's future.

She still couldn't sort out her feelings for Johnny and Ben. One minute she remembered the love she felt for her former schoolmate, and the next she contemplated the way Ben's hair glowed in the sunlight and the depth of feeling in his brown eyes.

Johnny didn't seem to be aware that Laurie saw Ben outside of work. She had an instinct that told her if he did, he would do something rash, like dashing off with another girl. She didn't think she could handle it after so many years of dreaming. Her jealousy lurked just beneath the surface, a trait she couldn't purge from herself.

The two sides of Ben never ceased to intrigue her, his intensity as a reporter on one side and his warm, easy manner on the other when the corners of his mouth twitched in private humor and a glint of amusement twinkled in his eyes.

She recalled last year's Christmas, the memory of Will not too far from the surface. Her family didn't plan a big celebration but at different times on Christmas Eve, Johnny and Ben dropped by. She hadn't thought to get either a gift but they each had something for her. Johnny gave her a name plaque for her desk, and Ben presented her with a cameo to pin at the neck of her blouse.

Laurie, thrilled with both, found the thought of Johnny's gift tarnished when she found he had given a plaque to Jenny Hunt as well. Maybe that's why she accepted a date with Ben for New Year's Eve.

She had agreed to go on the spur of the moment then realized she didn't know what awaited her or what to wear.

"How fancy is this ball?" she had asked Ben a day or two after his invitation.

"Pretty high-toned," he smiled.

"I haven't anything to wear," she wailed.

Ben laughed. "You women have said that since you first came out of the cave."

She stamped her foot in consternation. "It's true, Ben, I can't go. And I won't go if you laugh at me."

"I was teasing you, Laurie." Ben sobered. "A simple ball gown would be fine. With your mother's expertise with a needle, she could whip up something appropriate."

Her mother made a long, flowing dress for her to wear to the elaborate affair. Laurie didn't ask where the money had come from but she knew the sugar bowl still received a few coins every week and she contributed her share.

The dress, the blue of a summer twilight sky, mirrored her eyes. An egret's white plume anchored her pompadour. And at her throat, she wore the cameo Ben had given her.

Dressed in a dark suit, white shirt, and tie, Ben's impeccable grooming delighted Laurie, another new aspect of him. His formal attire fostered a formal attitude. He called for her in a horse-drawn carriage and handed her into it with aplomb.

They swayed in gentle rhythm with the trotting horses as they headed toward the Hotel Tower on the corner of Hewitt and Rucker where the ball had already begun. Laurie's nervousness about meeting all the socialites at the party didn't diminish her thrill in going. Someday she'd be one of them.

Ben had told her some of the personages who'd be present. It sounded like a Who's Who list for Everett.

She had practiced dancing in her room and in the kitchen with her mother. When she slipped into Ben's arms for the first dance, she knew she needn't have worried. His natural grace blended with hers and they danced nearly every dance. Because of her high color, her dignity, poise, and grace, many eyes followed her as she circled the floor with Ben.

It was pretty heady stuff for a girl raised in Riverside whose father was a drunkard, and who worked to help eke out the family income. Someday I'll be here because of who I am and not because someone brought me, she swore. She noticed how all of the people nodded and spoke to Ben. She knew he couldn't have done stories about all of them.

Laurie detected that several young women acted as if they had a more intimate knowledge of Ben than she. Their knowing glances prompted her jealousy. Now I'm jealous of Ben, she thought. Will I ever be free of it?

Ben loved holding Laurie in his arms. He basked in the envious stares of other men. He shielded her from them and hoped she didn't realize what an impact she had on the opposite sex.

He wrapped his arms around her in a more proprietary manner as bells rang and shots sounded to usher in the new year. His passionate kiss was that of a lover. Laurie responded just as passionately.

As she still pondered at her desk, she recalled nothing had been said since about the New Year's kiss but it lay between them like an intimate treasure. Laurie knew when Ben looked at her with that certain glint in his eyes that he thought of it too.

Laurie remembered the several lunches she and Alice had enjoyed together during the year. Alice told her about Ben. He had been the only child of parents killed in a boating accident on Puget Sound. His great-aunt Maud had raised him strictly and encouraged him to read and write. An Everett pioneer, she moved in its social circles.

So that's why Ben knew everyone at the New Year's Eve dance, Laurie had concluded, he was raised among their ranks.

Alice and Aaron had set their wedding day for May. She asked Laurie to be her maid of honor, her only attendant at the small wedding. Aaron chose Ben as his best man.

Laurie emerged from her reverie when she heard the presses start to rumble. Soon she would see her name in print. Excitement and apprehension did battle inside her. What if no one agreed with her? What if she hadn't written it well enough? Would her mother be ashamed of her?

"So that's what you were doing," said Johnny as he brought the new edition to her and to Mr. Hunt. He seemed to be a little out of sorts. Maybe seeing her name in a byline before he had been able to launch his journalistic career caused resentment. All he had done were a few obituaries and meeting notices, none with his name attached.

There it is; Laurie Krafft. She caught her breath and her stomach churned. With her passion cooled, she wondered if she had said anything in the heat of the moment she might regret. She read it through and it reflected her feelings perfectly. Mr. Hunt came out of his office and said, "You did all right, girl. We'll wait and see what kind of a response you get."

She hurried home to share the news with her mother. Before she even took off her hat, she launched into a tale of the day's events.

Her father lumbered out of the front room, and asked with a slur, "What's goin' on?"

"Laurie's written an article for the paper and it was printed," Lydia said proudly.

"Oh, is that all," Karl said and went back to lie on the couch. He had said he was too sick to go to work that day.

Laurie could hardly hold still while her mother read what she had written. With bated breath she watched Lydia's face as she scanned the article.

"Oh, Laurie, I'm so proud of you. I know you write in your journal all the time but I didn't know you had this kind of talent," she said as she got up and threw her arms about her daughter. "Your secret wish has come true, and the written word is so powerful. Writing will give you power, too."

No matter what anyone else might say, the support from her mother would sustain her. As she hung up her skirt and waist on her clothes rack, she hugged this new feeling to her, a feeling of having contributed to a cause, of making a difference. How fulfilling!

She hoped this was a beginning and not a once-in-a-lifetime experience. She drifted off to sleep.

CHAPTER 12

❀

"So you finally got to write," Mrs. Kirby mused. "How did the readers react to your article, my dear?"

"Oh, even before I took off my hat and coat, the phones rang," Laurie continued her story.

The first caller, a man, launched into a diatribe against women voting, his anger palpable as his voice increased in volume.

The attack startled Laurie at first, and then hurt her. Even if he disagreed with her he had no right to talk to her like that. Her old fear of violence surfaced and she started to shake. As she hung up the phone, tears trembled in her eyes and fell as Mr. Hunt came down the hall. He took off his black bowler and told her to come into his office.

He told her to ignore the ringing phones. "I want to talk to you." He put a fresh cigar into the corner of his mouth and asked, "Now what did you hear over the phone that upset you so?"

Laurie twisted her hands together as she stood in front of Mr. Hunt.

"Sit down, girl, and tell me," he urged.

She did as she was bid, and tried to control her voice and her weeping. She told him of the angry caller who had read her article.

"That's all right, Laurie, it happens in the news game all the time. No matter what you write, someone disagrees with you, and that's their privilege. If you really believe what you write, then you have to be prepared for the brickbats as well as the bouquets. You can't let yourself be too vulnerable to that kind of harassment," Mr. Hunt said earnestly. "I'll get just as much abuse for taking the other stand, just wait and see. And you wrote well."

Clumsily, he arose from his swivel chair, and laid his arm across Laurie's shoulders as he comforted her.

She gave a big sigh that ended in a sob, and said, "Thank you, Mr. Hunt. I'll learn. It'll take a while, but I'll do it, that is if you let me write again."

He didn't reply.

When she got back to her desk, the phones continued to ring and she learned the truth of what Mr. Hunt had said. Some, mostly women, thought what she had written was outstanding and so true. They balanced what those who disagreed with her said. Some of her opponents' remarks were said pleasantly even though they thought her wrong.

A mound of letters filled Laurie's desk when she got to work the following day. She started to sort them and open the ones for Mr. Hunt. With surprise she saw that some of them were addressed to her. Not knowing if she should give them to Mr. Hunt, she knocked on his door.

He growled his usual "Come in" and asked what she wanted.

"There are some letters here addressed to me and I don't know if you want to read them or not," she said with a question in her voice.

"After you read 'em, let me see 'em," he answered.

As she read them, she realized they reflected the same opinions as the phone calls. Some agreed with her, and the same number disagreed. As long as she got some support she could manage writing for the public. She hoped Mr. Hunt would give her another assignment.

In the lunchroom, staff members dropped by their table as she and Johnny talked between bites. Here again, the opinion of her article was divided, but no one had said she didn't write well. That sustained her through the controversy and she began to enjoy the attention.

Laurie sensed Johnny suspected something special existed between her and Ben who had just come into the lunch room. Laurie saw a calculating look come into Johnny's eye as he laid a proprietary hand on her arm. She looked into his eyes. Ben saw Johnny's possessive manner and the way Laurie gazed at him. He turned abruptly and left the room. Laurie caught a glimpse of his retreating back. Johnny's smug smile baffled her.

As Ben entered the hallway of the house where he lived with his great-aunt Maud, he took off the coat he wore to work, and donned the shabby sweater with the leather patches on the elbows. The frayed cuffs barely reached his wrists but putting the sweater on was like shrugging into a pair of comfortable slippers.

Aunt Maud held his hand for a moment as he kissed her waxen cheek. Her habitual black attire emphasized her transparent skin where the blue veins showed through the flesh. She always held herself erect even though she was in her seventies.

Ben opened the newspaper to read before dinner but the lunchroom scene filled his mind.

"What's wrong, Ben, dear?" his aunt asked.

"There's nothing wrong, Aunt Maud," Ben answered as lightly as he could. "Why?"

"You've been reading the same page upside down for the last half hour," his aunt said, with a hint of humor in her dry tone.

He rose from his chair and settled on the floor at her feet as he used to as a youngster. He had been seven when his parents drowned leaving Aunt Maud as his only living relative. He had thought many times how difficult it must have been for a maiden lady to assume the raising of a young boy.

He did not want for anything because his parents had left a trust fund for him. Aunt Maud had been strict but fair. She saw to it that he was brought up in the Davis tradition but allowed him room to grow.

The stately old house on Rucker had been both a refuge and a steadying influence on the boy as he grew to manhood. In his solitary life, he became friends with many people living in the books of his aunt's large library. As he grew older, there was no doubt he wanted to write. The focus of his writing had to be current news. That's where he felt excitement.

Ben leaned against Maud's knees, and began to unburden himself. "I'm in love with a girl who loves someone else," he began. "I fell for her the first time I saw her when she came to apply for a job at the paper. I've told you a little about her. She's Laurie Krafft. She's the one who wrote the article about women's suffrage."

"Quite right," Maud murmured.

Drawing a deep breath, he continued, "At first, she'd jerk away when I tried to hold her arm. She seemed disturbed by my touch. Then she grew comfortable with me and we've had some good times together. She was beautiful at the New Year's Eve dance and everyone envied me. I really felt proud, and when I kissed her, I could feel her respond. I thought we were getting closer but now she seems to be under Johnny Stevens's spell. They were schoolmates."

"What makes you think she's under Johnny's spell?" Maud asked quietly, trying to get at the crux of the problem.

"Whenever I see them together, he's holding her hand or gazing into her eyes, and she seems to glow," Ben said with a sigh.

"Why don't you talk to her about your feelings?" countered Maud.

"I don't want to rush her," said Ben, "especially if she has eyes only for Johnny. I keep hoping time will change things. She's got some powerful feelings against drinking and fighting, too," he added. "She's only eighteen but she seems older. Her father drinks too much but her English mother is a real lady. She reminds me of you."

"Why, thank you, Ben, that's quite a compliment," his aunt said. "Why don't you invite Laurie for dinner next week and let me get acquainted with her?"

Ben got up on his knees and put his arms around Maud. "I know it's no secret to you I've had lots of women friends," he said wryly. "None of them affected me like Laurie does. Thanks, Aunt Maud."

The lovely old home where Ben and his aunt lived impressed Laurie. The house, sided with dark brown shingles, had white pillars and window moldings. The deep porch gave the house graciousness, and as the two walked across it, the door opened and there stood Maud.

"Welcome to our home, my dear," said Maud with dignified cordiality.

Laurie was awed by the tall, stately woman in her bejeweled black dress with the high neck. She sensed the strength in the woman even though her countenance seemed frail. Maud's hair was now silver but Laurie could see how she must have looked when it was the color of Ben's. She's still a striking woman, decided Laurie.

"Laurie, this is my great-aunt Maud," Ben said with pride, circling his aunt's shoulders with his arm. "She's been wanting to meet you."

"I'm glad to meet you, Miss Davis," Laurie said as she bobbed her head once in deference. She had been apprehensive about meeting the older woman because of Maud's inherited wealth and her place in Ben's life.

"Don't stand on ceremony, my dear. Call me Maud, please," said the gracious lady with a flip of her blue-veined hand.

Laurie saw that the modest entry hall gave a feeling of affluence and permanence. Dark polished wood paneling reflected the light from the chandelier. To the right of the door stood the mirrored coat rack. A holder in the corner held the umbrellas needed in this rainy climate. The broad stairway to the upper floor rose majestically from the end of the entry.

When Ben saw her look at the banister, he laughed, "I polished that many times with the seat of my pants."

Maud led the way into the parlor. The quiet magnificence of its decor astounded Laurie. It was comfortable and rich, not garish like the Baker mansion. Maud settled into the upholstered rocking chair that fit her form exactly, and Ben ushered Laurie to a seat on the sofa across from his aunt. He asked Laurie if she'd like a glass of wine before dinner.

"No" she said abruptly, and then followed it with a polite "Thank you."

I shouldn't have asked her, Ben thought, I know how she feels about alcohol, but hindsight doesn't help much.

"Tell me about your family, dear," Aunt Maud said as she attempted to put the girl at ease.

"My mother is a seamstress and my father works at the Clough-Hartley mill," Laurie said nervously.

"I read the article you wrote about women having the vote," Maud said.

Laurie, still more jittery, asked, "What did you think of it?"

"You said what you had to say with great courage and obvious writing talent," Maud began, "and I agree with you. Women have been too long suppressed by men who are afraid they'll discover just how bright and capable we women are." Her strong opinions came through her gentle, patrician manner.

Laurie relaxed and the three chatted until dinner. As Ben escorted the two women into the dining room, Laurie caught her breath at the candlelight shimmering in the polished table. The crystal goblets flashed pinpoints of fire. The multiple spoons and forks bewildered Laurie who had never seen more than one of each by her plate. She followed the lead of her hostess. When Maud picked up a spoon, she did the same masking her lack of knowledge. She felt she had acquitted herself quite well without any embarrassing moves.

Even in March, the table held fresh flowers. The scent reminded Laurie of her visit to the Baker mansion. Again she compared the two homes, one furnished to impress others and this one made for living graciously.

As the meal progressed, the three talked with animation. Slowly and skillfully, Maud extracted Laurie's convictions from her. The parlor conversation after dinner deepened Laurie's regard for this courtly woman.

"It's time I went home," began Laurie. "Tomorrow is a workday and it's getting late."

"I'll ride home with you on the streetcar," Ben said as he went into the entryway for their coats.

"I've thoroughly enjoyed your visit, my dear," said Maud as she clasped Laurie's hand. "It's made me feel twenty years younger to see your enthusiasm. You're an articulate, lovely and dignified young woman."

"The evening has been very special for me, too," said Laurie surprised at her own sincerity. Her misgivings at the dinner invitation had evaporated and left only the enjoyment.

As the streetcar rumbled out Hewitt, Ben held Laurie's hand. They talked of Aunt Maud. "She raised me from when I was seven years old," said Ben, "and as I've grown older, I've appreciated her wisdom, her wit, and her youth, even though she's in her seventies."

"She's a dear woman," Laurie replied.

Ben walked her from the streetcar to her home. "I don't want anything to happen to you," he said lightly. Actually, he wanted to prolong the evening as long as possible. As they stood on the bottom porch step, he held both her hands and looked intently into her eyes. He could smell her sweet essence as he bent to kiss her lips.

Again, Laurie felt he restrained himself.

She inhaled the smell of his wool coat and felt its roughness as she leaned her cheek against it.

"I want you to come to our house again, Laurie," Ben said with intensity. Next time he'd ask her about Johnny.

"I will, Ben," Laurie replied with the same warm fervor.

CHAPTER 13

❀

"What a turmoil you must have been in with two men vying for your favors," the elderly Mrs. Kirby said. "I imagine there are any number of women who would have liked to be in your place. I hope you chose Ben, but tell the story in your own way, my dear."

Outside, the frozen plain heightened the warmth between the two women. As they nibbled cookies from Mrs. Kirby's bag, Laurie said, "I'll start the next chapter in 'Laurie's Life' with Alice's wedding."

Laurie preened herself in front of the mirror. She and her mother had just finished sewing her dress for Alice's wedding. It was the same blue as her eyes, simply and elegantly made. The soft material floated around her thighs like a diaphanous blue cloud. She and Alice had pored over magazines for weeks to find just the right style for each of their gowns.

Lydia looked at what they had chosen and said she could finish both of them with time to spare. Excitement built as the dresses took shape and the day of the wedding neared. Alice, at the house a great deal, became like a member of the family. She helped with the dishes, stoked the fire and sewed hems.

Alice and Aaron had rented a small parlor at the Hotel Virginia for the ceremony and had invited just a few friends to share the event besides their attendants. They included Lydia, Mr. Hunt, Jenny Hunt, Aunt Maud, some of the teachers at the business school, and the families of the bride and groom. Lydia expressed delight at her invitation. Although she had relationships with many society women because of her sewing, she seldom attended social functions. Karl had been asked but declined the invitation. Laurie heaved a sigh of relief at his refusal.

When paper staff members heard the guest list, some wondered why they had not been invited. Aaron explained that limited space allowed only a small wedding. Most accepted his explanation philosophically but Johnny acted as if he had been snubbed. He made biting remarks to Laurie about his lack of an invitation but all she could do was repeat what the couple said. His sullenness did not fade away and it bothered Laurie because she had not completely shed her feelings for him.

A warm sun welcomed the wedding day. Laurie kept thinking of the old saw, "happy is the bride the sun shines on." She hoped Alice would be happy, although it bothered her that Aaron tended to exert his will on Alice rather than treating her as a partner. Alice always gave way to what Aaron decided. She was not as independent as Laurie had at first thought even though she earned her own living.

Ben came by to fetch Laurie and her mother for the wedding, right on time. The carriage rolled up to the house and he bounded up the stairs to knock on the door.

Lydia, already dressed in her beige gown, answered him regally at the door. "Laurie will be right down," she said with a welcoming smile. "The day is lovely for the wedding, isn't it?"

Karl had come in very late the night before and slept soundly on the couch. His snores punctuated the pleasantries exchanged by Lydia and Ben.

Laurie had heard the buggy and knock on the door. She took a last look at her image in the mirror and floated down the stairs in her excitement.

Ben caught his breath when he saw her. Her figure had filled out during the year he had known her and she seemed more beautiful to him than ever. He had felt closer to her after the dinner they had shared with Aunt Maud and he dared to hope she felt the same closeness in spite of what he suspected about her fondness for Johnny.

Laurie sensed how he reacted to her as he gazed. Rosiness began in her neck and traveled into her cheeks.

"You're lovelier than you were on New Year's Eve," Ben said affectionately, "and that's saying a lot."

"Thank you, Ben," said Laurie brightly. "You look distinguished. Mother, do you think we can match our escort's polish today?"

"We'll try not to embarrass him." Lydia laughed. Her dress had a high neck that nestled under her ears and emphasized her aristocratic bearing.

Ben helped the two women don their wraps and escorted them to the carriage with a special pressure on Laurie's arm. He didn't know if she felt it or not, but she didn't draw away.

As they entered the hotel lobby, Ben clasped an elbow of each woman and felt proud to escort them. Eyes turned in their direction as they made their way to the parlor where the ceremony and buffet were to be held.

Both Laurie and Lydia went to Alice's dressing room. Alice's mother fussed around as she complained about the size of the room, the warmth of the day, the cost of the parlor, and anything else she could think of. Laurie hoped it was due to nervousness but she instinctively knew this is what Alice escaped from.

The ivory satin gown glowed and so did the bride. Her blonde hair, caught up into a pompadour, was covered by an ivory lace cap holding the short veil in place.

Laurie pinned the cameo Ben had given her for Christmas on Alice's bodice and kissed her on the cheek. "There, that's something borrowed. The gown's new so what's old and what's blue?" asked Laurie.

With a mischievous flourish, Alice pulled up the flaring skirt of her wedding dress and showed a blue garter. "There, that's both old and blue," she laughed with a lovely blush.

Laurie thought, she has been a very special friend to me, about the only real one I've had, except for Ben, of course.

The opening strains of the wedding march on the parlor piano told them it was time to gather in front of the minister, the Rev. John Fowles. Neither Alice nor Aaron attended church regularly so they didn't know whom to ask to officiate. Laurie had suggested Rev. Fowles.

As they entered the parlor, they saw Aaron and Ben look toward them on the other side of Rev. Fowles. Alice held Aaron's eyes but Laurie's gaze locked with Ben's. She thought she saw a yearning in them. It unnerved her and excited her at the same time. He looked distinguished in his suit and white shirt, she thought, and really very handsome.

Rev. Fowles was expansive in this element, his voice both mellow and commanding. He delivered his cliché-filled prayers with rolling tones. After the couple exchanged rings he pronounced them man and wife, and told the groom he could now kiss the bride.

Aaron, tall and rangy with sandy hair smoothed to perfection, lifted the veil from Alice's glowing face and perfunctorily kissed her. She sighed as she looked into his face. Laurie could sense Alice was more enthralled with Aaron than he was with her.

As they turned to greet their guests, the slight Mrs. Fowles played heartily on the piano. She appeared to love weddings and her husband was so good at ceremonies, she had told Laurie.

Often the thought of Mrs. Fowles brought to Laurie's mind the Biblical verse, "The meek shall inherit the earth." Actually Laurie felt that all Mrs. Fowles wanted was her husband and that she had him confused with God.

Mr. Hunt came up to Laurie with a new light in his eye. "I didn't realize my secretary was so pretty," he said, giving her a very warm hug. "Pretty soon, all the fellows'll be hanging around your desk and I won't get any work out of you."

Jenny Hunt congratulated the newlyweds and then turned to Laurie. "I'll tell Johnny what he missed," she said with a smirk. "He was so disappointed not to be invited but I'll tell him how pretty you looked and how handsome Ben was."

Somehow, I don't think Johnny wants to hear that, Laurie concluded as she went over to her mother. She took her arm and led her to Mr. Hunt. "This is my mother, Mr. Hunt," she said proudly. "I've told her a lot about you."

"I hope it wasn't all bad," Mr. Hunt replied with a grin.

Laurie could tell he was quite taken by her mother.

"You don't look old enough to have a daughter the age of Laurie," he said gallantly.

It had been a long time since someone had been so complimentary to Lydia, Laurie thought. She saw a pink tint suffuse her face.

"Thank you, Mr. Hunt. I'm very proud of my daughter."

Alice took hold of Laurie's arm and asked her to help her get ready for the honeymoon trip to Seattle. The couple was leaving from Everett on the afternoon train. They had reservations at the Olympic Hotel. Laurie helped her into her going-away suit, the same ivory color as her wedding dress. The high necked, pink silk blouse reflected her blooming cheeks.

I hope I'll be as pretty a bride as she is, thought Laurie. She gathered up the wedding dress and veil and put them into a bag to take home to keep for Alice until she got back from her honeymoon.

Amid rice and good wishes the young couple left the hotel and Ben drove them to the imposing Great Northern railway station near the waterfront. The cement building teemed with activity. The great steam locomotive stood on the tracks next to the long covered passenger walkway. Ben hurried the couple through the throng to get them to the train on time. They already had their tickets and luggage for the short trip.

Ben watched as the train slowly chugged southward along Puget Sound gathering speed as billows of white smoke poured from the engine. He saw the caboose disappear around the curve as he went back to the carriage. Once back at the Hotel Virginia, he escorted his two companions home. *I hope one day Laurie and I stand before that minister and board this train as man and wife*, he wished fervently with a knot in his stomach.

As Ben walked Laurie from the streetcar to the office on Monday, he asked her if she'd go out to lunch with him. He decided he could ask her about Johnny then.

"I'd love to," she said. Ben, so strong and yet so gentle, had been in her thoughts more than ever after the wedding. Although he put on a show of being relaxed and flippant, he was truly an earnest young man. She knew he cared deeply about his aunt and about his job. She hadn't quite determined how he felt about her, but her feelings had changed. She now thrilled to his touch, and looked forward to being with him.

"I'll come by your desk at noon to pick you up," Ben said as he went down one hallway and she down the other.

Late in the morning, as Ben dashed out the door on a breaking news story, he met Johnny. "Tell Laurie I can't take her to lunch today because I'm on a story. Tell her I'll talk to her when I get back," he said hurriedly as he put his arms into his coat sleeves. He ran down the street.

"Sure, Ben," Johnny called after him. In the lobby, he turned toward the press room instead of Laurie's desk.

Laurie's stomach told her it was time to eat. Glancing up to the clock on the wall, she saw the hands stood at twelve-forty-five. Ben hadn't come by to pick her up. She was puzzled and hurt.

Johnny came up to her desk and asked, "Are you going to eat in the lunch-room?"

"Well, I guess so," she said doubtfully. "I had a lunch date but it seems to have been canceled."

She angrily picked up her lunch bag and walked to the lunchroom with Johnny.

"Tell me about the wedding," he said. "Was Alice a beautiful bride?"

Laurie told him all about the ceremony, the buffet, the people and the young couple. She said little about Ben.

When Ben came hurriedly up to her desk late in the afternoon, she was decidedly cool toward him.

Why is she shutting me out, Ben wondered? He had Johnny tell her he couldn't take her to lunch. "Have you eaten?" he asked.

"Yes, I ate with Johnny in the lunchroom," she said and turned her swivel chair away from him to her typewriter, stifling further conversation.

After work, he tried to take her arm as he walked her to the streetcar but she pulled away from him. He puzzled about what caused her manner to be so frosty. He believed they had reached a new level of togetherness at the wedding and now she behaved as if his presence angered her.

When Laurie walked into the house, the kitchen fire was about out and a chill filled the kitchen. She didn't know if it were the lack of heat from the stove or her bleak day that caused the chill. She realized the bleakness came from the fact Ben broke his lunch date with her without telling her and then acted as if nothing had happened. He can't toy with me like that, she swore.

A note on the table told that her mother was over at the cribs caring for some sick girls.

She coaxed the fire into a blaze and started to get a meal for her father. She heard him come up the steps to the front door and bang his boots on the porch to get rid of the sawdust.

As he wearily sat on a chair to take off his boots, he asked, "Where's your mother?"

Laurie handed him the note and began to set the table for dinner.

"She's always taking care of other people," Karl said plaintively. "She's got enough to do here at home. Her heart's too big."

As he drained his last cup of coffee, Karl said, "I'm so tired I'm going to bed. Your mother ought to be home soon."

Laurie wiped the table and washed the dishes as she waited for her mother. I need to talk to her about Ben, she thought. And I want to remind her she was going to tell me something about the past.

In bed, she read until nearly eleven o'clock as she waited. She finally closed her book and slipped deeper under the covers. I need to talk to her soon she thought as she settled into troubled sleep.

The next day was a difficult one for Laurie, distracted from her work by thoughts of Ben and the broken lunch date. She decided to talk to him and ask him what had happened. He hadn't been at the corner to walk her to the office this morning, either. Anger and curiosity merged.

As she walked toward the lobby, she met Johnny and he fell into step with her. "Have you seen Ben this morning?" she asked.

"Yeah," Johnny replied with a malevolent gleam in his eye that Laurie puzzled over. "I saw him leave with Jenny a little while ago. She was hanging onto his arm."

Laurie turned abruptly saying she had work to do, and went back to her desk miserable at the thought of Ben with Jenny. Jealousy raged just beneath the surface. She hoped her mother would be home so she could talk to her.

She felt a pang of relief when she saw smoke curling out of the chimney. Her mother was home, thank goodness. She needed to unburden herself.

She hung her coat and hat in the hallway and asked, "What's wrong with the girls over on Hewitt, Mother?"

"They have typhoid fever, I think," Lydia said. "They've got all the symptoms and about all I can do is sponge them with cool water, give them a little laudanum, and comfort them. There are five sick girls and I'm not sure they'll get well. Their fevers are very high. I was there today for awhile and I'll go back tomorrow. It's no wonder it's spreading with the open sewers and the lack of clean drinking water."

Laurie waited for Lydia to sit down after starting dinner. "Mother, I don't know what to think about Ben," she started hesitantly. "I thought he was becoming quite fond of me and at the wedding, I felt he might even love me, but he broke a lunch date yesterday without telling me and he wasn't at the streetcar this morning."

"Have you talked to him about it, Laurie dear?" her mother asked.

"I was going to this afternoon because I couldn't stand it," Laurie said dejectedly. "I couldn't find him so I asked Johnny if he had seen him and he told me he had seen Ben go out the door with Jenny on his arm. Johnny had a strange look in his eyes."

"Has Ben paid any attention to Jenny recently?" Lydia asked quietly.

"Not that I've noticed," said Laurie, "but that doesn't mean he hasn't. I've dreamed for years that I loved Johnny but now I'm not sure of that any more."

"I've wondered if you had a special attachment to Johnny. But about Ben, when the opportunity presents itself, ask him what happened about lunch and see how he acts and listen to what he says," Lydia counseled. "He strikes me as being an honest and forthright man. I, too, thought he was especially attentive to you at the wedding."

"All right, that's what I'll do," Laurie sighed, and then she remembered the talk her mother promised so long ago. "Remember some time ago you wanted to talk to me?" Laurie asked. "I wrote it down in my journal and we've never had the talk. What was it about?"

As her mother drew a breath and started to speak, Karl pushed open the door and asked, "Is dinner ready?"

"It will be in a few minutes, Karl, come let me help you off with your boots," Lydia said. "We'll talk another time, Laurie, and you have a chat with your friend."

CHAPTER 14

"Did you follow your mother's advice?" Mrs. Kirby asked kindly when Laurie lapsed into silence.

"Yes, I did, but that was after going through a lot of anxiety," Laurie answered.

"Did you realize what a scoundrel Johnny was?"

"Eventually I did, but that took a while, too."

Ben again failed to meet Laurie at the streetcar the next morning. He really has changed his mind about me, she thought, just as I began to look at him with more feeling. This sudden change hurt her more than she cared to admit.

She opened the mail for Mr. Hunt and answered the phones as she worked. The editor strolled down the hall in an expansive mood, removed his black derby, and asked Laurie, "How are you?"

"I'm fine, Mr. Hunt," she replied without her usual enthusiasm.

"When you finish opening the mail, bring your pad and pencil and come into my office," he said with a courtly bow as he meandered through his door.

As she went into his office loaded with mail in one hand, and her pad in the other, he turned from the window and asked, "Is something bothering you, Laurie? You act as if you've lost your best friend." Mr. Hunt's piercing gaze locked on Laurie's face.

"Maybe I have," she said.

"Can I help?" he asked. He sat down in his swivel chair and motioned Laurie to sit.

"It's a personal matter," she said sadly.

"Well, I want a smiling face to greet me in the mornings," he laughed. "Is Johnny giving you a bad time? I thought you might be a little sweet on him. Or maybe you miss Ben since he's been sick."

"He's been sick?" she repeated as her head jerked up. "I didn't know that. I hadn't seen him around but I thought he was on assignment or just busy somewhere else."

"His aunt said he's been quite ill with influenza," added Mr. Hunt. "She said it might be several weeks before he comes back to work."

As Laurie transcribed Mr. Hunt's editorial, Johnny came up to her desk. "Is it about ready?" he asked as he lounged against the wall.

"Just about," answered Laurie. "Did you know Ben was sick, Johnny?"

"It seems to me I did hear something about that but you don't have to worry about him anyway, he just used you and now you won't have to put up with him for awhile," he sneered.

"How did he use me?" Laurie asked. A frown puckered her brow.

"Well, he always had you taking notes for him, for one thing," Johnny said. "A reporter is supposed to do that himself."

"But the times I helped him were when Mr. Hunt asked me to, not because Ben asked. It was faster that way," Laurie replied, still unsure in her own mind. Maybe a grain of truth existed in Johnny's words.

When Laurie got home that night, she noticed her mother looked very tired. She just sat in the kitchen chair. Her hands, usually busy with housework or sewing, now lay idle in her lap.

She gave Lydia a calculating look and asked, "What's wrong, Mother, you look worn out?"

"I'm all right, dear, just a little tired. I spent the day over at the cribs. Typhoid is spreading there I'm afraid," she said wearily. "There's not much I can do but try to make them comfortable. Fixing a broken arm is easier than curing typhoid." She leaned her head into her hand as her elbow rested on the table.

"Well, you can't take care of them if you get sick yourself," Laurie admonished and busied herself getting dinner.

Karl came home, and Laurie put the meal on the table. Lydia tried to eat but just picked at the food on her plate.

"Are you sick, Lady Lydia?" asked Karl.

"No, I'm just tired," she said with a feeble effort at a smile, not telling him she'd spent the day at the cribs.

Laurie's concern for her mother drove Ben from her mind. I'll have to help her more, she decided. She sent her mother to bed and cleaned the kitchen herself.

As she trudged upstairs she thought she might write a short get-well note to Ben. She donned her flannel nightgown and brushed her hair as she mentally composed her note.

Propped up by a pillow at the head of the bed, she tried to write Ben's note. She realized how Johnny's words had hurt her. She didn't realize how much Ben's friendship meant to her. Those were special times they spent together and the way he treated her after the wedding made her melt just like the thought of Johnny used to. She couldn't be so mistaken about that. Of course, she used to feel that way about Johnny, but didn't any more. His childishness was so apparent now.

After many tries at writing the note and surrounded by crumpled papers, her words said simply and impersonally, "I am sorry to hear you are ill. I hope you are well soon. Laurie."

The next few weeks passed drearily for Laurie. She did her job but the spark had gone out of it because of Ben's absence. An unfamiliar emptiness lodged inside her. He finally answered her note saying he was getting better and would be back soon. He thanked her for her message. It doesn't have a hint of emotion in it, thought Laurie. Maybe Johnny was right.

As the days went by, Laurie could see that her mother failed to recover her usual verve. Lydia reached the point where she could hardly get out of bed.

Soon, Laurie realized the seriousness of her mother's illness. She squelched all other thoughts and when her job was finished for the day, she rushed home to take care of the house and her mother.

Rosie from the cribs dropped by on a Saturday to find out why Lydia had not come back to check on the girls. When she found out how ill Lydia was she offered to stay with her during the weekdays until Laurie got home from work. "After all, she was takin' care of us when we needed her and now she needs us," Rosie said, frowzy in her fake finery. "If I can't come, I'll send someone else."

Laurie, heartened by this poor girl's obvious devotion to her mother, said with genuine gratitude, "I would appreciate that very much. She's really very ill."

"Can I see her?" asked Rosie. Laurie led her into the bedroom and Lydia mustered a smile of welcome.

Laurie bathed her mother's face to cool her. The rising fever and headaches were the same symptoms as the crib girls had. She refused to let herself believe her mother had typhoid.

Rosie confirmed it, though. "It's just like the girls," she said, and Laurie faced what she had suspected all along.

Laurie could tell Lydia tried to hide the severe stomach pains by the way she clenched her jaw and held her breath. After Rosie left, she brought warm water to bathe her mother. As she lifted the flannel nightgown, she saw rose-colored spots on her mother's body.

On Monday, Rosie came by as Laurie left for work. "I'll be back as soon as I can," she said hastily. "I've fixed her some breakfast and made some soup you can give her for lunch. If she needs me, send someone to the paper. And thanks again, Rosie." Like a revelation, she realized these girls were filled with the same emotions she had. She touched Rosie's arm, the one her mother had set when it had been broken, and then went out the door.

Ben came back to work looking wan and weak. He smiled at her without his former warmth and she kept her mind on her work and her mother.

In a reserved manner he asked, "May I come by and see you some evening?" He had to find out what had gone so wrong between them.

"My mother is very ill," she droned.

As the week wore on, Lydia became progressively weaker. On Friday, Laurie told Mr. Hunt about her mother. "If she's no better on Monday, I'll stay home with her. I hope you'll give me some time off. I need my job but I also need to help my mother."

He had been quite smitten with Lydia at the wedding and instantly agreed. "Take next week off, Laurie, we'll make out here. And your job will wait for you."

Nursing her mother and running the house absorbed all of Laurie's time. She could hardly bear the stench of Lydia's diarrhea and had to change the bedding frequently. Her mother's weakness made it impossible for her to get out of bed.

Laurie, numbed with fatigue with so much to do, fixed Will's bed for her father. She moved a cot into her mother's room to be with her all the time. Heating water for the frequent laundry kept the house so warm Laurie took in deep gulps of fresh air when she did the wash on the back porch.

She realized her mother's mind wandered and sometimes she failed to recognize her daughter. Laurie refused to face the fact her mother might not survive. She sent for Dr. Long to come although Lydia told her not to bother him, she'd be well soon.

Dr. Long ushered Laurie out of the bedroom before his examination. "Do you know who I am, Lydia?" he asked gently.

With an effort she focused her eyes on him. "Yes," she murmured feebly.

"Have you had abdominal pain?" he asked. She nodded. He took her pulse, listened to her chest with an ear trumpet, and put a thermometer in her mouth.

"You know you have typhoid fever, don't you, Lydia?" She nodded. "Laurie said you got sick a couple of weeks ago and that you've had diarrhea."

She blinked her eyes in acknowledgment.

"I gave you the examination only to confirm my diagnosis. Now I have to tell your family. I don't relish this part of being a doctor." He locked his teeth in a grimace then added, "If you haven't started to get better by the end of the week, you'd better make your peace with God." He took her hot hand in his big fist trying to give her strength from his hold.

When he went out and put his medical bag on the table, he asked Laurie, "Where's your father?"

Just then Karl, bleary eyed and unsteady, came through the door from the living room. "Howdy, Doc," he said with a wave of his mangled left hand. "Lady Lydia's getting better, isn't she?"

"Both of you sit down," Doc Long said. He drew a deep breath and continued. "Lydia is in the third week of typhoid fever. If she doesn't get better by the end of the week, prepare yourselves for the worst." His grave manner left no doubt that he believed what he said.

In her fatigue and anguish, Laurie put her head onto her folded arms and sobbed. I can't face life without my mother, she screamed internally. I have no one else who cares about me.

Karl slammed his fist onto the table and turned his head away. "She can't die," he shouted in his torment. He twisted out of his chair and stormed out of the front door.

Doc Long kept his arm around Laurie as she sobbed. Finally, she raised her tear-stained face to him and asked, "What can I do to help her?"

"Keep her as comfortable as possible and if she seems in pain, give her some laudanum. Don't be alarmed if she doesn't know you. She'll be in delirium sometimes but that's one of the symptoms," he sighed as he shrugged into his coat. He continued to shake his head as he trudged out the door.

As the week wore on, Lydia's condition worsened. The nursing, housework and lack of sleep began to tell on Laurie. The hour or two of sleep she snatched were full of nightmares about her mother.

Early Saturday morning, she jerked awake to find her mother looking at her with compassion. The dim lamplight failed to mask the emaciated form under the quilt. Lydia had not known her for two days. She's going to get better, rejoiced Laurie.

"Laurie, will you send for Rev. Fowles, please, and then come back here?"

Puzzled by why her mother wanted the minister, she woke her father to send him for the pastor.

"There's something I have to tell you, dear, something I should have told you a long time ago," she said weakly. Laurie knelt on the floor at the side of the big bed, and bent her head to catch the barely audible words.

"When I was very young, I lived in England as you know," her mother began with obvious effort. "My father was a minor nobleman and life was wonderful. When I was sixteen, I fell in love with the son of a count. He courted me and said he loved me."

Her voice faltered and she was quiet for a while. Laurie laid her head on the quilt. She's gone to sleep, she thought, and smelled a lovely rose scent permeate the sickroom. There are no flowers here, she realized in wonder. She picked up her head again and saw her mother's eyes open and Lydia began to speak again.

"I'll never forget how happy I was that summer. I was pretty and I was loved. My sweetheart became my lover. Such passion we shared. Does that shock you, Laurie?" she asked weakly.

"No, Mother, I'm not shocked," she said aching inside.

After awhile Lydia gathered strength to speak again. "The unthinkable happened. I got pregnant and suddenly the whole world changed. Because of family pressure, my lover left me. I was not a suitable person for his wife. My parents were shocked and embarrassed. They wanted to send me away to have the baby and then give it away." Again her voice faded away for a time.

"I couldn't face that because I wanted the baby even though it had no father. They gave me enough money to live on and booked passage for me on a ship leaving for America. The crossing was terrible for me. I kept thinking I would have a child of my own to care for so I endured it. I was sick most of the time, retching into a basin."

Lydia stopped talking and closed her eyes, her breathing very shallow, and her stomach contracted in pain.

"I'll get you some laudanum," said Laurie as she started to rise from her knees.

"No, don't go, I want to tell you the rest. On the ship was a seaman who took care of me. He held my head when I vomited. He wiped my brow. He brought me food. He made me eat to keep up the strength I would need for the baby. When the nightmare was over and we landed in New York, the same seaman found lodgings for me and still cared for me.

"The baby girl was born and she was beautiful. The kind seaman wanted to marry me. He said he worshiped me and I believed him, so we were married and moved to Minnesota to start a new life. The seaman is Karl and you are my beautiful baby."

Tears squeezed out from beneath Lydia's lashes. Laurie wrapped her arms around her mother and cried gently.

"Do you hate me, Laurie?" her mother asked barely above a whisper.

"No, Mother, I love you more than ever and it explains so much," Laurie smiled through her tears.

"If anything happens to me, I want you to take care of your father," Lydia said. "He kept me alive and was there when I needed him most. And although he isn't your natural father, he has been a father to you all these years. Will you promise me?"

"Yes, Mother. Now I know why you always defended him," Laurie said as she wiped her eyes.

Just then a gentle tapping sounded at the door. Rev. Fowles entered. Lydia told Laurie she wanted to talk to the minister alone. Laurie went out to make some tea hoping it would revive her mother.

Rev. Fowles jerked open the bedroom door and called for Laurie and Karl to come quickly. They knelt on each side of the bed their faces filled with pain. Lydia struggled one more time to reach her husband and daughter. She smiled as she greeted her God. The fragrance of roses still clung to the room.

In shock Laurie went out into the kitchen and stood staring at the stove. She went through the ritual of making the tea and started to fix a tray for her mother. A knock on the door brought her back to reality and in despair she went to open it. There stood Ben. "Oh, Ben, she's gone and I can't live without her," she cried.

He came in, closed the door and took her in his arms like a comforting brother.

CHAPTER 15

Small Mrs. Kirby stretched to put her arm around Laurie as the girl cried quiet tears for the dear mother she'd lost.

"What a terrible tragedy for you, my dear," said the elderly woman. "You and she were so close." She paused while Laurie dried her tears then added, "You finally found out what she was going to tell you."

"Yes, I did. I really didn't mind I had no legal father until later."

"And you still had the turmoil of Ben and Johnny besides your father's drinking."

"That's true but I was too numb to think of those things at the time. I don't know how I got through the next few days."

She scrubbed, cleaned, cooked and scrubbed some more to cope with her catastrophic loss. She exhausted herself. The numbness of fatigue put her to sleep at night.

Ben came every day and his mere presence comforted her. The neighbors dropped in with solemn words of sympathy and Rev. Fowles made the arrangements for Lydia's funeral. Written words of condolence arrived from Lydia's sewing customers and the Hewitt Avenue girls came by in twos and threes.

Sally Jenson appeared frequently but every time she started to speak, she'd cry and Laurie, so filled with tears herself, found it difficult to retain her outer composure.

Although friends and neighbors brought food for Laurie and her father, the two ate little. After Karl's first outburst and drunken binge, he stayed at home, usually with his head in his huge hands. The stubble grew on his cheeks making his pallor all the more noticeable. Laurie began to fear for him, too.

Mourners filled the church pews at Lydia's funeral. Most everyone had wet eyes as Rev. Fowles conducted the services. The entourage followed the casket to the cemetery where Lydia was put to rest next to Will. At least they're together now, Laurie thought, with little comfort and feeling her loss all the more.

A gathering at the Krafft home followed the interment. Neighbor women fixed and served the food. Subdued voices murmured sympathy and Laurie didn't know if she could stand it until they all left. She acknowledged their remarks and went through the motions of being grateful even though she drowned in a sea of anguish.

Eventually everyone left except Ben and her father who had cleaned himself up for the funeral. His clean-shaven face reflected his pain. Only his broad black mustache remained. Laurie could hardly stand to look into his grief-stricken eyes.

As Karl slumped at the table with his cup full of cold coffee, Ben and Laurie moved into the living room. "I really appreciate your support over the last few days," Laurie began in a monotone.

"Don't mouth platitudes to me, Laurie, you're angry at the loss of your mother and you hurt like hell," Ben growled.

Laurie's tears coursed down her pale cheeks and she nodded.

"I know how you feel, honey," Ben said soothingly. "Even though I was very young when I lost my parents, I remember how angry I felt and how full of pain I was. All the sweet mutterings did nothing to help at all. Sympathy made it worse."

Ben held Laurie for a long time until her sobs dwindled into gentle crying and finally to a few shudders. She raised her head, eyes red, hair tumbling out of her bun. She wrapped her arms around herself. "Maybe in time the grief will go away," Laurie began.

"It never will," replied Ben, "but it will lessen and soon you'll be able to get on with living. Write it all down in your journal. Getting it out will help. Aunt Maud and I want you to come stay with us for awhile until you're better able to cope."

"I can't, Ben," Laurie sighed. "I'm going to stay here with Father and we'll make it together. This isn't a platitude; you don't know how much I appreciate your concern and your invitation. I'm pleased that Maud came to the funeral, and Mr. Hunt, too." She remembered that Johnny hadn't even come by.

"If you're sure you'll be all right, I should be going," Ben began. "I'm still trying to get my strength back from that dratted influenza."

After Ben left and Laurie felt more composed, she sat next to her father at the table. She reached for his hand and he grabbed hers convulsively. She tried to keep from crying.

He shook his big head from side to side as he moaned, "What are we going to do without Lady Lydia?"

Laurie knew he needed her above all else. "We'll be fine as long as we're together, Father," she said.

"I know how you feel about me and my drinking," he said with self-disgust.

"Things are going to be different now," Laurie began. "You're right, I didn't have much respect for you when you drank and I was impatient with Mother for allowing it to happen."

She sighed and continued, "Mother told me about her past and how you helped her when she needed you. You have been a real father to me when in truth you didn't need to be and I love you for that."

Karl got up from his chair, pulled Laurie to her feet and they clung to each other as they shared their grief.

"All right, that's enough," Laurie finally said as she pulled away and wiped her eyes. "We'll always miss her but we have to go on from here. We have each other."

Karl nodded and heaving a big sigh said, "I'll go back to work tomorrow."

Laurie echoed, "I will, too."

In early August, Mr. Hunt asked Laurie to come into his office. "Have you ever been to a circus, Laurie?" he asked.

"No, not really. One came to town in Minnesota just as we were getting ready to leave for Everett, but I didn't get to go," she said tentatively.

"Well, Ringling Brothers' circus will be in Everett on the twentieth. How'd you like to write a story about going to the circus for the first time?" Mr. Hunt asked, a fond twinkle in his eye. "This one won't be as controversial as the last article you wrote. I'm going to send Johnny with you."

Swallowing the nervous lump in her throat, Laurie said, "I'd like to give it a try. Father works on Saturdays, so I don't need to worry about being home." He had not stopped at the saloons since her mother's death and genuine warmth had sprung up between father and daughter.

Laurie gloried in the balmy day and could barely wait to go to the circus. She anticipated a real newspaper assignment with delight. She briefly wished Mr. Hunt had asked Ben to go with her.

She met Johnny in front of the circus gate and together they went into the grounds where a huge tent billowed. Gaudy signs told of the treasures to be experienced inside the big top and among the small tents lining the perimeter of the field. The yellow straw covering the ground made walking shaky on the slick surface.

As they entered the big tent, dust kicked up by many feet tickled their noses. Laurie could see Johnny's excitement although she knew he wondered why he wasn't the one assigned to do the story.

They found seats several rows up from the center ring. The noise of the crowd blended with the blaring music of the circus band, and the reedy sound of the large calliope. The aroma of roasted peanuts mixed with the animal smells.

A man dressed in tight tan breeches, frock coat and top hat dashed into the center ring with a cracking whip to emphasize his announcement of each act. People cheered, children gazed with wide eyes, and vendors sold all sorts of food as they went up and down the stands. Others hawked brightly-colored balloons.

Flying bodies on high trapeze swings left Laurie's palms wet with fear for them. Big lions and tigers roared with feigned fierceness as their trainers shot blanks and cracked whips to subdue them. One giant blond man put his head into the mouth of a Bengal tiger and then bowed to acknowledge the admiration of the roaring crowd.

Laurie took notes as fast as she could but sometimes her pencil remained poised while she lost herself in the excitement of the show.

A huge elephant trundled around the center ring with a beautiful rider astride just behind its head. The lady swayed to the motion of the pachyderm. A large pink feather, the same color as the tights she wore, adorned her loose flowing hair.

Clowns pulled long strings of handkerchiefs out of their baggy pants and threw imaginary water into the audience from a pail amid screams of anticipation.

Laurie tried to watch the acts in all three rings and found herself bewildered by all of the activity. Johnny, just as excited, kept a possessive arm around her shoulders. She hardly noticed.

After the show, the human stream flowed out of the tent. Laurie and Johnny strolled around the field, ate sausages and drank lemonade. Even though they could eat no more, the heady odors of cooking food made them wish they could start eating all over again.

Filled with the satisfaction of an enjoyable day, Laurie allowed Johnny to escort her home. As they rambled along, Johnny asked sulkily, "I wonder why Mr. Hunt asked you to do the story instead of me? He knows I want to be a reporter."

"Have you ever been to a circus before?" Laurie asked. When he said he had, she continued. "Well, he wanted a story from the viewpoint of a person who had never seen one before, sort of a fresh outlook, and he might have decided I needed something exciting to do after Mother's death." She could say that now without tears filling her eyes.

"I hope he doesn't wait too long to give me a break because if he does, I'll go work at another newspaper," Johnny said with vehemence. He glowered for awhile as they caught the streetcar for the ride to Laurie's house.

Her father hadn't come home from work yet and she needed to start dinner. Johnny came into the house without an invitation and straddled a chair as she started the fire in the kitchen stove.

"I didn't know you could cook, Laurie," he said idly as he bit his fingernails.

"There're just the two of us now," she explained. "Father takes care of the garden and gets the wood, and I do the housework and cooking. We're getting along pretty well."

The heat of the cook stove produced a lovely rose in Laurie's cheeks as she stirred the stew.

"It sure smells great, Laurie. Is there enough for me?" Johnny asked.

Laurie really didn't want him to get the idea he was part of the family but her mother's training prevailed and she said, "Sure, Johnny, we'd enjoy having you."

The biscuits came out of the oven just as Karl banged open the front door. He had lost some weight but he'd also lost the pallor that followed Lydia's death. Without the false refuge of alcohol, he was a much gentler man and he radiated affection when he saw Laurie. The relationship they had built sustained them through the first few weeks of the loss they both felt so deeply.

Johnny and Karl talked in the front room while Laurie cleaned up the kitchen after dinner. When she walked into the living room pushing back the stray strands of her hair, her father got up and said, "I'm very tired so I'll go to bed now. Goodbye, Johnny. Come again." He shuffled down the hall to the bedroom he had shared with Lydia.

Johnny pulled Laurie down on the couch beside him and spoke about his grandiose dreams of the future. As he talked he gathered Laurie closer and closer. He took her head and pushed it down on his shoulder.

She realized in wonder that her secret love for him was gone. She couldn't believe she had really felt that way about him. How foolish she had been.

His hands moved to the buttons of her waist and he started to undo them.

"Stop, Johnny," Laurie protested but he continued.

"I bet you let Ben get fresh with you just because he's older and a real reporter," Johnny mocked.

Laurie tried to push him away but he persisted. One hand fumbled at her buttons and the other pulled up her long skirt.

"I knew your legs would be pretty," Johnny leered. "Now I want to see those beautiful breasts you hide underneath that blouse." He gave a mighty tug and ripped it open. He stuck his hand inside her camisole and grabbed her breast.

The shock of his hands on her thigh and on her breast jolted Laurie. The embarrassment of the touch brought a bright red to her face. She jerked away from him with a mighty thrust and ran. She straightened her clothing and asked him to leave. Her haughtiness left no doubt she meant it.

"I'll go," said Johnny, "but you liked it, Laurie, I know you did. There'll be another time and you won't pull away from me. I'll show you I'm as good a man as anyone, even Ben."

With Johnny's taunt ringing in her ears, she put out the lights and made her way upstairs. As she wrote in her journal that night, she wondered how she'd feel if Ben were the one caressing her.

"That Johnny's a rat, an absolute rat," exclaimed Mrs. Kirby. "I hope you saw through him."

"That I did a little later," remembered Laurie.

CHAPTER 16

"Now, let's forget Johnny and you tell me about your assignment," Mrs. Kirby stated.

"I felt wonderful when I wrote it, so exhilarated," the young woman said.

As Laurie wrote about her circus experience, she lived the excitement of it all over again. The words she poured out on the blank sheets of paper in her typewriter reflected her delight, her awe, her exhilaration. It may seem naive, she thought, but it's what I felt and that's what Mr. Hunt wanted.

She read her typed pages over again, and then retyped them with the changes she wanted to make. She took the finished article in to Mr. Hunt and left it on his cluttered desk while he talked on the phone.

Soon his door burst open and he said, "This is great, Laurie, just what I wanted. I've done a little editing and added a note about your byline. Have Johnny take it to the backshop."

Laurie didn't really want to talk to Johnny although she knew she couldn't avoid it. She didn't see him in the lobby and started down the hall to the backshop.

Ben came out of the press room and asked, "How was the circus, Laurie?"

"Read it in the paper," Laurie laughed, and did a quick two-step down the hall.

As she waited with suppressed excitement for the day's edition of the paper to be printed, she straightened her desk. Johnny came along and chatted in his normal easy manner. He didn't allude to the tussle they'd had in her living room but she knew he thought about it by the way he looked at her.

"How about me coming by tonight?" he asked casually.

"Sorry, Johnny," she replied. "I have something else planned."

"I bet it's with Ben and you're going to let him use you again," snarled Johnny as he swung on his heel and stomped down the hall to the lobby.

"What's wrong, Johnny," asked the laconic Charlie Shaefer from under his green eyeshade. "Someone put a burr under your saddle?"

Johnny ignored him and strode to the backshop.

Laurie's plan for the evening did include Ben. He said he wanted to talk to her where they wouldn't be interrupted. Curious, she invited him for dinner, without fear this time because she knew her father would be home on time, sober.

The aroma from the oven made Ben's mouth water. A pleasant ambience wrapped around the three of them as they ate. "I didn't know you were such a good cook, Laurie" commented Ben. "You could have another career as a chef."

She laughed and asked, "Can I write and cook, too?"

They lounged at the table after the dishes were cleared and talked of the lumber glut and the growth Everett experienced. Laurie finished her second cup of tea and the men drank their coffee.

Finally, Karl drained his cup and said, "I'm going to leave you two young people now and go to bed. Goodnight, Ben, I hope you come again. I really enjoyed your visit."

Ben wiped the dishes as Laurie washed them and together, they put them into the cupboards. It created an intimacy Laurie wanted to prolong. She felt Ben wanted it to continue, too.

The temperate evening drew them out onto the porch. They sat on the steps and Laurie wondered when Ben would broach the subject he wanted to talk over with her. She had imagined all sorts of things.

"Do you remember the day I invited you out for lunch?" he asked.

"Yes, I do," she replied reluctantly although she would have rather forgotten it.

"You were very cool to me after that and I have to know why. Didn't Johnny tell you I had to go on assignment and that I'd see you later?" he asked earnestly.

"He didn't tell me anything," she answered. "If he had I'd have understood. And when you were sick, he said you had gone out with Jenny hanging on your arm."

All of a sudden it became perfectly clear that Johnny had done everything he could to destroy the special affinity between Ben and Laurie. She recalled

Johnny's accusations and turned to Ben. "Have you been nice to me just to use me?" she asked.

"Oh, Laurie, of course not. I've treasured every minute we've spent together," he said as he pulled her closer to him. "Is Johnny so special to you that you believe everything he says?"

"For years I secretly loved him, I thought. When we were in school, he used to come over sometimes and occasionally walk me home from school," she began. "I can remember how special I felt when he put his arm around me."

"Do you still feel the same way about him?" Ben asked quietly. He dreaded what the answer might be.

Laurie turned her head toward him and looked directly into his eyes. "No, Ben, I don't," she said openly. "The day of the circus he came home with me and invited himself to dinner. After Father went to bed we sat on the couch and talked. He got familiar with me and I knew then that I was over my fixation. It was like I had a great load lifted off my shoulders."

"I'll beat him to death," Ben swore as he got up and paced up and down the walk. He clenched his hands into fists.

"Sit down, Ben, it's all over and nothing really happened," Laurie placated him. "It was worth it to know I no longer felt anything for him."

Ben calmed down and sat again by Laurie. He put his arm around her. "I don't want any other man touching the woman I love," he said heatedly.

Laurie pulled away and looked at him, her excitement mounting. "What did you say?" she asked.

"I love you, Laurie," he replied. "I wasn't going to press you about it so soon after your mother's death but I lost control when you told me about Johnny. I've loved you from the very first moment I saw you come into the paper office. Ask my Aunt Maud if you don't believe me, she knew from the beginning."

Laurie basked in the warmth of his revelation. It felt so right and spawned a depth of love she had not felt for anyone else. This was not a secret love but a full, encompassing love. This is what she had read about most of her life.

She reached for Ben as eagerly as he reached for her. Their lips met in thirst for each other. Passionately and gloriously they clasped one another. "Oh, Laurie, I didn't dream you'd feel the same way about me," Ben breathed.

"I think I knew it all along but didn't dare acknowledge it," sighed Laurie still stunned by the emotions she felt.

Reluctantly, Ben said he had to leave. "I'll see you tomorrow at work, honey," he said as he gave her one last lingering kiss filled with the hunger of his love.

"Oh, Ben, I do love you," Laurie said as she reluctantly pulled away from him.

Laurie's article about the circus brought calls and letters. People remembered they had felt the same as she the first time they'd gone to the circus. Filled with Ben's love and the approval of her readers, Laurie soared. She felt a pang that her mother couldn't share her triumphs. But she knows, Laurie thought, she knows.

Mr. Hunt called her into his office for his usual editorial and after he had dictated it, he settled back in his swivel chair chomping on his unlit cigar. He had quit smoking but he couldn't bring himself to abandon the cheroot in his mouth.

Laurie waited for him to dismiss her but he mused to himself about something. She started to leave when he motioned her to sit again. She studied the expressions that flitted across his heavy face and wondered what he thought. The folds around his mouth deepened. Her curiosity nearly got the better of her, but she forced herself to wait patiently.

"How would you like to write a column a week about the social events in this town?" he asked thoughtfully. "Our reporters seldom have the time to delve into the sociable scene unless there are political implications."

Laurie pondered a moment, just a moment, and said, "I'd like to try it. What if occasionally I included something important, like women's issues, and new businesses, for instance?"

"Social stuff is important. If you don't feel that way, your readers will know it. We'll have to see how it goes. Write it up each week and we'll talk about it. Anything that comes in the mail that you could use I'll give to you," Mr. Hunt thought out loud. "It might not work but Everett's cosmopolitan enough now to be interested in lighter activities. There're forty fraternal lodges with most of 'em having women's auxiliaries, reform clubs, political clubs, women's clubs, historical societies and professional organizations here and that's part of the news we need to cover. And don't forget the forty churches. Your deadline will be Thursday afternoon for publication Friday. Now get out of here, I have work to do."

Laurie was overwhelmed with this new challenge. She had always wanted to write regularly and now she had her chance. The first thing she must do is organize a file to record all the clubs and find people to contact, she decided. Some of her mother's former sewing customers would help her, she knew.

Her first column included bits and pieces of Everett's social scene with a few kernels of thoughtful comment to balance it.

Mr. Hunt frowned a bit at the comments but finally shrugged his shoulders and said, "As long as your name's on it, you'll have to take the consequences. We'll go ahead and run it. What do you want to call your column?"

Laurie had thought long and hard about that. "Is it all right if we call it 'Happenings'?"

Hunt tentatively agreed and a column was born. She saw the pride Ben had for her in her new endeavor and Johnny's sulkiness. Laurie avoided him as much as possible.

After the second column appeared, Laurie started getting phone calls and letters with suggested topics. A few thought she'd better get married, stay home and raise a family. To herself she thought, I will someday, but not now. This is really what I want to do.

Laurie coped both with her secretarial duties and her writing but the work at home drained her energy. She noticed her father also seemed progressively more exhausted as the weeks passed.

One night after dinner he sat lost in thought for a long time and Laurie settled down at the table with him after she finished the dishes. She heaved a big sigh then drank her cup of tea.

"You're tired, too, aren't you, honey?" he began.

"That's true, Father," Laurie said as she covered his big hand with her smaller one.

"I've thought a lot about keeping this house. It's a lot of extra work for both of us and it's a long way from both of our jobs," he continued. "One of the guys told me about a rooming house near Bayside that was pretty nice, not fancy, but comfortable. What do you think about selling the house and moving into it?"

"It's a new idea, Father," Laurie said as she wondered if she could leave the home her mother had made. "Let me think about it for awhile. I'm tired now and my head's too woolly."

The next day she asked Mr. Hunt if she could talk to him about a personal matter. As she closed his office door he asked, "What's put that sparkle in your eyes lately, Laurie? Is it Johnny?"

With an embarrassed blush she said, "Not Johnny, Ben."

"That's much better. Ben is a fine young man. I'd be proud to have him as my son," Mr. Hunt said expansively. "For awhile I thought he might get together with Jenny but that didn't happen."

"What I wanted to talk to you about is my father and me," Laurie began, a little flustered by her temerity in broaching a private matter to her boss.

She explained her father's idea of selling the house and moving to a rooming house. She explained how difficult it would be to leave the home that held so much of her mother. "Neither Father nor I are knowledgeable enough to make the decision without someone wiser helping us," she sighed, "That's why I'm asking your opinion."

Mr. Hunt dropped his chin for a moment or two and then looked into Laurie's eyes intently. He said, "I think a lot of you, Laurie, and I wouldn't presume to tell you and your father what to do. I can tell you a few things to help you think it through before you decide. First, would your mother want you to stay in the house merely because she had lived there? Would it be easier for you and your father to live closer to your jobs? Would you and he lose the feeling of family if you moved into a rooming house? If you decide to do it and sell the house, make sure the money is put in the bank in both your names."

"You've given me a lot to think about, Mr. Hunt. It sorts out the problems we have to consider," Laurie said.

The two talked a while longer. Mr. Hunt suggested other avenues of thought. "And talk to Ben about it," he said as Laurie got up to leave.

At lunchtime, she told Ben about her father's suggestion and Mr. Hunt's remarks. "What do you think, Ben?" she asked.

He thought for some time before he replied. "I think you have too large a burden with a full time job and taking care of the house and your father. It sounds like Karl needs to get away from the extra work and the weight of memories, too." He really wanted her to marry him then she wouldn't have to worry so much but he knew it was too soon to talk about that.

As she wrote in her journal that night, Laurie pondered about the move to a boarding house. What would Mother have wanted us to do, she asked herself? She didn't want to betray her mother's memory by leaving but eventually she realized that Lydia would have wanted what was best for her daughter and her husband. And I'll make sure we keep the feeling of family, she pledged as she drifted off into dreamless slumber.

Laurie and her father visited the rooming house suggested to them. In the big, square house, not elegant but comfortable, they brushed through the tasseled curtains which shielded the sitting room entry where Mrs. Forbes awaited them. The heavy furniture was upholstered in horsehair except a rocking chair with hand-carved arms. Laurie looked at the lawn-like green carpet. A potbellied stove heated the room, and a small table loaded with plants bathed in filtered light from the large window covered with lace curtains.

Books filled the imposing secretary in one corner of the room and the opened desk revealed the pigeonholes where neatly filed papers lodged.

Mrs. Forbes stood as the two walked into the room. Karl had his hat in his hands and Laurie loosened her coat. "We're interested in a couple of rooms next to each other," began Karl. "My daughter and I have decided to sell our house and move into a boarding house."

Mrs. Forbes' dark hair, peppered with gray, formed a pompadour on top of her head. Her ample form filled her dark dress nearly bursting the seams. Kindly she asked, "And what of Mrs. Krafft?"

Laurie replied, "She died of typhoid fever several months ago and there's just Father and me left." She tried not to show her emotion.

"Well, I have two rooms on the second floor with a connecting door. Would you like to see them?" she asked. With nods from both Laurie and her father, she led them up the carpeted stairway. With a flourish, Mrs. Forbes unlocked one of the doors halfway down the long hall.

They followed her into the room, spacious but impersonal. I could fix that, Laurie thought to herself. Then Mrs. Forbes opened the door between the rooms and preceded the two into the room further down the hall. Same as the first, it held a clothes press, large bed, easy chair, and night stand. The wallpaper seemed drab to Laurie but again with personal things in the room, it would be fine.

Turning to Mrs. Forbes, she said, "What about meals? We both work and would need only breakfast and dinner with a packed lunch for work."

Mrs. Forbes said, "That can be arranged. Several of my boarders follow the same pattern."

"And how can I do our laundry?" Laurie continued.

Mrs. Forbes answered, "A woman comes in twice a week to do washing and ironing for a small fee. The bathroom is at the end of the hall."

As they discussed the big step, the Kraffts walked around the neighborhood of the rooming house. They decided the move would be best for them. The relief Laurie experienced surprised her. No longer would she have to do tedious housework and fall into bed so tired she couldn't move. They went back to the rooming house and told Mrs. Forbes they'd move in the first of December and paid the first month's rent for both rooms.

Mrs. Kirby said, "That was a wise move on your part. It's what your mother would have wanted, I'm sure."

Both she and Laurie brushed engine soot from their coats and looked at the snow along the tracks they traveled. The snowfall continued to deepen on the ground.

CHAPTER 17

As the conductor passed down the aisle, Mrs. Kirby asked him how long before they arrived in Spokane.

"In about two hours, ma'am," the man answered.

"That should be time enough for you to finish your story, my dear," she said to Laurie. "Was it difficult to move from your family home?"

"Indeed it was," the young woman replied.

Laurie paused amid boxes erupting with all sorts of family possessions. She found it hard to decide what to store, what to take to their new quarters and what to give away. She had covered herself with a huge apron and tied her hair back carelessly with a hank of ribbon. Overwhelmed by her task, she heaved a big sigh as she heard someone on the porch.

The interruption pleased her no matter who it might be. Rev. Fowles stood at the door. "Oh, I'm so glad you dropped by, Rev. Fowles," Laurie said with genuine enthusiasm. "There's something I want to talk to you about."

She ushered him into the living room and sat on the overstuffed chair as he chose the couch. "Father and I have decided to give Mother's clothes and other usable things to the church for distribution. Can you arrange for someone to come by to pick them up?" Laurie asked. Her breath caught in her throat as she consigned her mother's things to strangers, but Lydia would have wanted it that way.

"Of course, child, just tell me when they'll be ready and God bless you for your charity," Rev. Fowles said piously. "The reason I dropped by was to tell you the result of my research into the matter you spoke to me about at church."

"You mean about the smell of flowers in Mother's room when she died?"

"Yes, my dear child. As I told you then, I didn't smell the roses but I learned that the world of the spirit mingles mysteriously with the physical world in very rare moments," Rev. Fowles explained.

"The sweet essence was sent as a sign that God was with your mother as her soul prepared to separate from her body, a sign for you alone. This is the reason you were aware of the fragrance and I was not. This gift was given to you so that you would remember forever that God's hand was on Lydia as she departed from this earthly life."

Bowing her head, Laurie wept a few quiet tears then derived comfort in the knowledge her mother was so blessed. "Thank you, Rev. Fowles," she said. "You've relieved my mind and I will always remember it as you said."

Laurie regularly attended church services on Sundays, and without urging, her father accompanied her. "Father and I will be living at Bayside, and we might not make it to church as often," Laurie said, "but we'll try."

"Remember, child, that we'll always await you with open arms when you can come to church and you will be in our hearts the rest of the time," Rev. Fowles intoned. With an affectionate pat on Laurie's shoulder, the minister ambled out the door to continue his church duties.

Laurie pulled some boxes into her father's bedroom and began the heart-wrenching task of sorting her mother's possessions. Karl had asked his daughter to do it because he still missed his wife so terribly. At least I can spare him this, she thought. Her mother had asked her to watch out for him.

Nothing hung in the clothes closet Laurie wanted to keep so she boxed it all up for the church. Drawer by drawer she went through the dresser, emptying each one onto the huge four-poster bed.

Spilled out of the drawer with Lydia's undergarments, she saw the mementos her mother had saved through the years; coils of baby hair, school report cards, the newspaper notice of Will's death, and some letters tied with a yellowed ribbon which had once been white. Laurie hadn't recalled her mother getting any correspondence and her curiosity intensified as she undid the ribbon.

She could see by the return address that all of the letters had come from England. As she read, she realized her grandmother had written them. They told how she missed her daughter, and her granddaughter whom she had never seen. A lump of unshed tears grew in Laurie's throat as she read. This woman's pain in losing her daughter reached as deep as Laurie's ache in losing her mother.

She wondered why there were so few letters to span all the years her mother had been gone from England. The last letter, written in a bolder hand, informed Lydia that her mother had died and Lydia would be receiving no more letters from home. It was signed by Lydia's father. Some of the ink that formed the letters was smudged and Laurie realized her mother's tears caused the smudging. Why didn't she tell me, Laurie asked herself in anguish? I would have helped her.

She retied the letters with their old ribbon and carried them upstairs to put with her very special treasures. These letters will be with me always, vowed Laurie, and I'll share them with my children. They will need to know about their ancestors. I wish I knew more about them, too.

It took a week or so for Laurie and her father to feel comfortable in their new home. Pictures on the walls, quilts handcrafted by Lydia on the beds, and items from the home they had both known helped soften the starkness of the rooms in which they lived.

Before they went to bed each night, they left the door between the rooms open and freely entered one another's domains. Sometimes after dinner with the other roomers, they'd sit and talk. Laurie had brought her mother's rocker for her room, and Karl's easy chair was moved into the corner of his.

They had never talked so freely with each other. Laurie hadn't shared much of her inner emotions with her father but now she felt comfortable in talking about her job, Ben, the future, the past, and her dreams.

Karl, in turn, explained how his drinking had taken hold of him. "I wanted Lady Lydia to have the very best of everything like she had been used to at home," he told his daughter. "I tried but I just couldn't make enough money. When I couldn't provide the kind of life she was used to I started drinking to wipe it out of my mind and then I couldn't stop. Every time I felt I had failed her, I stuck my head in a bottle."

With a flash, Laurie realized why Karl had called her mother Lady Lydia, it all made sense now. And she understood what had driven him to drink.

They exchanged pleasantries with the others who lived in the house at breakfast and dinner, but spent the rest of their time together in their rooms. Ben visited frequently and Mrs. Forbes allowed him upstairs only because Laurie's father was there, too.

Father and daughter had talked about Christmas and its painful memories. With Will and Lydia both gone, it promised to be a cheerless holiday until in mid-December Ben solved their problem.

"Aunt Maud insists that you two come to our house for Christmas Day," he launched with a determined set to his jaw. "She refuses to take 'no' for an answer. And if you could see how excited she is about the arrangements you won't refuse her invitation. Of course, I'd be very disappointed if you didn't come, too," he added as an afterthought with a meaningful look at Laurie.

Laurie felt both excited and apprehensive about the Christmas arrangements. Her father appeared nervous, too. She wondered about gifts since nothing had been said so she bought a flowing plant for the house; not too personal but an acknowledgment of the season.

A large Christmas tree in the living room and festoons of holly on the front door made the Davis home very festive. Mistletoe hung in the archway to the front room and Ben took full advantage of it as Laurie entered. She blushed beautifully with a quick glance at Maud to see her reaction. A bright smile told her it was perfectly fine by the straight-laced older woman.

"Aunt Maud baked some of her special Christmas cookies," Ben said, glowing. "She's always made them for me herself. Try some with your eggnog."

Karl pulled at his collar and shrugged his shoulders into his coat continuously. His voice cracked in nervousness. Soon he relaxed as Maud's graciousness put him at ease.

Animated chatter circled the dinner table. Both Laurie and her father needed the frivolity to dispel the aching void left by Will and Lydia.

"Let's go for a walk and let the old folks get to know each other," Ben begged Laurie with a wink at his Aunt Maud.

"Do you mind, Father?" asked Laurie.

"Of course not, honey, I think Maud and I can fill the time very well."

The two young people emerged from the house into the gloriously bright and crisply cold weather. A thin layer of snow reflected the sparkle in their eyes.

They meandered toward the waterfront drinking in the sheer perfection of the day. The cold weather did little to cool their love. Sitting on a discarded beam, they silently wound their arms around each other as they watched the brilliant blue bay with the snow-capped Olympic Mountains beyond. Even the sight of the garbage barge moored for dumping in the bay didn't dim the golden aura.

Ben took his arms from Laurie and she felt a twinge of disappointment as he started to rise. Is it going to be over so soon, she asked herself? Is he restraining himself again?

Instead of pulling her up and walking away, he knelt in the snow and clasped her left hand. "Laurie, I love you and want you to be my wife," he said solemnly.

"Oh, Ben, I love you, too," Laurie said with a catch in her voice realizing the absolute truth of her statement, "but I have to take care of Father. I wish I could marry you but I can't right now." On a solemn note she added, "Besides, you need to know about my past."

"Nothing you have to say would change my mind," Ben said vehemently, "And I don't mean we should get married right away. I was thinking of being engaged and maybe getting married on your nineteenth birthday in August."

Before she could say any more, Ben pulled a small package out of his pocket and gave it to Laurie. Curious, she opened the parcel to find a jeweler's padded box inside.

"Open it, darling," Ben urged.

She did and astonishment swept away her breath. There lay a ring so beautiful it brought tears to her eyes. Ben lifted it from its satin nest and slipped it onto her ring finger.

She started to protest but he stifled her comments with a passionate kiss. Sitting side by side for a few minutes, they held each other's hands tightly. Finally Laurie turned to Ben and said, "I can't accept this ring until you've heard about my birth," she began sadly.

"All right, if you think it's necessary, I'm ready to listen, my sweetheart, but it won't change anything," Ben vowed.

Laurie told him of her mother's deathbed revelation; the mad affair she had gloried in, the pregnancy, the decision her parent's had made and how Karl had rescued both Lydia and her newborn daughter. "I suppose that makes me a bas..., a bas..., a fatherless child," she concluded with a stifled sob and she hung her head. "I will understand perfectly if you want to take the ring back," she sighed woefully.

"Do you think the circumstances of your birth could possibly diminish the depth of my love?" cried Ben. "It's you who are important and not how you were born." He pulled her up to him and tried to kiss away all of her doubts.

"But, Ben, what would Aunt Maud say, and your friends, if they knew?" She had hesitated to tell him about her past for so long and worried it would end their relationship. "Would you want the mother of your children to be illegitimate?"

"What kind of a man do you think I am? I want you and to hell with what others think. And my children couldn't have a better mother."

She thrilled to Ben's reaction. "Yes, Ben, I want to be your wife," she whispered into his ear.

"You should know I've done some things I'm not especially proud of. I guess everyone has things in his past he regrets. But those, ah, indiscretions happened before I met you."

"I understand, Ben. I've done things I'd rather forget, too."

"Let's go tell Aunt Maud and your father," Ben said as he pulled her along the street excitedly.

"I don't want Father to be upset," she began. "Maybe we ought to wait for awhile before telling anyone."

"You can't hide that ring or the look on your face," Ben said, "and besides he'll be happy for us, I know he will."

They pushed through the front door of the Davis house and rushed into the parlor. Maud looked at the pair with knowledge of what had happened on her face. "When are you two going to be married?" she asked sedately with a half-smile.

A frown started to crease Karl's heavy brows but Laurie ran over, knelt beside him, and told him she and Ben were engaged and planned to marry late next year. "Be happy for me, Father," she begged.

"I am, honey," he said as she searched his face. "You know I mean it, don't you?"

She nodded her head and clasped him with gratitude.

"That calls for more eggnog," said Maud as she headed to the kitchen. "I'm delighted for you both, and for Karl and me, too."

Late in March, Laurie came home from work and went directly to her room because she was so tired. Although she felt exhilaration with her work, weekly deadlines and furious activity drained her. She took off her coat and sat in her rocker to think about the events since Christmas.

She and her father went to the Davis house often for dinner. Maud and Karl had established a friendship both seemed to cherish. The depth of her father's knowledge surprised Laurie. She had never thought of him as a learned man. She realized his education came from the seafaring life he had led. His travels had taken him to many foreign lands and his stories fascinated Maud who had traveled abroad in her younger days.

The easy routine at the rooming house left time for Karl and Laurie to share their evening hours except when Ben invited her to a moving picture or out for dinner. Karl never seemed to mind and he always waited up for Laurie so they could talk a bit before they went to bed. They had retained the feeling of family and that affection grew with each passing day. Laurie no longer cautioned herself against the day when Karl might drink again.

She thought Mrs. Forbes had taken a special interest in her father but he seemed unaware of it. He paid no attention to her other than being polite. Laurie could see how an older woman might be drawn to Karl with his rugged good looks, the thick thatch of black hair that sprung from his forehead and the mangled left hand which a woman might find romantic.

Startled out of her reverie by the dinner gong, she wondered why her father hadn't appeared. He's usually here by now, she thought. Maybe they had to work late at the mill.

Dinner was over and still her father had not come home. Her brows drawn into a scowl, she tried to think of where he could be. Please God, don't let him be drinking again!

As she lay in her bed with the adjoining door ajar, she continued to wonder why he had not come home and had not sent word to her. She dozed off a time or two but real sleep eluded her.

As she dressed for work, she hoped Karl had come in late and hadn't wanted to disturb her. She looked into his room and saw the bed had not been slept in.

She pushed her breakfast around on her plate but ate little. She picked up her lunch and headed for work distracted by worry.

Ben met her as she entered the lobby and saw her frown. "What's wrong, sweetheart?" he asked solicitously.

"Father didn't come home last night, Ben, and just when I was sure he wouldn't drink again. Even when he drank, he always came home," she said her voice choked with tears.

"Don't worry, Laurie, let me make a few calls and see what I can find out," reassured Ben.

Laurie went back to her desk to start the work day unable to decide what else she could do. I'll depend on Ben, she told herself, and settled down to work.

CHAPTER 18

Worry nearly drove Laurie out of her mind. She didn't know what she would have done without Ben and Mr. Hunt.

Ben used all of his skills as a reporter and all of his contacts to trace Karl's movements on the day he disappeared. Mr. Hunt agreed he could be spared for the day after Ben explained that Laurie's father had failed to come home.

Ben talked to the mill manager on the phone and dashed away to meet him in person. He had used Robert James as a news source several times so talking to him would be easy.

He went into Mr. James' office and the small, nervous man with the abbreviated dark mustache shook his hand. The manager's suit coat hung on the back of his swivel chair, and his gnarled hands told of his background as a mill laborer.

"My fiancée's father, Karl Krafft, didn't come home last night and we're trying to find out what happened to him," Ben started. "We were wondering if something had occurred at the mill that might explain his absence."

"Well, Ben, the workers got some bad news yesterday," Mr. James explained. "We're shutting the mill down for awhile. The shingle weavers' union is giving us grief and we're having a tough time selling our shingles. This isn't for publication but it might explain Karl's disappearance. He might have been very upset."

"Who's his foreman?" Ben asked. "Maybe he knows what happened to Karl."

"That would be Don Hendry. He should be around here somewhere. I'll send for him," Mr. James said and went to the door to relay his message. As he sat down again he made pleasant conversation. "So some young girl has hooked you, Ben. She'd better be on her toes to keep track of you."

"She's beautiful and intelligent, and I'll have to keep track of her. She works at the paper, too. You might have read her column in the paper called 'Happenings.' She does have a mind of her own," Ben said. Some of the girls he had dated, even debutantes, hadn't been known for their mental acuity.

A bold rap on the door announced the foreman and he pushed his way through the opening. "You wanted me, boss?" he asked. He was a bull of a man with a gruff manner. Ben felt his strength and could see how such a man might be needed to control the men on his shift.

"We need to find out what Karl Krafft did yesterday, Don. Can you remember the last time you saw him and who he was with?" Mr. James asked.

"Let's see, we told the men at noon the mill was closing," Don said as he stroked his chin in thought. "There was almost a fight but I stopped it. I sort of remember that Karl took off with a couple of his former cronies. They hadn't spent much time together for a long time since Karl quit drinkin'. I thought at the time it could lead to trouble but I was lookin' for problems anyway so maybe I read too much into it."

"Thanks, Don. What were the names of those two old cronies?" James asked his foreman.

"Nels Hanson and Stan Carlson, a couple of shingle sawyers," answered Don. "They're pretty heavy drinkers so a good place to start lookin' would be the saloons. Those two will stay soused until their money runs out." He braced his shoulders and added, "I hope they didn't go to Seattle to spend it."

Ben thanked Mr. James and pondered what he had heard as he walked out of the office and down the road leading away from the mill. It will hurt Laurie very much if her father started drinking again, he thought. He hoped there'd be another explanation. He called Laurie to tell her he still followed some leads, not wanting to upset her with what he'd learned.

While Ben moved from saloon to saloon looking for Karl's two friends, Laurie headed for Riverside. Maybe someone had seen her father. Leaving a note for Ben with Charlie Shaefer, she caught the streetcar toward her old home.

Full of doubts she plodded down the wooden sidewalks hoping for some revelation about her father. As she passed their former home she thought how much she had changed since she had lived there. She was so opinionated then, she mused, everything so right or so wrong, no middle way. How much pain she must have caused her mother when she spoke so badly of Father. She always said he did the best he could for us, and she was right.

So much has happened to change me. I've found out things aren't as right and wrong as I thought they were. If you listen with your heart as well as your mind, you learn so much more, she concluded as she went up the steps to the Jenson house.

In response to her knock, round Sally answered the door with the twins clutching her skirt. "They're so cute," Laurie said grabbing one of them and twirling around. "It's hard to believe it's been two years since Mother and I delivered them," she said with a catch in her voice. The twins were round like their mother and chortled with glee at Laurie's attention.

"It's good to see you, Laurie. You haven't been around much since you and Karl moved to Bayside," sighed Sally. "We've missed you. How about some coffee?"

"Thanks, no, Sally, I dropped by to see if you'd seen Father yesterday or today. He didn't come home last night and I'm worried about him," Laurie explained.

"Well, no, I haven't but I'll call Henry in from the back yard to see if he knows," she said as she went to the back door to holler at Henry. "The mill shut down yesterday and maybe that has something to do with it. We're just about out of our minds with worry. These five kids take a lot of money and the old man has his needs, too. Oh, here's Henry. Henry, Laurie is looking for her father. She hasn't seen him since yesterday."

"Gee, I'm sorry, Laurie. When we got laid off yesterday, he was real mad. He took off with Nels and Stan but I don't know where they went. I came home," Henry said apologetically. "If I hear anything, I'll sure let you know."

"Do you know where Nels and Stan live?" Laurie asked.

"They're both single and live in a rooming house here in Riverside," Henry said giving her the address.

"Well, I'm going to walk around the neighborhood for awhile and then see if those two men are in their rooms. Maybe someone can tell me something. I have to find him."

Laurie hugged each of the twins again and went out the door dejectedly. She walked slowly and queried people along the street she had known before. She went up the broad steps and knocked on the door of the rooming house where Nels and Stan lived.

When the landlady answered the door, Laurie asked, "Are either Nels or Stan here?"

"Nope, haven't seen 'em since they went to work yesterday but I heard the mill closed down so they're probably dead drunk somewhere," she sneered as she scratched under one arm. With her lips in a permanent pucker, she said, "You don't look the type to visit the likes of them two. What do you want 'em for?"

"My father works at the mill, too, and he didn't come home last night. I was told he was with them," Laurie explained with a sinking heart.

The woman shook her head as she clicked her tongue and closed the door.

Laurie turned and went down the stairs on her way back to the streetcar. She couldn't think of anywhere else to look and she couldn't go into the saloons. Ben planned to canvas them, he had told her.

If I can just find him, I don't care if he's drinking, Laurie said to herself, I want him to be with me. He's all the family I have left.

Laurie asked Mrs. Forbes when she got home, "Has Father come in yet?"

"Come into the sitting room," the landlady said as she drew the weary girl between the portieres into the cozy room. "No, dear, I haven't seen or heard from him and there are no messages for you."

Laurie could see her distress. She does have some affection for Father, she thought. She's worried about him, too. She settled heavily into the rocker with the carved lions' heads. The girl put her hands over her face and started to cry.

"Where can he be and what's happened to him?" she moaned through her fingers. "Ben's looking through the saloons for some news about him but I'm still worried sick. He could be lying hurt somewhere."

"Go up to your room, dear," Mrs. Forbes said, "and I'll bring you some tea. That'll help."

Laurie thought that's exactly what her mother would have said and done.

Laboriously, she climbed to her room hoping her father might have come in unnoticed but she knew better. No one ever came or went without Mrs. Forbes's knowledge. She glanced into his empty room before she took off her coat and hat. The raw March day had left her cold and miserable.

Tea soothed her sore throat and calmed her raveled nerves a little. What do I do now, she asked herself? She and her father had become so close since her mother's death. She yearned for him. She had wasted so much of her time being angry with him when she should have appreciated him, she thought. If he were only here now, she'd tell him how much she loved him and how sorry she was it took so long to realize it.

Exhausted by her sleepless night and her journey to the old neighborhood, Laurie dozed in the rocker. Mrs. Forbes tucked the quilt around her and tip-toed from the room.

She didn't know how long she had slept but she awoke with a lurch when she heard footsteps in the hall. Maybe that's him, she thought eagerly. She pushed the quilt aside and ran to the door jerking it open. Ben took her into his arms and held her for a moment. Mrs. Forbes followed right behind him. A young male visitor was not allowed on the second floor without a chaperon and Laurie didn't have one now.

They both came into the room and Ben gently pushed Laurie down into the rocker once again. Mrs. Forbes sat primly on the edge of the bed. Kneeling beside Laurie, Ben told of his trek through the saloons without finding the two men who had been with her father.

"I was told they'd probably gone to Seattle for more booze and women," Ben continued. "I went to see Chief Kraley down at the police station to see if he knew anything. He called the hospitals but your father hadn't been brought in, and he sure wasn't in jail. The chief said he'd make some inquiries and let me know tomorrow."

"Did you get my message at the *Herald*, Ben?" asked Laurie. When he said he had, she told of her visit to the rooming house, the Jensons and about the others she had talked to in the old neighborhood, all to no avail.

"I think you ought to stay home tomorrow, sweetheart," Ben said, worried about the drawn look on Laurie's face. "Mr. Hunt can get along without you for one day."

"Oh, Ben, I need to keep busy. I can't sit around doing nothing, I'd go crazy with worry," Laurie cried. "At least I'll be where something is happening, and maybe the chief will have some news."

Ben knew it was useless to argue with her.

At work the next day, Laurie tried to keep her mind stuffed with other things but she became distracted anyway. Mr. Hunt, in blunt kindness, told her the paper would do everything it could to trace her father. Even Charlie Shaefer stopped her in the lobby and peered out from under his green eyeshade as he told her in his taciturn way that Karl would turn up soon.

Ben went by her desk into Mr. Hunt's office with a grim, "I'll see you in a few minutes, sweetheart, I have to see Mr. Hunt first, then we'll talk."

Laurie could hear the murmuring voices in the inner office. What are they talking about, she asked herself? She wondered if it had something to do with her father.

Soon, Mr. Hunt came out of his office and summoned Laurie. She sat in her usual chair with her pencil poised ready to take dictation. "You don't need to take notes now, Laurie," Mr. Hunt said kindly. "Ben has something to tell you."

She gripped her hands together in her lap as she looked at Ben with dread. "What did you find out, Ben?" she asked needing to know but afraid of what he might say.

"The chief asked me to come over to the station this morning. He had sent some of his boys to the saloons. They found out more than I did," Ben said and then paused as Laurie waited with fear gnawing in her stomach.

"They traced your father to the saloon at the east end of Hewitt that's right on the river. The bartenders remember Karl very well; he had been a frequent patron at the place before he quit drinking. There's no mistaking him for anyone else with that left hand of his," Ben continued his solemn story. "They admit he was there and had gone down the hallway to the bathroom sometime after midnight but they didn't see him come back again. Nor did anyone else see him after that."

"Is that the same saloon Sally Jenson told me about a long time ago where drinks are drugged and the guys lowered through a trap door into a waiting skiff then sold to the sailing ships?" Laurie stumbled over the words. "I think they call it shanghaiing."

"I'm afraid so, honey," said Ben worried about how this would affect her. "No one can prove what happened but we do know for a fact it was the last place he was seen."

Laurie looked at Ben and Mr. Hunt in horror. "Oh, no, that couldn't have happened to him. I can't lose him now that I've just found him. He's all I have left."

Ben suppressed his resentment that she didn't remember she had him. He knelt beside her and put his arms around her. She couldn't control her trembling.

Mr. Hunt said, "I'm sorry, Laurie, but it looks as if that's what happened. I've assigned Aaron to do a story on the practice so we can at least discourage it from happening again. The chief said he'll use all of his resources. I know that's little comfort but at least we can assume your father is still alive."

Laurie got up from her chair with a shudder and said, "I appreciate what you've both done for me. I have to get back to work."

"Take the rest of the day off, Laurie," Mr. Hunt said but she shook her head.

Now all my family is gone, she cried inwardly.

"How terrible for you, my dear," Mrs. Kirby sympathized as she patted Laurie's clenched hands.

"It's painful to relive it," the young woman said.
"But it's also cleansing," the wise elderly woman counseled.

CHAPTER 19

Laurie continued with her job although the disappearance of her father remained a dull pain in her heart. More and more she realized how much she loved Ben and how much he loved her. It helped relieve the deep ache she felt.

When she returned to her rooming house every day she hoped there would be a message from her father, and each day her hope proved fruitless.

Late in May, she entered the rooming house with the usual hope in her heart and Mrs. Forbes greeted her in the entry way. "My dear, there's a letter from Japan waiting for you. Maybe it's from your father," she said excitedly.

Laurie took the letter from Mrs. Forbes's hand and raced upstairs. She wanted to be by herself when she read it. She didn't see the look of disappointment on the older woman's face.

To prolong the moment, she took off her coat and hat, and opened the window a trifle to absorb the warm May day. The envelope had strange oriental markings on it and she carefully slit the top.

A money order for two hundred dollars fell into her lap as she took the letter out of its envelope. The letter explained. "Dear Laurie, I know you must be worried about me but I want you to know what happened. As you've probably already found out, the mill closed and I went out of my mind. I started boozing with my two buddies and the saloon at the end of Hewitt by the river is the last I remember. They must have put something in my drink because the next thing I sensed was the motion of the ship on the high seas. At first I thought I was just a young man again feeling the salt air on my face and the lift of the ship but I soon realized I had been shanghaied and pressed into service aboard a lumber schooner.

"We're in Japan and will be leaving here today. I had to write you so you'd know where I am. Life aboard ship isn't too bad and because of my experience the captain has made me second mate so my billet is comfortable.

"We got some of our pay and I am sending it to you to put in our joint bank account. I will not drink again so have little need for money. My board and room are included on the job." Laurie could see her father's wry smile as he wrote that.

"We're about ready to shove off now, honey, but I want you to know I love you very much and I'll see you as soon as we reach port again. I'll probably stay with the ship, though, it's more permanent than the shingle mill.

"I hope I get home in time for your wedding. I have to give the bride away, don't I? Your loving Father."

Laurie sat back and clasped the letter to her as if it were her father she embraced. What a relief it was to know for sure. She had to share the news with Ben right away. Mrs. Forbes just happened to be in the hallway when she rushed down the stairs. "It is from him," Laurie said happily, "and what we thought happened really did. I've got to call Ben."

Just as she reached for the phone, the door opened and Ben came in. He saw her joyful look and his face broke into a smile. "You've heard from your father," he said.

"Oh, yes, Ben, and it happened just the way we thought it did. Here, read it for yourself," Laurie said. She flung her arms around Ben and then hugged Mrs. Forbes. "There's enough money to pay for his room until my wedding with some left over," Laurie said. "Then he'll probably go back to sea. He seems to like it. He gave it up for Mother when they were married."

After Ben read the letter, Laurie handed it to Mrs. Forbes to read. "Why is it, darling, that every time I really need you, you show up?" Laurie asked Ben. "You seem to appear whenever I need to talk to you."

"I hope that's the way it'll always be, sweetheart," said Ben, "and now we'd better be planning our wedding. We've only got a couple of months."

Amid the flurry of wedding arrangements, Ben and Laurie had their jobs to do. They met in passing and tried to have lunch together as often as they could.

One brilliant day near the end of July, Mr. Hunt called them both into the office. Clearing his throat he asked, "If I sent you both to the Alaska-Yukon-Pacific Exposition in Seattle, could you behave yourselves and bring me a couple of good stories?"

Both said they could be trusted and jumped at the chance to visit the fairgrounds. The exposition celebrated the riches of Alaska which now belonged to the United States.

"Snohomish County Day is August third and most of the communities will send delegations. The county and Everett have a stake in the exposition. That half-mill levy raised over twelve thousand dollars for the county's booth," Mr. Hunt said refreshing their memories. He gave them the train tickets and the press passes they would need.

"Ben, I want you to talk to the dignitaries like Teddy Roosevelt, William Jennings Bryant and President Taft. Laurie, I want you to do a piece like you did on the circus; what you see and what you feel," Mr. Hunt explained. He pressed his fingers together in a pyramid thoughtfully. "And I'd like to hear how appropriate you think it is to have the exposition on the University of Washington campus. Be sure to spend some time at the Snohomish County booth and find out how the money was spent. You'd better be on the job the day after, too."

Suppressed excitement filled both Ben and Laurie as they boarded the morning train to Seattle. Decorated cars from different towns were hooked onto their train and everyone was agog with anticipation. People from all over the county staggered with the movement of the train as they greeted each other in the aisles. Ben and Laurie joined in the jostling and finally sat side by side as they watched the watery expanse of Puget Sound.

"I've always wanted to ride the train again," said Laurie. "I barely remember how excited I was when we came here from Minnesota. The scenery was so impressive, as I recall."

"I wish we had time to take the train back where you were born for our honeymoon but there just isn't time now. We'll go later after we're old married folks," Ben said.

The train wound around the Puget Sound shoreline to the Union Station on King Street. All the county people paraded up Yesler Way to Third Street where they took the crowded streetcar out to the fairgrounds. Laurie could see the glistening white domes in the distance. As they went through the entrance, sounds, smells and sights became a feast for the senses.

Mr. Hunt had given them money for food, rides, and sideshows. They clapped in time to marching bands, craned back their necks to observe the carnival rides, and watched as fairgoers tried their hands at games. Ben stopped at the shooting gallery.

"Your writing is much better than your marksmanship," Laurie told him. A grin softened her comment.

For ten cents, Ben took the Aero Plunge but it frightened Laurie. She noted that the boys wore knickers, young girls had on calf-length dresses and most women were dressed as she was, in long skirts and high-necked waists. Most wore big hats while her small one perched precariously atop her pompadour. A few daring women sported new pegged hobble skirts. She wondered how they could get into a streetcar wearing them. They might be stylish and show a delectable ankle but they'd be so inconvenient.

The Streets of Cairo Oriental Village intrigued Laurie the most with live camels, Egyptian music on strange instruments, and obelisks flanking the entrance. Both Ben and Laurie were impressed by the realism of the simulated battle between the iron-clad Civil War ships, the *Monitor* and the *Merrimac*. Cloth of varying blue colors waved behind the two ships giving the illusion they really floated, and lights flashed amid sounds of bursting artillery adding to the realism.

They bought strange food and strolled through the formal gardens as they ate. People continually crowded the Snohomish County booth that extolled the vast array of natural settings, good economic times, and pleasures awaiting fairgoers.

"I have to go listen to what the dignitaries have to say now, sweetheart. Where shall I meet you afterwards?" Ben asked.

"I'm going with you," Laurie answered. "After all, I want to know what they say, too. They might talk about women's suffrage."

Later, many of the Snohomish County people joined the throng dancing in the Washington Building, Laurie and Ben among them. She delighted in how closely she fit into Ben's arms and how gracefully he danced.

After the glorious day together, the two got on the streetcar again headed for the railroad station. Glaring lights, loud music and excited voices launched them on their trip home.

On the train, Ben put his arm around Laurie and she rested her head on his shoulder. The lights in the railroad car dimmed and they felt alone. Their fatigue did not diminish their love.

As Ben walked Laurie to her rooming house, he'd stop once in awhile and gather her into his arms. He kissed her passionately and she responded just as ardently not caring if people saw them. Her reserve crumbled bit by bit.

At her door, he again enfolded her and kissed her. His impassioned embrace and kisses left Laurie breathless. She raised her arms and put them around

Ben's neck and pressed her body to his. He hungrily pushed his own body against hers lost in his longing for her. He suddenly released his hold and stepped back.

"What's wrong, Ben?" Laurie asked.

"I want to make love to you so bad I can barely stand it," he said. "It's very hard to control myself and I'm afraid one of these times I won't be able to stop and then you'd hate me."

"I don't understand, Ben. The books I've read didn't say much about passion except in flowery terms. You'll have to teach me," Laurie said wistfully, "and I could never hate you. I love you."

Their stories about the Alaska-Yukon-Pacific Exposition sparked a lot of calls asking for more information. People wanted to experience it for themselves. Mr. Hunt told the two reporters how wise he'd been to send them.

Laurie hadn't heard from her father again, but she knew he'd be home soon. Just in case he might not arrive in time, she asked Mr. Hunt to give her away at her wedding. He expressed his pleasure that she felt close enough to him to have him for a substitute father.

Laurie chose Alice for her matron of honor and Ben asked Aaron to serve as best man. The four of them had dinner together a month before the wedding to talk about the plans. Laurie noticed that Ben solicited her opinion whereas Aaron expressed what he thought without giving Alice a chance to speak.

"He treats her like a second-class citizen," Laurie exploded to Ben after they had left the Fields. "He doesn't appreciate what a warm, intelligent person Alice is. I've half a mind to tell him that."

"Now, sweetheart, you can't interfere in their lives. Be there if Alice needs to talk to you but don't pour your anger on Aaron," Ben said. "It's up to Alice to stick up for herself if she wants to. You can't make her."

"Of course you're right, Ben," Laurie said, divested of her exasperation. "You'll always listen to me, won't you?"

"I always have, haven't I? And I don't intend to change that. One thing I will have to change, though. I've always gone where I wanted, when I wanted and now I'll consider you first. It'll be worth sacrificing that freedom for a jewel like you."

She flung her arms around him and said, "There's so much I have to learn, dear Ben. I want you for my professor."

"I'm the best teacher in the world when it comes to you," he said softly.

The wedding day approached rapidly and Laurie anticipated it with both joy and apprehension. Would her father be home in time? She had wanted to share it with him so much.

One of the phones on her desk jolted her out of her reverie. "Everett Daily Herald," she began but before she could say anything else, Ben's voice came over the wire.

He sounded breathless and intense. "Sweetheart, put the receiver on the desk and go tell Mr. Hunt the courthouse is on fire then come back and I'll dictate the story to you," Ben said trying to catch his breath. "I don't want to let go of the phone."

Laurie did as he told her and picked up the phone again. "Mr. Hunt is sending Johnny out to help you, Ben. I'm ready with my pad and pencil."

He told her the details of the fire as he knew them. "It started this afternoon, August second, in the Iles and Newman Carriage and Wheel factory across from the county courthouse. The factory, a large frame building, is completely destroyed. Sparks and heat from the seething blaze soon ignited the roof of the courthouse. A mass of flame beyond the control of the firemen on the scene is leveling the county building. It looks as if the annex will be saved." Ben took a deep gulp of air and then asked if Laurie had gotten all of that.

"Yes I have, Ben," she answered. "Where are you calling from?"

"I'm in a store across the street at the end of the block," he answered.

"Be careful and come back as soon as you can. I'll have these notes typed up by the time you're back." Dear God, please don't let anything happen to him, she prayed.

The next day, she went with Ben to see the ruins of the courthouse. Only charred, wobbly brick walls remained with nothing but heaps of smoking ruin inside. It seemed just threads of masonry kept some of the teetering walls upright. Exhausted firemen slept on the lawn across the street from the smoldering hulk after their valiant fight.

What a shame, thought Laurie, especially after the city of Everett had donated the structure to the county following the county seat fight between Everett and the city of Snohomish. At least the firemen had saved the new annex finished last year. County government would continue.

Two days before her wedding, Laurie's old restlessness troubled her. She had not heard from her father. She insisted on working to relieve her anxiety. All the plans were made, the dress finished, food chosen, and honeymoon arranged.

Unable to eat her lunch, she walked disconsolately along Hewitt to Bayside. She gazed at the water in one of her last days as a single woman. The seagulls' raucous cries echoed her forlorn feeling. She saw a ship sailing into Port Gardner Bay under full canvas and watched as the crewmen furled the sails slowing the advance of the empty ship riding high in the water. Inch by inch it warped into the pier at the end of Pacific Avenue.

Its progress mesmerized Laurie. She couldn't take her eyes from it until it docked. She heaved a big sigh and wandered back to work. If only her father were on board, she thought pensively.

Her column had to be in to Mr. Hunt today for Friday publication. She made phone calls, read press releases and finally pulled it all together for 'Happenings.' It's wonderful to be part of the community's fabric this way, she thought with a smile. Ben knew how much her job meant to her. He agreed she should go on working, at least until they had a family. She thought fondly of the Jenson twins and how she felt when she cuddled them in her arms.

She heard a commotion in the lobby and raised her head in time to see a big, dark man stride down the hall toward her. She jumped up and ran to him. "Oh, Father, I'm so glad you're here. I didn't want to get married without you," she cried as tears of joy streamed down her face.

She caught her breath as she pulled away and looked at this man whom she had missed so terribly. His tanned face broke into a grin. His dark hair, sprinkled with white strands, hung over his forehead the way she remembered. He had trimmed all excess fat from his body. He looked wonderfully fit and happy.

"Laurie, honey, you've really grown up since I've been away. You're lovely," he said with pride. So many unspoken feelings hung between them. They'd sort them out later.

She ran in to tell Mr. Hunt her father had just arrived as she handed her copy to him.

"You don't mind if I'm a little disappointed I won't be giving you away, I hope?" he asked with a shy dip of his head.

"Oh, Mr. Hunt, you've been so much more than a boss to me," she said as she leaned down and kissed his cheek. She thought she saw tears in his eyes.

He said gruffly, "Take the rest of the day off" and swiveled around in his chair.

I understand you, you old softy, she said to herself.

Next, she pulled her father down the hallway to the press room to see Ben. Ben stood up with a delighted grin on his face. Karl reached out to shake Ben's hand but the young man pushed it aside and gave Karl a mighty hug.

"Thanks for taking care of my girl," Karl said. "She means everything to me."

"And to me, too," replied Ben.

Laurie absolutely glowed surrounded by the love of these two men.

"Father and I are going to the rooming house now, Ben. Are you going to drop by later?" Laurie asked.

Ben thought a moment and said, "Better yet, Aunt Maud and I want you to come to dinner."

"You haven't had time to talk to her, yet," Laurie protested.

"That's true but I'm sure my aunt will want to hear about Karl's adventures first hand. Dinner at six?"

CHAPTER 20

"Then you did marry Ben after all," Mrs. Kirby stated rather than asked. "I gathered that from your last name."

"Oh, yes," Laurie said. "I remember the day very well." She glowed with the recollection.

Today I will become Mrs. Ben Davis, thought Laurie as she luxuriated in her bed stretching her arms above her head. She jumped out from beneath the covers and raced to the window to see if the sun would shine on her. Indeed it would.

The dinner at Aunt Maud's had been delightful and her father had told of his seafaring adventures. Yesterday Mrs. Forbes had kept him occupied most of the day recounting what had happened to him. His every word seemed to enthrall her.

As Laurie brushed her long, shining hair, she looked into the mirror. Although it might be my imagination, she thought, I look older, more mature. Her cheeks reddened as she appraised herself.

Before donning her wedding gown, she'd have a luxurious bath with bath salts. She had bought some fragrant bath powder to pat on afterwards. She dreamed as she soaked among the bubbles.

When she got back to her room, she supposed she should eat some breakfast. A light knock sounded at the door from her father's room. She opened it in anticipation and he stood there with a breakfast tray.

"I thought we'd like to eat alone this morning, honey," her father said. "This is the last time we'll eat breakfast together for a long time and I want it to be just you and me."

"Me, too, Father," she said and pointed to the small table where he could set the tray. It held coffee for him and tea for her. She barely touched the hot biscuits and the eggs went uneaten. Both talked of Lady Lydia and how much they missed her. She should be here for her daughter's wedding. Although Laurie felt her there in spirit, her absence still left a void. "Will would have been fifteen now," said Laurie.

"I know, honey," said Karl. "You said what was in my mind."

As she nibbled a bite or two, her father reached into his pocket and brought out a small, white box. "I wanted you to have something special for this day and while I was in the Orient I found exactly what I wanted for you," he said as he handed her the box.

It reminded her of her treasured birthday locket which had come from a white box, too, so long ago.

She didn't think she could be any more excited but her enchantment grew. She carefully opened the box revealing a beautifully-carved jade necklace. Karl fastened the clasp for her and she relished the warmth of the stones on her bare neck. She dashed to the mirror to look at them and then ran back to kneel at her father's knee. "It is so lovely," she said as she kissed his cheek. "I will treasure it always and when you're away, it'll be our link. I'm going to wear it for my wedding."

Mrs. Forbes knocked on the door of Laurie's room and asked if she needed help dressing. "Of course I do, dear Mrs. Forbes," she replied and opened the door wide. "See what Father has brought me from the East?" she asked as she dragged the older woman into her room.

"I've arranged for a closed carriage in an hour," Karl said as he went through the connecting door to his bedroom.

Mrs. Forbes fussed around trying to help Laurie. Actually the young woman could have dressed herself but Mrs. Forbes was so eager to be part of the wedding. Although just a landlady, she acted as if she were the mother Laurie needed on her wedding day.

Karl let them know when the carriage arrived at the door and both ladies joined him in the parlor, Laurie in her wedding gown, and Mrs. Forbes in a soft mauve-colored dress with strings of jewels dangling from her aging neck.

The carriage carried them to the Davis house for the wedding. Karl went ahead before he helped the women alight.

"I want to make sure Ben doesn't see his bride before the wedding," he said, "not that I'm superstitious." He whisked his daughter and her helper up the stairs to the room the newlyweds would share after they were married.

Ben had asked if she would mind living in the Davis mansion, and Laurie had agreed it was the best thing to do. Some day they'd have a home of their own, with children, but right now, they decided they'd both be comfortable with Aunt Maud.

Soon Alice tapped on the door and joined in the excitement. Alice and Mrs. Forbes fidgeted around Laurie wanting to help but not really knowing what to do. The bride, used to doing for herself, carefully avoided offending either one of her two close friends.

Laurie looked around the large sitting room next to the bedroom she and Ben would share. She had packed most of her things already and her father would bring them over while the Davises were on their honeymoon. She asked him to especially bring her mother's rocking chair for the sitting room.

When the couple had decided to stay with Aunt Maud, the older woman had turned a bedroom into the sitting room so the young people could have a place of their own. Laurie had helped with choosing draperies, furniture and carpet. She liked the light, airy look they had created so even on wet, dreary Pacific Northwest days, it would be a bright spot.

Both she and Ben agreed they didn't want a pretentious wedding. A few close friends, family, and some coworkers would be present. They had chosen to have a buffet afterwards rather than a large dinner. Maud's cook seemed delighted she was to be the one in charge.

Flowers filled the gracious, stately living room. White lilies decked the mantel where Rev. Fowles stood. The organ in the corner of the room had once given a lot of pleasure to Maud but her arthritic hands no longer could roam across the keyboard. During the wedding practice, Mrs. Fowles caressed the keys. She told Laurie she had never played so grand an instrument.

After everyone assembled in the living room, Laurie descended the stairs on her father's arm. When Ben saw his bride enter the back of the room, his jaw dropped in wonderment. Laurie's ivory satin petticoat glimmered through the lace of her dress. The jade necklace nestled around the high neck, and the white orchids of her bouquet trembled as she walked. A satin crown held the lace veil on her head.

Exclamations of approval could be heard as she and her father walked slowly down the aisle between the chairs. Maud murmured to Mrs. Forbes, "I've never seen a lovelier bride. She's the daughter I've never had just like Ben's the son I didn't bear."

When Ben lifted Laurie's veil to kiss her after the vows, he gathered her to him passionately instead of mechanically touching her lips. Quietly he whispered, "I pledge myself to you for the rest of my life."

Unable to reply because of the unshed tears of joy in her throat, she nodded, and together they turned to greet their friends. Alice dabbed at her eyes and Mrs. Forbes teetered on the brink of sobs. Laurie noticed her father's damp eyes.

The wedding guests entered the dining room where the cook had laid out the buffet to perfection. She stood behind the kitchen's swinging door and pushed it gently so she could watch. She smiled at the "oohs" and "aahs" she heard.

Before guests loaded food onto their plates, Mr. Hunt made sure that everyone had a glass of champagne and then proposed a toast to the newlyweds. "Long life and happiness to my two favorite people," he said as everyone raised their glasses.

Laurie looked at her father with misgiving and his nod reassured her he just touched the glass to his lips to honor the toast. She had never tasted spirits before but maybe on this occasion one sip wouldn't hurt her. She raised the glass and with her eyes on Ben, took a little in her mouth. The bubbles tickled her nose and she laughed as she rubbed it. She found the biting taste refreshing.

The young couple cut the beautiful wedding cake the cook had baked and exchanged morsels of the confection. Laughter and warmth filled the room but the newlyweds eagerly awaited their honeymoon trip to Seattle. Ben had promised her they'd take a train trip to Minnesota in a few years, maybe on their fifth anniversary.

As Laurie started up the stairs to change her clothes, she tossed her bridal bouquet to the waiting women. A gleeful giggle erupted from Mrs. Forbes as she caught it, a certain gleam in her eye as she looked at Karl.

When Laurie came down the stairs to her waiting husband, she went first to her father. "I know you'll be gone when I get back," she said with a catch in her voice. "You'll never know how much it meant to me to have you here to give me away," she said as she hugged him close to her. "Remember you always have a home with us whenever you want it. You're my only link to the past and I treasure you."

"I'll always come back to you, honey," Karl said. Dashing a tear out of his eye he added, "Lady Lydia would have been very proud of you today."

Ben and Laurie looked forward to revisiting the exposition in Seattle while they stayed at the Olympic Hotel. As they entered the hotel lobby after the train trip from Everett, Laurie stood and marveled at the rich interior. Dream-like, she looked at her fairy prince beside her.

She was distressed about what would happen when they got to their room. Although she loved Ben with all of her heart, she didn't know exactly what to expect. The books she devoured usually ended at marriage with "and they lived happily ever after."

To delay the intimacy she expected, she suggested they have dinner in the dining room first. Puzzled, Ben agreed.

When they got to their room, the luggage sat on the floor. The large room had a big double bed. The window looked out over Elliott Bay and Laurie didn't feel the restlessness she usually felt when she looked at far horizons.

The setting sun cast a rosy glow into the room from behind the Olympic Mountains across the bay. They had not yet lit the lamps. Ben stood behind his new bride as they watched the orange orb descend and light faded in the room. Turning her to him, Ben lowered his lips onto hers and with a sigh murmured how much he loved her.

"Be patient with me, dear Ben," she said to him. "I really don't know what I'm supposed to do."

"Don't worry, sweetheart, I told you I was a good teacher," Ben said.

When Laurie started to unpack her bag, Ben took hold of her hands and suggested she take her nightgown and robe into the bathroom to change. When she hesitantly came back into the room, Ben waited for her in his robe. He picked her up and held her to him as she laid her head on his shoulder, her arms encircling his neck.

Slowly, he took her to the bed, removed her robe, and gently placed her among the soft blankets. He pulled the covers over her, and then took off his robe. He had nothing on underneath it and she blushed as she saw his body then quickly looked away.

Laurie, who had hated to be touched, abandoned herself completely to his lovemaking in joyous ecstasy.

Ben held his wife gently in his arms. A tear ran down her cheek. In alarm he asked, "What's wrong, sweetheart?"

"I'm just so happy I can't help crying. I've never felt so loved or loved so much in my whole life," she answered and pressed herself to him again.

The young couple rode the train back to Everett tired in a wonderful way, living again in retrospect their honeymoon. They bought a small silver spoon stamped with many symbols and pictures of the Alaska-Yukon-Pacific Exposition to remind them of the time spent on the grounds and their honeymoon.

As they went into the Davis house, they noticed some valises sitting in the entry way. Maud came out of the parlor, dressed for traveling. Ben and Laurie looked at each other then at Maud.

"Aunt Maud, are you going somewhere?" Ben asked somewhat shocked.

"I'm going to France to visit an old friend for a month," the stately lady said, "and besides, I decided you two should be by yourselves for awhile without an old lady looking on."

"You'll never be old, Aunt Maud, and this is your home," said Ben.

"It would never have been a home without you, Ben, dear," the older woman said. "I never married nor had children but you two are mine as if I had borne you. Now trust me to know what's best. I'm going and that's that."

With a warm embrace and kiss, both Ben and Laurie stood aside as Maud went out to the waiting carriage for her ride to the Great Northern depot. Ben picked up her bags and packed them beside her. "Write to us, Aunt Maud, so we know you're all right."

Maud told him, "I have left my friend's name and address on the parlor table so you'll know where I am." With a wave of her hand, she bid them good-bye.

Laurie and Ben looked at each other in wonder as they went into the house again. With a laugh he picked her up in his arms and ran up the stairs with her to their new home.

CHAPTER 21

When Laurie entered the *Herald*'s lobby after she and Ben had returned from their honeymoon, dour Charlie Shaefer told her marriage must agree with her. A slight hint of a smile lifted the corners of his mouth as he ducked behind his cage again.

Somehow, Laurie felt more confident and ready to meet the world head-on since the wedding. Only a short time ago she was a young girl from Riverside with nothing but determination and some writing talent and now she was a wife, secretary, and writer.

The delight she and Ben found in each other had deepened as they learned about one another. With Aunt Maud in France, the cook didn't come in until the afternoon and Laurie made breakfast for the two of them each morning, an intimate, domestic time.

It was not all sweetness and light, however. Laurie was still opinionated, especially about the equality of women, and Ben argued with her just to see the snap of her blue eyes as her consternation grew. In the midst of a tirade, she'd see Ben's grin and realize he just baited her. She'd pound his chest in mock anger and they'd collapse laughing together with their arms around each other.

During the work day, they each went their own way, both absorbed in the demands of their jobs. Mr. Hunt more frequently gave Laurie feature stories to do besides her weekly column and secretarial duties. While she was away from the office on a story, Jenny Hunt answered the phones. Johnny still worked as a copy boy but he also did news stories. His sneering attitude had mellowed somewhat. He hung over Jenny's desk at times and often lounged against the wall near Laurie's desk. He had little to say about Ben. She no longer felt twinges of jealousy when she saw Johnny with Jenny. Time does take care of things, she thought.

Mrs. Kirby said, "It surprises me that jealousy is such a strong emotion for you. You're lovely and live an exciting life doing what you dreamed of doing."

"It's an emotion that can devastate me, no matter how much self-confidence I have," the young woman replied. "I didn't think I could share this with anyone but you're about to hear the final chapter of my life."

Laurie dashed into the office after an interview as she raced against a deadline. She hadn't had a chance to tell Ben she'd be gone for an hour or so. She looked for him and found him leaning over Jenny's desk. She felt instant anger. Filled with unreasoning jealousy again, she turned and raced out of the door again. She strode with fury down the street. I will not tolerate that behavior from my husband, she swore to herself. He may have been a Romeo before he married me but he'd better not be one now.

Ben caught a glimpse of Laurie through the window and ran out the door. He shouted at her but she ignored him. Why does she have to run away when she gets angry, he asked himself? All he could do was wait for her to come to her senses. She'll realize she has a deadline and she'll be back, he hoped.

Laurie's headlong dash down the street slowed as her anger cooled. She stopped, took a shuddering breath, and decided she'd better go back and write her article. With a sniff she thought, at least she had her job.

She didn't' see Ben when she entered the paper office but as she wrote her story, he came back to tell her he was off on an interview and would be home in time for dinner. He noticed her coolness but didn't let it bother him. He'd been through her jealous rages before.

I just bet he's off to do an interview, Laurie thought. I wonder what she looks like. She tried to put her resentment aside as she wrote her story but it lurked just under the surface.

As they sat down to dinner served by the cook, Ben looked at Laurie frequently with a frown creasing between his brows. After the meal, the couple usually went into the parlor to read and talk. This night, Laurie went directly upstairs to their sitting room.

After a few minutes trying to figure out what had sent Laurie on her headlong dash, Ben followed her. "Sweetheart, what happened today that made you so angry?" he asked.

"I'm not angry," Laurie said firmly. Her mouth clicked shut.

"Well, if you're not, you're sure giving a good imitation of it. I thought we'd always be able to talk to each other about anything," Ben said just as firmly.

Laurie exploded. "What is so captivating about Jenny? I saw you hanging over her desk this afternoon when you thought I was gone."

"Just a minute, Laurie. She had some messages for me," Ben started. He wouldn't stand for her false accusations. His patience wore thin with her jealousy.

"I can just imagine what those messages were, the way you were mooning into her eyes," Laurie snapped.

Ben turned his back, took a deep exasperated breath, and started to explain. "Jenny answers the phones while you're gone, doesn't she? If there are messages, she's the one who takes them and distributes them. That's all there was, and I wasn't mooning into her eyes. You must have me confused with Johnny."

Complete silence reigned as Laurie saw the truth of what he said. Her blind jealousy had taken control again. She hung her head and tears started down her cheeks. "Oh, Ben, of course you're right. I'm sorry. I did it again, didn't I?"

He took the few steps between them and gathered his wife in his arms. "At our wedding I pledged myself to you forever. Since I first saw you, there's been no one else for me and there never will be." He tilted her face to his and kissed her very tenderly.

Laurie wiped her tears away and added, "And I never confuse you with Johnny. He hasn't mattered to me for a very long time."

Laurie earned a reputation for her newspaper writing and when she mentioned her name on the phone, people knew her immediately. Some of the men she talked to disagreed openly with her view on women's suffrage and equality for her sex but she knew she spoke for many others who agreed with her.

She attended women's meetings in the afternoons as part of her coverage with Mr. Hunt's encouragement. Although his point of view differed, he stoutly defended the freedom of the press and printed what she wrote. Her "Happenings" column had grown steadily since its inception, partly due to the town's growth and also to the column's popularity. The number of phone calls for her increased as the weeks went by. Some wanted newspaper coverage, others gave opinions.

Laboriously she built a list of sources to whom she could refer and who trusted her with information. She now had many people who served as a foundation for her writing.

When Ben covered night meetings, Laurie and Maud would talk in the parlor for awhile. Maud's month-long trip to France had tired her but she had endless stories to tell of her travels. Her dry humor made her a delightful conversationalist. When she retired, Laurie would wander into the library for a book to take up to her sitting room. Reading still gave her special pleasure.

When Ben came home, he usually peeled off his clothes down to his underwear and told her all about what had happened. I think he's really a nudist at heart, she thought, as she enjoyed the look of his lean muscular body, and remembered how it felt next to hers.

They not only had their love to share but their careers as well. Both understood the challenges of reporting the news, meeting deadlines, and taking the opinions of their writing in stride. How lucky we are, thought Laurie, we have so much in common now, even though our backgrounds are so different.

Life was not idyllic, however. Laurie's jealous rages still baffled Ben. One night he came home from covering a town meeting.

"You've been drinking," Laurie accused.

"I went with a couple of the guys to the saloon after the meeting to get some further information," he said patiently. "I had to have a couple of beers so they'd feel like I was their buddy and talk to me."

"I think I smell toilet water, too." Her voice became strident.

"I'm sick of these accusations, Laurie," Ben said, his volume rising, too. "I trust you when you're out on a story. Why can't you trust me?"

"Well, I don't have men hanging around me like women flock around you."

"That's just your imagination, sweetheart. Come on now, relax and think it through. Have I ever really given you any reason to be so jealous?"

Laurie sat on the edge of the bed, took several deep breaths, and thought of all the times she had railed at Ben for the same thing. She realized none of those occasions proved Ben to be a philandering husband.

"I'm sorry, honey," she said quietly. "I just love you so much; I can't bear the thought of you being with another woman. And I know what drinking does to men and what goes on in saloons. I guess I always assume the worst when I smell beer."

"I've told you a thousand times how much I love you and that I would never do anything to jeopardize our marriage. Please believe me."

"I do, Ben," she answered. "I'll try harder, really I will."

The raw day spawned wind-swept snow swirls around Laurie as she walked into the doctor's office late in February, the weather unusual for this time of year. She had taken the morning off with Mr. Hunt's permission although she had not told him of her mission.

She explained to the doctor how she had been slightly ill each morning and felt out of sorts. It had been going on for a month or so. She had not told anyone else and did her best to hide it from Ben.

She found it difficult to talk to Dr. Long even though their friendship went back a long way. He left her with his nurse who helped Laurie disrobe and put a gown on for an examination. Although a modern woman, Laurie became embarrassed at the doctor's touch.

After she donned her clothing again, she joined the doctor in his office. He picked up her hand and gazed into her eyes. "Your mother would have been so happy for you," he began. "You are going to have a baby, I'd say in about seven months."

Laurie had already come to the same conclusion but hearing someone else verbalize it startled her. She felt tears in her eyes as she thought of her mother, and what Lydia had been through to give birth to her.

"You're right, Dr. Long, she would have been thrilled to be a grandmother. I miss her so much."

The doctor gave her a list of things to do and to refrain from doing until the baby came. "Does Ben know he's to become a father?" he asked.

"Not yet, but he will soon," Laurie said as her excitement mounted. She'd have to wait to tell Aunt Maud who stayed in Seattle with a terminally-ill school friend. She'd tell Ben right away.

She ignored the cold wind as she rushed back to the office to find her husband. Johnny told her he was on a story down on Hewitt near Bayside, he didn't know just where. Laurie hurried out again. She couldn't wait to tell Ben about the baby. They had talked of having one but not so soon. Even though the day was cold with blowing snow, Laurie hugged the thought of the baby to her just like she had hugged the Jenson twins to her when they were born. The idea of having one of her own was glorious.

Laurie looked into store fronts and even through saloon doors as she searched for Ben. At the saloon in the Marion Building, she saw him through the big front windows. He stood at the bar with one foot on the brass rail. A woman dressed in a frowsy knee-length soiled satin dress had her arm around his shoulder and looked imploringly into his face. Her feather boa hung around his chest.

I don't believe it, thought Laurie, how could he come here to meet a cheap woman like that when I'm carrying his baby? On a blind impulse, she strode into the saloon and stood glaring at Ben.

One whiff of his breath told her he had consumed at least one beer and his failure to recognize her right away told her he'd had more than a couple.

"What are you doing here with that woman?" she screamed.

Ben looked at her stupidly, and then realized his wife stood there enraged. "I'm sorry, sweetheart. I'm on a story," he said as he shrugged his shoulders.

"What kind of story? One about cheap women?"

Ben bristled. "Clara's not cheap, she's a good news source." Clara tightened her possessive arm around Ben and smirked at Laurie.

"I want you to come home now, Ben, I have something important to tell you," Laurie said sternly.

"Can't yet, have to get my story," Ben said distractedly. "I'll be back to the office as soon as I get it."

Laurie whirled away blinded by tears, the hurt she felt made her physically ill. It keeps happening, she thought. I find him with other women all the time. Despair filled her.

I have to get away from here, she said to herself in panic. I cannot abide this. She hurried home, up the stairs to the sitting room, packed a bag, and angrily wrote a cryptic note that she was leaving Ben to his cheap girlfriend.

Mrs. Kirby said, "How wonderful you're going to become a mother, Laurie dear, but are you sure you saw a romantic assignation between your husband and the cheap woman? Could you have been mistaken?"

The question prompted Laurie's careful thought. How could I be wrong? Clara's arm circled him possessively. Ben had been drinking and he knows how I hate it. Maybe he didn't have any feelings for the frowsy woman but she certainly had romantic ideas about him. Could I have jumped to the wrong conclusion again? Remembering Clara's look, I don't think so.

As the train steamed across the frozen prairie, she leaned her head back against the headrest and let her mind wander through the events in her life. She thought about how wrong she had been about her father. He might not really have wanted to drink but could find no way out once he started. Her mother had been grateful for his love and for his support. She had understood him and forgiven him whatever pain he caused her. She never judged him, just accepted and loved him.

She remembered the conclusion she had jumped to about Johnny and his casual friendliness with Jenny. She also painfully remembered her accusation of Ben when she had seen him in the same position with Jenny.

Maybe I'm wrong again, she conceded. She hadn't even given Ben a chance to explain. With wry amusement at herself, she thought she'd break her neck one of these days jumping to wrong conclusions and fervently hoped this was one of those times. In a flood of memory, she recalled her mother's admonition as she lay dying. "Don't run away," she had urged. "Stay and face whatever it is."

When Ben finished getting the facts for the story he worked on, he went back to the paper in a haze not quite grasping the seriousness of the scene his wife had created. Laurie wasn't at her desk and no one had seen her. He knocked on Mr. Hunt's door and at the surly invitation to enter, he asked if the boss knew where Laurie had gone.

"She said she needed the morning off but didn't tell me why," Mr. Hunt explained. "She didn't come back and she didn't call, either. I had to write my editorial out in long hand," he added testily.

Ben left the paper office and hurried home with alarm. Maybe she was sick. As he came in the door, he shouted for Laurie. The cook poked her head out of the kitchen and told him his wife had been there and then left with a valise without saying a word.

He raced upstairs and burst through the sitting room doorway to look for some explanation for Laurie's departure. He saw the white square of paper propped on the mantel and grabbed it.

He buried his face in his hands with despair after he read the note. She's gone. Why can't she understand?

He recalled the saloon scene and winced when he heard her screaming at him again, even though she had gone. What did she say? Something about coming home, she had something to tell him? He regretted his cavalier dismissal of her. Had he destroyed his marriage in one great swoop?

With the pain evident in his voice, he called to tell Mr. Hunt that Laurie had left him and was on her way to St. Paul. His boss didn't probe the reason behind the flight and Ben was grateful. He couldn't bring himself to talk about the whole affair now. He'd tell him later, he thought.

CHAPTER 22

Mrs. Kirby's eyes filled with tears at her new friend's visible anguish. Laurie cried for several minutes, raised her head, wiped her cheeks and said, "Talking to you has helped me see things a little clearer. I think I need to give Ben a chance to explain. Maybe he had a good reason for being with that woman and drinking although it had better be a good one."

"You've made a wise decision, my dear," said the stately little Mrs. Kirby. "I'm sure that's what your mother would have wanted from what you've told me about her."

"It's best to go back and find out what really happened. I'll send Ben a telegram from Spokane and then take the next westbound train," Laurie said with mounting enthusiasm. "I won't tell him about the baby, though. I'll do that when I see him face to face."

"You'd better ask the conductor if he can get your luggage off in Spokane so it can go back with you," said the practical lady.

Laurie flagged the conductor as he made his way through the cars. "Can I get my valise off in Spokane?" she asked earnestly. "I'm getting off there and taking the next train back to Everett."

"Yes, ma'am," the conductor said courteously. "You'll have to arrange for a refund on your ticket to St. Paul at the Spokane depot, too."

As they traveled across the two hundred miles of snowy plains in eastern Washington, the two women chatted and dozed. Laurie, now convinced she might have put the wrong interpretation on what she had seen, was anxious to get back to Ben.

Increased activity filled the cars as the train pulled into Spokane. Impulsively, Laurie hugged the frail Mrs. Kirby and said, "Thank you, Mrs. Kirby. But for you, I might have ruined the rest of my life."

"You'd have thought it out eventually, my dear. You're a smart girl. And don't forget your baby needs its father." Mrs. Kirby settled back in her seat as Laurie left the car.

Those last words startled Laurie. So far, she'd thought of the baby as hers. Mrs. Kirby had opened a whole new avenue of thought.

The conductor had Laurie's bag ready for her and pointed the way to the ticket counter. She exchanged her St. Paul ticket for a return trip to Everett. She asked where she could send a telegram and the ticket agent indicated the forms and the telegraph window.

She knitted her brow in thought as she wondered just what to say in her wire to Ben. She didn't want to write too much yet let him know she was coming back to hear what he had to say. It finally read "Ben stop. I was wrong to leave without talking to you stop. I'm on my way back on next train leaving Spokane Tuesday p.m. stop. Laurie."

The darkness outside the depot and the alien town intimidated Laurie a little but she had to face it to find a place where she could stay and sleep before her return trip.

The colored porter pointed to a hotel a couple of blocks down the street that would probably have a vacancy. "In fact, ma'am, I'll just call to see for sure," he said. "What's your name?"

The two-block jaunt gave her a chance to stretch her legs and get some fresh air even though the snow continued to fall in great flakes. The wind, not as severe here as on the west side of the Cascades, didn't feel as cold.

Although it was past nine o'clock, the night desk clerk welcomed her warmly and after she registered, a bell boy showed her to a second-floor room. It didn't contain the luxury Seattle's Olympic Hotel did but it would serve her needs.

She slept soundly until late the next morning. Her emotional ordeal and traveling had exhausted her. She delighted in the soft, cozy bed as she thought of the moment she would tell Ben he would be a father. Facing him again would take a great deal of courage. Her face turned red in embarrassment as she thought of the scene she had created. When did she change from a dignified young woman to a fishwife?

She had no morning sickness to contend with when she awoke and was ravenous. After she washed herself in the bathroom at the end of the hall, she went down to the dining room for breakfast. People came through the door stamping the slush from their boots. Snow fell from their coats as folks hung them on the rack.

The train didn't leave until evening so Laurie went back to her room to rest. The trip home would be lengthened by her impatience to straighten out her life. She vowed she'd never run away again. She'd follow her mother's advice. She bought some books to read on the train.

Ben found it impossible to focus on his work at the newspaper. Mr. Hunt told him, "Go home and straighten yourself out Ben. It's not the end of the world and you have to go on."

"Yes, sir, I will." This is one time he'd like to get roaring drunk, he said to himself. If she accuses me of being a rake, by God I'll be one.

He started down Hewitt toward the saloon where it had all happened. He placed his foot on the rail determinedly and ordered a beer, then another, and still another, until he was indeed roaring drunk. Clara put on her most sympathetic manner. She had passed on many tips to Ben and he considered her his friend. She had told him how his lean good looks and his sandy hair curling over his high forehead appealed to her but he never treated her as anything other than a news source.

She draped her arm around his shoulder as she often had before. She asked, "What bothers you, honey?"

He mumbled, "Doesn't matter."

Clara became more affectionate and invited him up to her room above the saloon. He agreed and she helped the stumbling drunk up the stairs behind the bar.

She loosened his tie and unbuttoned his shirt. "It's just to make you comfortable, sweetie," she said. But she also started to take off her dingy satin dress. She put her arms around Ben who sat stupidly on the edge of the bed and began to kiss him.

Startled even through his alcoholic haze, he pushed her away. "No, Clara, I can't," he said with a shamed face. "I wish I could but I love my wife too much, even if she left me," he slurred.

"So that's what happened, eh Ben?" Clara said her face breaking into a knowing smile.

Together they buttoned his shirt and retied his tie. "You're going home, Ben, my friend," Clara said firmly. "I'll get one of the guys to make sure you get there safely."

Clara's friend guided Ben home and walked him up to the door. As Ben fumbled with his key to unlock the door, the other man picked up a yellow envelope that had been slipped under the door.

Ben thanked his escort and stumbled into the empty house with the yellow envelope in his hand. Miraculously he made it up the stairs and into his sitting room where he sat in a stupor for some time. As the intoxicating fog lifted he looked at the envelope he clutched. It's a telegram, he realized. Anxiously he tore it open and read what Laurie had written.

"Oh, yes, please let me explain," he said vehemently. "I can't live without you." He cried like a forlorn child.

Laurie gathered her belongings and headed to the Spokane station early. She wanted to make sure she didn't miss her train. She checked her bag and sat in the waiting room. She took a lively interest in those who would be her traveling companions, a distinct contrast to her numbness as she waited for the eastbound train in Everett.

A short, broad woman firmly planted herself next to Laurie on the bench. "You going to Everett?" she asked brusquely.

"Yes, I am," Laurie replied. "I'm going back home."

"Well, my name's Maggie O'Hara and I'm out to see what the west is really like for a magazine article I'm writing," the woman said. She appeared to be in her late twenties with brown hair and sparkling brown eyes. An untidy bun clutched her hair at the back of her head. Her stubby ink-stained fingers picked at the fabric of her brown coat.

"Are you really a magazine writer?" Laurie asked excitedly. Without waiting for a verbal reply but noting Maggie's nod, she added, "I'm a writer, too. I write a column and features for the *Everett Daily Herald*. My husband's a reporter there, too."

An instant kinship sprung up between the two women and they chatted easily with each other. Laurie was impressed by the humor and spontaneity of the older writer. She's so natural, Laurie thought.

An ambulance pulled up at the depot door and a young man put into a wheelchair for his ride to the train. A young, pretty nurse with blond hair and blue eyes accompanied him. The nurse carefully pushed the chair up the ramp to the waiting train. They boarded early because of the young man's cast from foot to hip. The porter met them and helped get the young patient into his bunk on the sleeper.

When the porter returned to the station, Maggie asked, "How was that young man hurt?"

Laurie thought, she's as curious as I am.

"Oh, that's Harry Davis. He works for the railroad here in Spokane. He fell off the back of a boxcar and broke his leg so now he's going home to Seattle to mend. His nurse is Katy Jones. She works at the hospital here."

"Thank you," said Maggie looking to see if Laurie had heard the answer.

"He reminds me a lot of my husband," Laurie said. "He has sandy red hair like that and is just about the same height from what I could tell."

As the number of the people in the waiting room grew, Laurie and Maggie made their way out onto the platform for some fresh air amid the falling snow-flakes. They walked the length of the waiting train, No. 25.

Maggie counted, "Two day coaches, two sleepers, a mail car, a baggage car, and an observation car at the end. This is quite a train." The two sleepers were the Winnipeg and the Similkameen. Laurie wondered which one Harry Davis rested in. She'd like to know if he knew Ben. They really did resemble one another.

Wrapping their arms around themselves for warmth, the two women sighed with relief when they were told the train would depart in ten minutes and they could board now. Eagerly they went into one of the coaches and found seats side by side. They watched some of the other passengers as they chose their places.

An older couple picked a spot just in front of the two friends. They both appeared to be in their sixties. The tall and rangy man had a thatch of gray hair and his bushy brows overshadowed his small gray eyes. His wife, nearly a duplicate of her husband, was shorter and had smaller eyebrows. It's strange, thought Laurie, how two people who live together for a long time come to look alike. I wonder if Ben and I will look like each other in thirty years, that is if we stay together. The thought prompted her anxiety again. Please hurry, train, she urged silently.

As if in response to her thought, the conductor called a last "All aboard" and the steam engine started to churn away from the station platform pulling its seven cars behind it through the swirling snow. Here I come, Ben, Laurie said to herself.

CHAPTER 23

A local, No. 25 train, stopped at all the depots along the way across the white expanse of eastern Washington on its trip west. Close on its heels came No. 27, a four-car fast mail train from St. Paul.

Laurie caught a glimpse of the train that followed them. She stopped the conductor and asked, "Why is there another train behind us?"

He explained, "It's a mail train. Usually it highballs its way to the coast but this time snow slowed it in the Bitterroot Mountains of Idaho. It's late so we're traveling together."

Laurie wiped her finger along the windowsill and felt the grit from the coal used to power the engines. She looked at Maggie and said, "I'm glad we won't be on the train too long, we'd all be covered with soot."

As the train steamed through the falling snow, the two had become acquainted with the older couple in front of them. They were Carlton Mayhew, a retired millworker, and his wife Jennifer. They were on a return trip from Montana.

A man and a child joined the group in the parlor car. Robert Andrews, a widower, cared for his five-year-old daughter named Pearl. The task seemed too great for him. Slim, short, and dark, he moved his restless hands along the creases in his trousers. He was taking Pearl to stay with his wife's parents in Seattle for awhile. He acted overwhelmed by the loss of his wife to typhoid fever. Laurie felt instant empathy for him.

Everett Blackman, a middle-aged bachelor with a heavy beard and mustache streaked with gray, boarded last. Laurie wondered why he chose to ride in this car when smokers usually chose the observation car. Maybe he needed to sleep, she conjectured.

Maggie asked Laurie, "How long have you worked for the newspaper?"

"I started when I got out of business school. I was seventeen. That's where I met Ben. Are you married?"

"No, my friend. I never found a man who could put up with me. I'm an independent soul, I guess."

"Sometimes I wonder if I'm cut out for marriage. There are times when I act like a screaming harridan."

"I can't believe that, Laurie," Maggie said. "Is there some reason you're beating yourself."

"Is it that obvious?"

"To me, it is. Remember, I'm a writer, and you know writers are more observant than normal people."

"That's true, but I seem to have trouble observing myself," Laurie said wryly. "You're right, of course. I created a terrible scene with Ben in a public place and now I'm beginning to realize I might have been wrong. I still blush when I think of the way I yelled."

"I take it you fled Everett to avoid facing him?"

"Right, again, but a sweet lady on the eastbound train helped me see the event in a different light so I'm going back to let Ben explain. I'm so anxious to get it all straightened out."

The snow continued to fall and stack up along the track. The new arrivals in Wenatchee brought the news that a monstrous snow storm enveloped the whole Pacific Northwest. No one had seen so much snowfall this late in the season.

As the train pulled away from Wenatchee, Laurie took out her journal to write about the people cooped together in this pocket of the train. The date at the top of the page read "Tuesday, Feb. 22, 1910."

Gregarious Maggie went up and down the car getting to know about the people and from them, about the west, the essence of her magazine story.

When the two trains pulled into Leavenworth before the climb into the Cascades shortly after midnight, they waited. Laurie awoke and pulled at the conductor's sleeve as he quietly walked by. "Mr. Jennings, why are we staying here? I need to get back home," she said, her urgency evident.

"Well, ma'am," Jennings began, "we're just a little behind schedule and there's a whole lot of snow in the pass."

Laurie asked, "We'll be able to get through, won't we?"

"There really isn't anything to worry about, ma'am. We'll be leaving soon."

Maggie awoke and asked Mr. Jennings, "Is there usually this much snow?"

"No, this weather is very unusual. We seldom have so much snow this time of year, but don't worry, we'll be fine."

Conductor Jennings had a broad, kindly face and smiled easily. He walked down the aisle gracefully, used to the train's lurching. In his fifties with gray hair, he sported a small mustache and well-trimmed gray eyebrows which formed a shelf for the care lines in his forehead.

At one-thirty in the morning, according to Laurie's lapel watch, the two trains moved on. Jennings explained to Laurie, "Both trains will doublehead over the pass."

"What's doubleheading?" she asked with her ever-present curiosity.

"Two engines pull the same train up the mountain," Jennings answered. "They've just backed a helper engine into place and after it's coupled we'll leave. We'll follow a rotary snowplow up the slope." He made his way through the cars. He reassured his wakeful passengers and answered their questions.

Eleven miles west of Leavenworth, the trains ran onto a passing track while the Oriental Limited roared by going east. Laurie, about to go in search of Jennings to ask why the train had stopped, saw the big engine and cars swish by amidst a flurry of snow and steam.

Laurie followed the example of the other passengers in the car as she leaned her head back against her seat and dozed. The warm air around her and the monotonous rumble of the train lulled her. She thought of what Mrs. Kirby had said about the baby needing a father. She realized that not only did the infant she carried belong to her, but to Ben as well. Had she the right to deny him that?

When the train stopped again, she startled from her doze. What's happening now, she wondered? She just wanted to get back to Ben.

Jennings made his way through the cars and told the roused passengers the train had run onto the passing track at Cascade just east of the two-and-a-half mile tunnel. The time was six o'clock on Wednesday morning and the blinding snow storm still gripped them. We should be nearly to Everett by now, thought Laurie impatiently.

Since neither train had a dining car, hunger began to plague the passengers and crew members. Some had food hampers with them and offered to share. Jennings' warm smile reassured them that everything was still all right.

The railroad made arrangements for passengers and crew to eat in the Cascade cook shack. The settlement was a small encampment established for railroad workers. The sick passengers remained on the train and food was brought to them. A few declined to tramp through the snow for breakfast and snuggled down for more sleep.

Laurie and Maggie gathered their coats closely about them and headed for the cook shack. They saw a little depot, some side tracks, a water tank, and a railroad turntable, all fast becoming lost in snow drifts. A few workers' cabins huddled on one side of the depot. An electrical installation stood to one side of the black tunnel opening. Laurie stopped a crew member and asked about the electrical works.

"We use power to pull the trains through the tunnel. Coal fumes are deadly," he answered grimly.

Passengers ploughed in single file toward the cook shack. The one big room made from raw lumber was as primitive as the site on which it rested. A number of rough wooden tables flanked by crude benches filled the center of the large room. The tables were dotted with white enamel plates and tin cups turned upside down at the top of each plate. The checkered oil cloth table coverings added splotches of color to the rough shack.

At one end of the room, a great potbellied stove gave out smelly warmth. The coal came from the supply held in readiness for the big steam engines. The slightly gaseous odor of burning coal permeated the room around the stove.

The aroma coming from the other end of the room enticed them more than the heat of the potbellied stove. Johnny Erickson, the cook, presided over a huge flat-topped stove reminding Laurie of the kitchen stove of her childhood. Erickson, a giant of a man, had thick blond hair perched atop his flushed face. His huge hands moved efficiently as he greeted his unexpected guests. He looked like a misplaced logger with a spotted white apron tied around his hips.

Pans and kettles hung from spikes on the wall, and dully reflected the light from the lamps and stoves.

A shy Ivan Wilson helped Erickson. Tall and thin, he shadowed the cook's every move. Together they wielded the knives, cleavers, mixing spoons and tin openers. They deftly made their way around the barrels and sacks of foodstuff which cluttered the floor.

Laurie said to Maggie, "I've never eaten a better breakfast."

"Well, dearie, when you're really hungry, most anything tastes good although I agree these guys can cook."

After the cooked cereal, they ate flapjacks and eggs, and then finished the meal with tinned fruit. With breakfast over, Laurie and Maggie helped clear the tables for the train crews who stamped the snow from their boots and brushed it from their coats.

The two women listened to the banter between the crews of the two trains. The mail train crew chided the passenger crewmen for blocking the track. The No. 25 trainmen said that class came before pack mules. Their good humor buoyed the spirits of the passengers.

"If they're so happy, can anything really be so wrong?" asked Maggie.

Back on the train, the passengers, eager to get on with their travels, commiserated with each other about the delay and tried to find ways to pass the time.

Laurie went in search of Harry Davis, the young man with his leg in a cast. She wanted to find out if he knew Ben. In the Similkameen sleeping car, she found Katy Jones, the nurse, who took her to Harry's berth.

"I'll keep him company for awhile, Katy, if you want to go get some breakfast," offered Laurie. The young nurse seemed grateful for a respite from tending the young man who hated his inactivity.

"My husband's name is Ben Davis. Do you happen to know him?" asked Laurie.

"No, ma'am, I don't," drawled Harry. "Sorry to hear you're married, ma'am."

Laurie, puzzled at his remark, asked, "I don't quite understand what you mean?"

"Nothing, ma'am, just talkin'."

"Please call me Laurie. Ma'am is so formal." She sat on the corner of his lower berth and they talked about the weather, his accident which he called "stupid" and Laurie told him a little about herself. "Would you like me to come back later and read to you? I have a couple of books with me you might enjoy."

"I'd love that, Laurie. Time is hangin' pretty heavy on my hands, all right," Harry said.

"I have a traveling companion who's going to write an article about the west. Her name is Maggie and I'll bring her back with me sometime," Laurie added.

Carlton Mayhew, like everyone's grandfather, did his best to comfort and placate the other travelers. His wife, Jennifer, performed a like service for she was like everyone's grandmother.

Robert Andrews's daughter Pearl was a quiet shy girl reluctant to join the boisterous children running up and down the aisle. Laurie sat beside the Andrews and talked to the girl about her own childhood. Gradually the girl warmed toward her. She could see that Mr. Andrews tried to cope with his wife's death. Laurie told him how her mother had succumbed to typhoid fever.

"So you see, I understand how bereft you must feel." He, too, began to relax and warm toward her. Grief has a way of building walls and we have to break them down, thought Laurie.

Both Laurie and Maggie, as good writers do, kept notes and wrote in journals. Some of the men went back to the smoker to relieve their boredom. When they returned, reeking of smoke and whiskey, they told about the Irish lads entertaining in the smoker with songs from their homeland, slightly tipsy from the liquor that had slaked their thirst.

An Alaskan musher, Jeb Rawlins, had kept the men spellbound with stories of the frozen north and of course, this little snow storm was nothing compared to what he had experienced in Alaska.

Still on the sidetrack at noon, the hearty travelers made their way once again to the cook shack for a lunch of stew and home-baked bread. Some sent wires to tell families of the delay but Laurie chose to wait until she could see Ben in person to tell him all about this incredible trip, that is, if they could still talk to each other.

The trains had still not moved at dinnertime, so once more the passengers sought the cook shack's glowing warmth and savory food. This time Erickson served roast beef, lots of potatoes and more thick slices of home-made bread. His biceps bulged when he carved the big roast as if it were mashed potatoes.

As Laurie and Maggie sat idly about after eating, they heard someone standing at the uncovered window say, "I can see a rotary snowplow working its way down the passing track."

They ran to the window, rubbed a spot in the steam to look through and watched section workers dig snow away from the trains. "Maybe we're going to leave now," suggested Laurie with delight. "Let's get back to the train!"

Jennings doused their hopes about leaving and said maybe they'd depart tomorrow. Some of the passengers let their wishes get the better of them and passed the word they'd be on their way to the coast first thing in the morning. Everyone felt buoyed by the news and eagerly awaited the next dawn.

In the meantime, at dusk, they felt the passenger train jerk to life as it was pulled inside the east portal of the tunnel.

"This isn't the trip to Wellington," Laurie observed. "We've stopped again just inside the tunnel."

Jennings heard her remark and explained, "We've moved the mail train engine up to fill its water tank."

By nightfall, both trains occupied their original positions. The false start did not deter the lighthearted passengers, however. They knew they'd be off in the early morning.

Laurie heard the chugging of the snowplow with its pusher engines as it entered the tunnel on its way to Wellington just beyond. "I wish we could at least get to Wellington," she told Maggie.

"The snow plow is taking on coal and water at Wellington for the night's work," Jennings said.

Laurie appreciated his readiness to explain everything that happened and she busily wrote his explanations in her journal. What a story all of this would make.

With the windows of the parlor car now plastered with snow, those inside did not know that the storm worsened at nightfall. The vicious wind whipped the white blanket into huge drifts and it swirled around the stalled trains as it pelted them in sheets of snow so thick and hard it glued the rotary to the tracks almost as fast as the shovelers could dig it out.

Laurie saw the warmth of the car had melted a little snow from the top of the window. She got on her knees and cupped her eyes so she could see. She told Maggie, "It's a living nightmare for those crewmen. Just when they get enough track cleared to maneuver the rotary engine, the snow covers it again." It was well after midnight when she heard the rotary finally chug into the tunnel.

CHAPTER 24

❀

Tuesday was frightful for Ben. Four cups of strong, black coffee did little to assuage the terrible hangover from his angry binge the night before. He could not abide the thought of food.

He went directly to Mr. Hunt's office when he got to work. He paced down the hall, carefully moving his body as he held his head immobile. He knew if he turned it or nodded, it would fall from his neck.

Ben entered his boss's office and sat down in the chair usually occupied by Laurie. He slowly explained yesterday's events and about the telegram awaiting him last night.

"So she's coming back," Mr. Hunt said as he ran his hands through his scant hair, a sure sign of disquiet. "I really miss that girl. I've grown so used to her managing everything; I guess I've taken her for granted. Well, she should be back early Wednesday so I expect her here on the job bright and early Thursday morning. She's a firebrand all right, but we need that kind of gusto around here. Don't squelch it too much, Ben."

The day stretched ahead of Ben but he did his best to cope with the two interviews he had planned and the follow-up of another story he'd already done. He hoped those with whom he talked didn't notice his lack of enthusiasm. He finally ate a few bites at lunch and by the time he went home for dinner he did justice to the meal the cook prepared. God, how I miss my wife, he agonized.

Late in the day he called the Great Northern depot to ask when the Spokane train would be in the next morning. The station agent replied, "Six o'clock, sir, as far as we know now."

"Since the weather's still so bad down here, how is it in the mountains?" Ben asked.

"Snow's falling pretty heavily but so far the tracks have been kept open. The crews are working around the clock and Mr. Lindsay is up there with them."

Ben knew Harold Lindsay, the superintendent of Great Northern's Cascade Division, from several interviews he'd done with him. He found the tall, slender man in his late thirties intelligent and intense. They had met socially a few times and Lindsay always appeared well dressed, his dark hair neatly trimmed and his mustache a tonsorial delight. Even though Lindsay's sophistication attracted women like honey draws bees, he remained a bachelor.

Ben read late into the night to make the time pass more quickly. He gulped a couple cups of coffee the next morning and hurried to the station. Several others huddled in the depot waiting for the same train.

At seven o'clock, the station agent called for everyone's attention. "Ladies and gentlemen, we've had a wire from Cascade just east of the Cascade tunnel. The track is blocked by a slide at Windy Point a few miles west of the tunnel so No. 25 was held there in Cascade last night. Everyone is well and eating at the mess hall. The tracks should be cleared later today and the train will be in tomorrow afternoon at the latest." With a frown crinkling his forehead, he turned back to his desk virtually dismissing those waiting in the depot.

They looked at each other then slowly dispersed. Ben went to the paper office and when Mr. Hunt came in Ben told him about the train's delay.

"I heard that, too," Mr. Hunt said. "This is the worst series of storms this country's ever seen so late in the season but Lindsay's a good man so you don't need to worry."

That's easy for you to say, Ben thought, but I can't forget Laurie's up there in the middle of it all. He threw himself into his work to make the time go faster but it crawled along like an unsteady infant.

Ben had left a message at the depot to call him if any news came through. He used his press credentials as a spur. He had called Aunt Maud in Seattle the day before and told her what had happened. When the weather continued to be so wild on Wednesday, she called him at the office but he reassured her and said that the train had been delayed because of a slide but there was nothing to worry about. He wished he believed it himself. He tired of that phrase, "nothing to worry about."

Passengers awoke Thursday morning with eager anticipation. They'd be on their way today. They trooped to the cook shack for another breakfast.

Erickson moved his huge hands as he welcomed them into his warm cook shack. They enjoyed his hearty friendliness. Shy young Wilson added his greeting as he bustled about putting the enamelware on the tables.

After the diners returned to their cars they were told that the trains would be dug from the snow and moved to Wellington and with luck, they'd be off the mountain later in the day.

Passengers, full of joy throughout the train, clucked like busy hens as they looked ahead past their enforced idleness.

"Erickson told me the food in the cook shack is about gone with all these extra mouths to feed," Maggie said to Laurie when no one else could hear her words. "It's good we're moving on."

Laurie tried to read Maggie's feelings behind her words. She felt her friend worried about what would really happen. Foreboding became Laurie's companion.

A double rotary came out of the tunnel eastbound and the passengers cheered when Jennings said, "It's here to break the two trains loose so we can move on to Wellington."

Laurie saw a man in his late thirties outside the passenger train. His intensity reminded her of Ben. He directed the activities of the crew and they hurried to obey his orders.

As Jennings came through the car, Laurie asked, "Who's that man leading the workers?"

"That's Harold Lindsay. He's the superintendent of this railroad division," he explained. "If anyone can keep the track open, it's him. The men will work their hearts out for him. He won't ask one of his crew to do anything he wouldn't do himself."

Laurie could see the conductor greatly respected his boss.

The chore before the workmen was gigantic. Another foot and a half of snow had fallen during the night, drifting to more than three feet deep and burying the trains up to the windows. Each car had a snow cap draped over its ridge. The roaring winds had driven wedges of ice between the rails and under the wheels freezing them to the tracks.

Each wheel had to be cleared down to the tracks and then one by one they had to be freed. The men worked all day as the storm continued.

"I'm impatient to get going, but I feel so sorry for the workers," Laurie said to Maggie. "They're trying very hard to free the train."

Everett Blackman, the middle-aged bachelor, kept running his hands through his hair in agitation, just like Mr. Hunt, Laurie thought, although Mr.

Nellie E. Robertson   161

Blackman had much more hair to fumble through. He often sat by Laurie and talked of his past and philosophized about the future. Full of curiosity, she was a willing listener.

The inhabitants of the whole parlor car tried to keep the youngsters amused and in doing so, kept themselves busy too. Young Pearl had finally joined the other children in running up and down the aisle.

Laurie went down to the sleeping car to talk with Harry and to read to him. He seemed to thoroughly enjoy the stories Laurie told about her job.

"You're so young to have such an exciting career," he told her and asked, "Do you have to talk so much about your husband?"

"He's a wonderful man and I love him very much. Why shouldn't I talk about him?"

"Sorry, Laurie, just wishful thinking, I guess. Any more at home like you?"

"I'm all that's left, Harry," she said as she smiled pensively.

Maggie filled her time by talking to everyone in all the cars, even the smoker where the liquor supply seemed to have been depleted. She took copious notes all the while of the things she needed to know about the west for her magazine article. She told Laurie, "With all that's happening, my article could very well become a series."

Again, Laurie felt the sense of foreboding emanating from Maggie. What lurked beneath Maggie's surface good humor?

Maggie told Laurie about the three Irishmen in the smoker and how they shouted and danced jigs down the aisle when they heard they were moving on. She also repeated the bizarre stories the old musher had to tell.

The rotary snow plows began to move again. Laurie could see one entering the tunnel and another waiting with the two trains. No. 25 started to move into the tunnel with the throttles just barely cracked to keep the smoke and fumes to a minimum. The electric power had gone out in the storm and only steam could take them through the tunnel.

Laurie checked her watch. It was a little after eight o'clock. Darkness enveloped the train.

Just inside the west portal of the tunnel, No. 25 stopped. Again the passengers' hopes were dashed. "What can be wrong, now?" Laurie asked Maggie who responded with a shrug.

For an hour they waited while the rotary ahead of them worked through the snow drifts caused by the monstrous storm. Shovelers busily dug out the switches at Wellington. Finally the train moved into the small railroad town where the snow reflected a few lights. It passed the depot and ran onto the No. 1 passing track next to the main line.

An hour or so later, Laurie could see the mail train pull onto the No. 2 passing track on the far side of the passenger train. Laurie questioned, "Why are we stopping again? I thought we were on the way down the mountain." She received no answer.

So many extra railroad workers strained the facilities at Wellington. A number of them found nooks and crannies on the two trains where they could snatch a few minutes of sleep.

Bill Eddington, a trainmaster in the Cascade Division, dropped into a berth on the Similkameen sleeper. He had not yet fallen asleep when Laurie went back to visit Harry. When she discovered Eddington's identity, she plied him with questions.

His voice boomed out of his barrel chest as his gnarled hands smoothed the sprouts of gray hair over his ears. His head, nearly bald, had a fringe around the back. He told her, "There are some bad slides at Windy Point. Some have been cleared but others have sloughed off the mountain."

She asked, "Are the trains safe here?"

"There's never been a slide here before and there's no reason to think there might be one now. It's down the draws and ravines where the slides occur," he said wearily.

Sensing his need for rest, Laurie left the sleeper and went back to record what he had said in her journal and to share it with Maggie.

Laurie saw Eddington climb aboard the rotary after a short time. It went through the tunnel eastbound. He had to keep the tracks open to Leavenworth, Jennings told her. In the other direction, another slide had covered the track in the same place it had taken eighteen hours to clear the last one. And still the series of storms raged.

As long as the engines of the two trains kept up steam, the passengers basked in warmth. The engines needed both coal and water to function. On the rotaries, the supply of water ran low every four hours although it could be augmented by shoveling snow into the tanks and running a live steam line into it. The coal might be enough for twenty hours under normal conditions, but in these harsh circumstances, they'd be lucky if it lasted fifteen hours. Wellington was the main supply depot for steam locomotives in the Cascade Mountains.

Laurie and Maggie tramped around in the snow outside the trains early the next morning with their heavy coats pulled tightly about them. They could see that Wellington sat high on the side of a narrow v-shaped canyon. They were appalled that the trains stood on a cramped ledge, fifty feet wide, where the passing tracks stretched side by side. The land dropped off into a chasm just beyond the mail train on the No. 2 passing track.

They looked up into the swirling snow to see the unbroken snow field rising nearly two thousand feet up Windy Mountain. The burned-over slope showed black remnants of tree trunks piercing the white snow.

The pristine blanket drifted so badly that the tops of the telegraph poles could barely be seen above the white field.

As they returned to their parlor car, the two women could see pain and consternation on the passengers' faces. "What's happened?" asked Maggie intently.

Clearing his throat, Mr. Mayhew said quietly, "During the night a big avalanche at Cascade wiped out the cook shack with Erickson and Wilson in it. If we'd have stayed there, we'd have been swept away, too."

The tragedy subdued the passengers. "I wonder if the same thing could happen here at Wellington?" Laurie murmured.

Although Jennings began to show the strains of the enforced delays, he assured everyone, "There's never been a slide off this hill. They don't happen on slopes like this." He tried to alleviate their fears but some doubted his assurances.

Now the full depth of their isolation became apparent with a slide to the east and at least one to the west. Their train, caught between the slides, sheeted in snow, remained trapped in Wellington. As Laurie put it all into her journal, the date she entered was Friday, February 25, eight a.m., the fourth day of their ordeal. She felt a premonition now, herself. Did the isolation cause it, or did hopelessness of ever going home?

CHAPTER 25

Bundled again in their heaviest clothing, the passengers made their way to Bailets Hotel for breakfast. Eddington's rotary had come back from the east to plow out the passing track and refuel. As it headed for the main line, the hardy passengers ran alongside it for protection from the blowing snow until they got close enough to the hotel to make a dash for it.

The hotel with an annex on one side and a saloon on the other, had a dining room much more cosmopolitan than the Cascade cook shack. Memories of the men who had lost their lives in the avalanche overnight sobered them. They had been such good hosts to their unexpected guests.

Although unpretentious, the hotel provided a warm dining room for the passengers. Wallpapered walls reached up to its high ceiling. The long tables had real tablecloths of blue and red checked material, and chairs to sit on rather than the crude benches they had straddled at Cascade.

The lace curtains spoke of the woman's touch provided by Mrs. Bailets, a small, thin-faced woman who moved constantly. She had covered tables placed about the hotel with crocheted and embroidered doilies on which sat potted plants.

Maggie, Laurie, and Katy, the nurse, helped the overworked Mrs. Bailets serve the passengers, their faces flushed by the warm room.

A mood of forced gaiety permeated the hotel. The passengers were impatient to get on with their journey and they still remembered the tragedy at Cascade. Trapped together as they were, they had come to feel close to one another. The underlying fear that an avalanche could engulf them as it had the Cascade cook shack added an undercurrent of uneasiness.

After the wreck of the meal had been cleared by the young women, Laurie and Maggie stayed to talk to Mrs. Bailets. They found she had come to Wellington as a pioneer and in true pioneer spirit cured her own ham and bacon, canned fruit and vegetables for use in the dining room, and baked her own bread. The smell of baking bread lingered as they talked.

She took care of all the hotel rooms, clerked in the store and post office, and did all of the laundry by hand. An old-fashioned woman, she seemed happy with the load she carried. Cheerfully content with her lot in life, she assured them, as Jennings had, that there had never been a slide where the trains were on the two passing tracks.

As they waded back to the train, the girls examined the cluster of workers' cabins crowded against the hillside beyond the hotel. The Hotel Bailets complex included a general store, post office, tavern and card room. The stub tracks curving into the canyon passed a motormen's bunkhouse, a roadmaster's office, a section house and a small depot.

The two women saw that the main line track, plowed only last night, was already badly blocked by blowing snow, the stub tracks heading into the end of the canyon nearly obliterated. Only the corners of a work train and a few boxcars poked through the heavy white blanket.

As they watched Eddington's rotary engine labor along the main line again toward the tunnel, the plow drove into a big drift and halted as if it had struck stone. The section crew crowded around and furiously started to dig it free. It finally backed down the main line and onto the passing track, too much snow, too many drifts.

Laurie stopped by the depot to send Ben a telegram. She ardently hoped he wanted her to come home. She had to cling to that belief despite her apprehension.

Back in the car, they asked Jennings what would happen to Eddington's snow plow. He answered, "The crew will dig out the helper engine from our train and use that as a pusher to get the rotary through the drifts. We won't need it going down the mountain, anyway," he explained. At last the pusher engine, coupled with the rotary, helped pull the plow back up on to the main track.

After it disappeared into the tunnel, the passengers felt as if they had been abandoned, like watching the departure of one's last friend. Somehow the presence of the snow plow and Eddington had been a comfort. The big man had given them a sense of security.

The children in the parlor car reflected the restlessness of the adults. People ransacked their luggage to find things with which to divert the children; picture books, bits of jewelry, trinkets. Some became spontaneous storytellers to help pass the time. Some of the older passengers went out into the storm to relieve the tedium. Laurie and Maggie had taken one of the older boys out into the snow but it became more of an ordeal than a lark.

Sometimes, a traveler would start singing and most of the others would join in, as they faked merriment. Laurie relieved Katy at Harry's bedside as often as she could and the young man seemed grateful for her presence.

"Katy's a pretty baggage," Harry told Laurie, "But you have a sparkle that I like."

Laurie didn't know what to say as she reddened with embarrassment.

While Maggie and Laurie tramped up and down the track late Friday afternoon, they saw the double rotary snow plow coming in from Windy Point. They went back to the train with hope in their hearts to see if they were going to leave.

Jennings said, "The slide isn't completely cleared away yet. The rotary came to refuel and take on water." As the crew trudged to the hotel to eat, the two girls plowed their way through the snow to help Mrs. Bailets, a woman they greatly admired and who would be one of the sterling characters with which Maggie intended to people her magazine article.

When they boarded the train again, Mr. Mayhew and Mr. Blackman had found out that Lindsay felt sure the slide would be out of the way by morning and that the trains would leave then.

Still worried about what had happened at Cascade, the more vocal passengers called for moving the train somewhere else for safety, like into the tunnel. If an avalanche started down the face of Windy Mountain, they'd be swept over the edge. Others, aghast at the thought of being trapped in the tunnel by yet another slide, were equally vocal.

They settled down that night to an uneasy sleep, still haunted by the Cascade avalanche, depressed at the forced delay and apprehensive about what morning would bring.

"It's hard to believe we'll be off the mountain tomorrow," Laurie said to Maggie. "We've been promised that before," her usual confidence undermined by what had happened so far and what could occur. Her imagination ran like an untamed stallion.

The two women talked quietly before settling down to sleep. "Does it snow this much in Everett?" Maggie asked. She seemed to have lost her exuberance and filled now with doubt.

"Not really," Laurie chuckled. "It rains, mostly. It's a wonder we don't have moss on our backs. Are you going through to Seattle?"

"That's where I'm headed, dearie. They tell me I'll find a thousand stories there and all I need is one. Of course, this trip will make a great series all by itself."

"I've just had a great idea, Maggie," Laurie said with enthusiasm. "Why don't you stay with us in Everett for awhile? You'll get a flavor of the west more there than in Seattle. It's still a fairly small town with stumps still in some of the yards. There are a lot of outdoor privies, too. My mother insisted on a water closet, however."

"A water closet?" Maggie knitted her puzzled brow.

"My mother came from England and our bathroom was always a water closet."

Laurie lost her train of thought as she remembered her mother and the hole in her life her death had created. Ben filled it partially. With sudden insight she realized her basic driving force was not to lose another loved one. She had lost her brother and mother, nearly lost her father, and she couldn't bear the thought of losing Ben to another woman so she ran away before it could happen.

"Where were you just now?" Maggie asked.

"Soul searching," Laurie replied, "and I think I've found my basic problem. Only time will tell. But getting back to my invitation, what do you say?"

"I know you have a problem back home. Are you sure I won't be intruding?"

"I'm sure, Maggie. Ben will thoroughly enjoy showing you his town and he knows every nook and cranny of it. You couldn't have a better guide."

"It's a deal, dearie," Maggie said with finality and a frown.

As they awakened Saturday morning after a bad night, the snow still swirled around the train filling the passengers with dejection. Their anticipation turned to worry.

Jennings assured them the rotary had gotten through the slide at Windy Point and that Lindsay wanted to push it around the point to see if the track were clear beyond it. "The snow plow came back to Wellington early this morning for more coal and water," Jennings told them. Laurie realized she had heard it when she had made her way back to check on Harry in the sleeper.

Unable to sleep herself, she had decided to spend a little time with the injured young man.

Jennings urged the passengers to go get breakfast at the hotel and then be ready to leave when the message came through. The trail to the dining room had been completely filled by another foot of new snow and the old snow had drifted with it. Wellington now had no rotary to plow the track.

Crew members, with the help of some male passengers who jumped at the chance to break the boredom, cut steps up the snow bank and made a shortcut path across the drifts to the hotel. Maggie, so eager to make the trek, tumbled off the path into a deep snow bank and laughed so hard she couldn't get herself back on the trail without the help of the men who howled as hard as she. The merriment helped break the tension although Maggie's laugh bordered on hysteria.

When Jennings announced there would be only two meals a day since the food ran low, Laurie again felt consternation.

"I thought we were leaving," shouted Mr. Blackman, speaking for all the rest who nodded their agreement.

"It's just a precaution," Jennings said as he tried to calm the passengers slumped into their seats with despondency.

When they heard the rotary return around noon, again they became cautiously excited about leaving.

Maybe we're really going to get off the mountain today, Laurie mused, or maybe not.

The engine took on coal and water, and then left again.

Much later, as they talked in snatches with each other, the passengers watched as Lindsay, dragging with fatigue, headed for his private car. It had been attached to the end of an eastbound train on Tuesday and left in Wellington before the slides closed the track.

The story filtered out of the private car and Jennings told his passengers. Lindsay's private secretary and his colored steward were in the private car with their boss and from them came the sequence of events.

"This series of storms is now over a hundred hours old and every hour the snow falls means a greater depth to fight with its added weight and danger," Jennings repeated. "Mr. Lindsay ordered the rotary back to Wellington to refuel but it was stopped by a big new slide filled with green timber." The tree trunks, boulders and heaps of hard-packed snow from the hillside made it an impossible mass for the snow plow to break through. The slide isolated the rotary from its coal supply.

Lindsay had consigned the rotary to the safest spot between the two slides and had four men stay with it to keep up steam. He then crawled over the huge slide and made his way into Wellington.

That's why he looked so exhausted, Laurie surmised.

On the train, where before there had been hope, despair reigned. With all of the rotaries out of commission; one disabled, two stalled between slides, and the fourth held up east of the tunnel, there appeared no way off the mountain still shrouded in snow.

Mr. Blackman shouted angrily, "We may be here until the spring thaw!" Up until now they had dealt with the delay as a temporary matter. Now it seemed a permanent one.

Laurie wrote disconsolately in her journal, her words reflecting the resignation of the entrapped passengers and her own private worry.

All day Thursday, Ben waited for a call from the depot but none came. He finally could stand it no longer and called the station agent. The agent told him of a further delay and the train would probably be in sometime Friday. Ben found it difficult to deal with his impatience but again, work solaced him.

Aunt Maud called him at the office to tell him her friend had died and she'd be home the following day. Concerned because of the storms that still lashed the Northwest, she asked about Laurie's arrival. Ben told her his wife would probably be home tomorrow, too, and then they'd have a proper celebration.

Friday morning, Mr. Hunt called Ben into his office. "I've just heard some confidential information you should know but it's not for publication," he began very seriously. "Laurie's train is trapped between two slides at Wellington. With the snow still coming down and causing slide after slide, they don't know how long it will take to clear the tracks. My source tells me the passengers are fine and in reasonably good spirits."

"Is there any way I can get up there?" asked Ben eagerly.

Mr. Hunt said, "As soon as I can get clearance from the railroad, I'll send you up there as a reporter. So far, they don't want to cause a panic by printing the story, and I agree with that."

Another day dragged by at a turtle's pace, Ben overcome with worry. Was she warm enough? Was she getting enough to eat? Was she well? All of these thoughts continually marched through his mind and he made an effort to shunt them aside as he wrote.

Just before he left to pick up Maud at the train station, a telegram arrived from Laurie. It said, "Dearest Ben stop. Stranded at Wellington until snow slides cleared stop. I am fine but eager to see you stop. Be home soon stop. With love, your wife."

Relieved to some degree, he vowed to send her a wire tomorrow to let her know he waited for her.

CHAPTER 26

Ben and his Aunt Maud talked late into the night on Friday, both worried about Laurie's entrapment. They had always been straightforward with each other and found no reason to hide their concern from one another now.

They reminisced about how the young girl had changed their lives and added so much texture to them. They discussed Karl and his travels. A letter from him awaited Laurie's arrival.

Exhausted by his emotional ordeal and the extra work he had done to stem the tide of worry, Ben finally went to bed and halfway through the night Maud roused him by shaking his shoulder.

"You were dreaming, Ben, and making frightful noises in your throat," she said with worry. He sat up, wiped the perspiration off his face. She sat on the edge of the bed in her dark velvet robe with her braided gray hair trailing down the back. She pulled Ben to her just as she had when he was a little boy after his parents were killed. He'd had nightmares then, too. She said, "Tell me about it, Ben."

Ben described his dream. "I was with Laurie on the train with snow all around and everyone moved in slow motion up and down the aisle." He drew a deep shuddering breath and continued, "There was a terrible roar and a great avalanche buried the train. I tried to save Laurie but I couldn't reach her. I was smothering and couldn't breathe."

"Your worry fostered that dream, Ben dear," explained the old lady. "It's not a premonition of what's going to happen. Now that you're awake, you can see the truth of what I say, can't you?"

"Of course, Aunt Maud, I know better than to believe a dream," said Ben although internally he wasn't certain at all. "I'm going to send her a wire in the

morning and then go down to the office to work for awhile. If you hear anything, be sure to call me there."

Marooned in a white wilderness filled a lot of the passengers with dread.
Their only hope of escape rested with the railroad crews who battled continually to clear the slides.

Word passed along the cars on Saturday that a meeting would be held in the
smoking car in the afternoon. Most of the men crowded into the cramped
quarters plus a few women including Maggie and Laurie.

Everett Blackman, the most vocal and critical, chaired the gathering and
each had his turn to speak about what course of action the passengers could
take. After a great deal of discussion, they elected a committee of three to meet
with Lindsay to discuss their very grave concerns.

The committee, with Blackman at its head, trudged to Lindsay's private car.
When Lindsay's colored steward told him of the delegation, the boss peeled off
his soaked boots and wet socks. He sighed and nodded his head. "It's the first
time I've seen my feet in a day and a half," he mumbled. He hadn't slept during
that time either. "And I'm just too tired to eat," he added to his steward. He'd
had only two full meals and a few bites of lunch during those stressful hours.

The men entered the car where Lindsay slouched in his chair. He looked at
them through glazed, red-rimmed eyes. Dark whiskers bristled from his chin
and his mustache straggled across his lip. Fatigue creased his face weathered by
the wind and snow.

As Blackman presented the passengers' concerns including getting through
to Everett and sustaining themselves in Wellington, Lindsay listened with
dejection etched on his countenance. At the conclusion of their list of concerns, he said wearily, "I've never forgotten my responsibility to the people on
these trains. My crews have worked without letup to open the main line so we
can get the trains off the mountain. No one, I repeat, no one cares more about
these stressful circumstances than I do. I've done everything I can think of and
I don't know what else I can do."

His work-roughened hands rubbed the stubble on his face, his tonsorial
perfection obliterated by exhaustion and hours of unrelenting effort in the
snow.

"No one remembers such storms," he said slowly shaking his head from side
to side. "Five days of constant snowfall has created problems we've never seen
before. Some parts of the track have been cleared three times, and slides are
coming down now where we've never seen them. I've never had a train stalled

this long on my division and it appalls me." A great transcontinental railroad stood paralyzed and it was in his Cascade Division. "The responsibility is mine," he told the men.

Blackman spoke up, "Wouldn't we be better off in the tunnel? At least an avalanche wouldn't sweep us over the edge like at Cascade."

Lindsay slammed his fist on the table next to his chair in a sudden spurt of energy. "That's out of the question! I wouldn't put an animal in that dismal black hole. It's cold and dripping in there. If we tried to keep steam up, you'd all be suffocated by fumes. If we didn't, you'd all freeze. And feeding the passengers would be impossible with the train in the tunnel."

"Then why can't we be moved to one of the spur tracks away from the edge?" asked Blackman while the other two men nodded their heads.

"If you'll take a good look at those spurs, the hillside above them is steeper than the one you're complaining about," Lindsay with a futile gesture of his red hands. "Part of that hill avalanches every winter and some of the snow hits those spurs. If you were on one of them, you'd be in far more danger than where you are now."

"Then what about the snow shed we heard about near Windy Point?" the trio asked.

Lindsay explained patiently that a few cars might fit into snow shed but not all of them. "The shed is built where slides most usually come down and the exposed cars would surely be swept away. I fully understand how you feel but you really don't know the demands of keeping a track open with such unusually heavy snowfall and what could happen." He paused in thought then added, "No, the trains are in the safest possible place. I've sent for more rotary assistance. One plow is coming from up the Rockies and another is on its way from Seattle to Scenic just down the bank from Windy Point."

He said, "Please tell the passengers I'm going to hike out to Scenic early Sunday morning. The telegraph lines are knocked out and I have to get down to Scenic to send wires and coordinate efforts to free the trains. And I personally will direct the rotary's work up the hill." He leaned his head against the back of his chair and closed his eyes.

The three men thanked Lindsay for his time when he was so completely exhausted and made their way back to the observation car where many of the passengers waited to hear what had happened.

Blackman said the trio believed Lindsay was doing everything possible to relieve their plight.

"What about pulling the train into the tunnel so we don't get swept away like those boys at Cascade?" asked the Alaskan musher.

"He said if they kept steam up to make sure the train remained warm, the fumes would choke us all, and if they didn't, we'd freeze. And they wouldn't be able to get food into the tunnel to feed us, either," explained Blackman. "I've been the strongest advocate for moving into the tunnel but now I can see how wrong I've been."

Both Maggie and Laurie listened intently as passengers posed questions and the three men gave answers. When everyone had spoken, a minister from one of the other cars stood up and very soberly intoned, "Tomorrow is the Sabbath and after breakfast I will conduct services in the first coach."

"Dawn on Sunday, Feb. 27, was just like the rest of the dawns on this hillside shrouded in white," wrote Laurie in her journal as she waited for Maggie to ready herself for breakfast. The snow continued relentlessly. Her eagerness to get to Ben had turned to anxiety. Please, God, let me be with him again, she silently prayed, and I'll never doubt him again.

She felt completely out of touch with him now because of the ruptured telegraph line which left no communication possible either eastward or westward. Even with a trainful of people with whom she'd become friends, she felt alone.

After breakfast, the passengers returned through the windswept drifts to the train. Some of the mail train workers joined them for Sunday services. The porter from the Similkameen sleeper had an usually deep voice and it plaintively echoed through the car as he sang a familiar hymn.

Jennings told the group that Lindsay had started for Scenic with a couple of men to break trail.

Blackman told his fellow travelers, "I hope the superintendent got some rest last night. He was completely exhausted. I believe Lindsay is the only one who can get us off the mountain."

When the word of Lindsay's departure passed throughout the train, a few of the men in the smoker wondered why they couldn't hike out to Scenic, too. "It's only three and a half miles away on the west side of Windy Point," one said.

Jennings heard the remark and said, "The drop-off at the point is eight hundred feet and there's no way down except on the seat of your pants. You'd be crazy to try it without proper gear."

"What about following the track to Scenic?" asked another.

Jennings replied, "That's another five miles to trudge while the track loses elevation."

The trainmen in the smoker agreed wholeheartedly. "It's insane to even try walking out," they told the passengers.

While a few of the men were adamant about tramping out of the entrapment, others tried to dissuade them. "Pay attention to those who know the mountains," the cautious ones urged.

Still intent on leaving, they cornered Jeb Rawlins, the Alaskan musher who ought to know about this weather and how to cope. They had collected twenty dollars among them and offered it to Rawlins for leading them to Scenic. He spat into the brass spittoon, looked contemptuously at the city clothes the men wore and said, "Nope, I could get down easy enough but I won't be responsible for any city folks who don't know what they're doin'." With another shot at the spittoon, he got up and left the smoker.

The men resolved to go. They bid their friends goodbye in high good humor. Some of those remaining thought they courted death while others wished they had the courage to go with them. Blackman led the hikers even though he had expressed great trust in Lindsay to get the trains out. A loud, impatient man, his decision might have been prompted by his forced inactivity.

Some time after they had gone, a couple of the younger men decided to try it too, and they followed the tracks of the first hikers.

Maggie and Laurie felt strong enough to attempt it too, but none of the men would let them go. In thinking about it again, Laurie decided it was best to stay. Vigorous activity might hurt her baby.

The hikers numbered five now as the two late arrivals joined the original three. They staggered over slides and in the snow shed they found linemen working on the telegraph line. The workers echoed the sentiments of the railroad men about the foolhardy attempt to get to Scenic but the group was too exhausted to go back to the train.

As they got to the peak of Windy Point, they could see Scenic Hot Springs in the hollow. Since no trail led down the steep hillside, they pulled their coats underneath them as they sat in the snow and took a wild ride down the mountain. They later said they couldn't breathe careening wildly down the hill but none were hurt. They picked themselves up and trudged into Scenic.

CHAPTER 27

A strange presentiment made Ben restless all day Saturday. Nearly alone in the press room, he tried to work. Finally, he plodded home to be with his aunt. She'll help buoy my spirits, he decided.

A pounding at the door as they finished dinner sent Ben eagerly to see who knocked but fright lurked just beneath the surface.

Mr. Hunt stood at the door shaking the wet drops from his coat.

"Come in, Mr. Hunt, and warm yourself," Ben said but what he really wanted to ask was, why are you here?

Maud came out into the entry and shook Mr. Hunt's proffered hand. "Will you have some coffee with us," she asked in her stately manner. He nodded and she told the cook to bring coffee into the parlor.

Ben barely throttled his impatience as the niceties of pouring the coffee took place.

After a swig of the black brew, Mr. Hunt satisfied Ben's curiosity. "I guess you found out the telegraph line to Wellington is down," he started.

Ben nodded dumbly and felt again the frustration at the inability to reassure Laurie.

"I've just had word a snow plow from Seattle is on its way through Everett to Scenic. They've given permission for you to ride along," the older man said seriously. "You'll be that much closer to Laurie and also you'll be in a position to do a pretty darn good story that we're going to publish on Monday. The telegraph works at Scenic and you can wire your story down."

Ben couldn't suppress his excitement. His nose for news twitched but that took second place to the thought he'd be closer to his wife. Maybe with a little luck he'd see her tomorrow and be able to tell her he was hers, no matter what.

"What time will the plow be through here?" he asked.

Mr. Hunt told him to be at the depot by six o'clock. The idle talk that followed between the three didn't penetrate Ben's awareness. He was lost in thought about Laurie.

After Mr. Hunt had given him a press railroad pass with his signature, he left. Ben, so impatient to start his journey to Scenic, paced the floor in the parlor, then in the entry way, and finally in the sitting room he shared with Laurie. He had no nightmares, he didn't even sleep.

Ben packed himself a lunch and slurped some coffee, impatient to be out of the house. He ran to the Great Northern station to wait for the rotary snow plow long before it was due. The railroad workers at the station knew he had permission to board the plow with them so he tried to relax as he waited. He talked to the men, one by one, and each of them assured him that there had never been an avalanche where No. 25 sat on the passing track at Wellington. Aunt Maud was right, Ben concluded, my nightmare came from worry and it wasn't a premonition.

Finally, the men swung aboard the snow plow as it paused only long enough to get additional water and coal for its mercy mission into the Cascades.

The noisy giant made talk next to impossible as it wound its way to Scenic Hot Springs. When they got to Scenic, Lindsay had not yet made it down the mountain although they expected him any time. He had called from the snow shed's telephone.

Ben talked to all of those he could find who could tell him about winter and the mountains, about what had happened and what could be expected. As he ate in the dining room, he organized his notes into some semblance of order. A commotion on the station platform jarred him out of his concentration.

Lindsay had arrived and with him, the five passengers who had hiked out to Windy Point and slid down the mountain. They had overtaken him while he covered the distance from the bottom of the hill to the settlement. One of the two railroad men with Lindsay, clothes torn and tattered, had a bleeding face and scratched arms. His slide down the mountain had been far from graceful.

The superintendent sighted Ben and raised his eyebrows in a question.

"I have permission to be here, Mr. Lindsay," Ben replied to the unasked query.

"Well, Ben, I don't have time to talk to you now. After I send some wires I'll be headed back up the mountain on the snow plow," Lindsay said dismissing him.

"I have another reason for being here besides my job, Mr. Lindsay. My wife is on that train trapped at Wellington," Ben explained. "Is there any way I can get up there?"

"Not unless you can climb a cliff in a blizzard," answered the superintendent gruffly, but laid a gentle hand on Ben's shoulder before he went to the station agent's office to send his wires.

Ben followed the passengers who had made the trek into the inn at Scenic Hot Springs where they collapsed from their ordeal. "Knowing what I do now, I'm convinced the other passengers couldn't make the hike," one of them muttered shaking his head.

When Ben sat down next to an exhausted Everett Blackman, the older man tried to shrug him away when the young man said he was a reporter for the *Everett Daily Herald*.

"I can't talk now, young fellow, I need some food and some rest," Blackman said wearily.

"Before you rest I need to know about my wife," Ben said quickly.

"And who is she?" asked Blackman.

"She's Laurie Davis. She works for the paper, too," tumbled the words from Ben's mouth.

"So that pretty young lady is your wife, huh?" Blackman sighed. "She's a very smart girl and did a lot to keep up the spirit on the train. And she's so impatient to get back to you." He looked deeply into Ben's eyes with compassion. "She was fine when we left this morning. And I have every confidence Lindsay can get those trains out. He's a very dedicated man and knows how to use the resources at his command. Rest easy, Ben, she'll be with you soon," Blackman added.

In Wellington, a new worry surfaced. The engines ran low on coal and without fuel, they would cease to function. The source of heat in the cars would be gone. Coal still sat in the chute but without a rotary to clear the way, the engines couldn't reach it.

The mail train still had a pretty good supply of fuel. Freed from its white sheet, it chugged up near the engine of No. 25, and the coal loaded onto the beleaguered passenger train. If the snowy travail continued, the engine of the mail train could be shut down and the coaches heated with its fuel in stoves placed in each car.

Another problem forced its way into the passengers' perception. Laurie asked, "Why are the railroad laborers with packs and bedrolls on their backs heading toward Windy Point?"

Jennings said, "They demanded higher wages and the railroad refused so they quit."

Even if the snow plows made it through to Wellington, who would dig each wheel out of its snowy crypt, Laurie asked herself?

The appearance of Eddington as he strode out of the tunnel's mouth added to their uneasiness. "What happened to his snow plow?" Maggie asked.

"His double rotary got stuck between two slides east of Cascade and ran out of coal," Jennings answered.

"Where's his crew?" asked Mayhew.

"All fourteen of them hiked eight miles to Cascade last night, and now Eddington's come to Wellington to report to Mr. Lindsay." With the telegraphic lines still out, the group asked how Eddington intended to do that. His patience wearing thin, Jennings said, "He didn't know Mr. Lindsay had gone to Scenic."

When Eddington heard that the other double rotary was trapped between two slides near Windy Point, he hiked along the track to help.

Strange rumblings in the mountains alarmed the passengers on Sunday afternoon but the trainmen assured them again how perfectly safe they were.

Mayhew made his way to the saloon next to Bailets to get some pipe tobacco and to stretch his legs. He looked down the spur tracks toward where the canyon sides met. The workers' cabins stood under the steep mountainside. As he neared the porch of the saloon, he heard a sound which arose from the mountain reaches above the cabins. He jerked his head around quickly. While he stared in shock, he saw part of the hillside fold and slide down with a deafening roar.

Snow-shrouded evergreen trees splintered with loud cracks, and the whole white river spread out onto the flat at the head of the canyon. Shaken with the enormity of what he had seen, he now knew what caused the sounds they had heard throughout the afternoon.

When Mayhew returned to the coach, Laurie could see his consternation. He tried to pass off his agitation but she knew something had happened to alarm him. He had been one of the passengers who supported the trainmen and had told his fellow passengers their fears were unfounded.

Laurie said quietly, "I can see the fright in your eyes, Mr. Mayhew. What happened?"

Speaking very softly he told her and his wife what he had seen in the canyon. He repeated what Lindsay had told them earlier. "The places where slides occur are in canyons and draws, not where we are stopped now."

Not really satisfied, Laurie and Maggie talked about things other than their isolation.

"I'm looking forward to experiencing Everett," Maggie said then added to herself, "That is if this white blanket doesn't become a shroud."

"I didn't catch the last thing you said, Maggie."

"It was nothing, Laurie. Let's get some sleep if we can."

Jennings' departure for Scenic on Monday added to their desolation. He needed to send for replacements for his rapidly depleting supplies. He had helped them cope with what had befallen them and they fretted about his absence. Ten passengers went with him which deepened the feeling of abandonment the remainder felt.

With snow drifts nearly six feet deep adding to the isolation, travelers found it more difficult to keep their spirits up and the children entertained.

Laurie took her journal back to the Similkameen and Harry. After she brushed the soot from his blankets she said, "I've kept a journal since I was a little girl. There are some things I'd be too embarrassed to read but there are events you might enjoy."

"I'd love to hear what you've written, Laurie," said Harry, his heart in his eyes. Laurie chose not to notice his amorous gaze.

She read him happy parts and sad parts. As she read about her mother, tears spilled down her cheeks. Even after all this time, she felt so deeply about her loss. Harry laid his labor-roughened hand on hers in a strong clasp. She gathered courage enough to tell him about her birth which sparked his interest.

"Maybe you're royalty," he exclaimed enthusiastically. "As soon as I get this cast off, maybe I better kneel to you, princess."

She laughed, glad to be lifted out of her gloomy despair. "When you're walking again, you'll have to come to Everett so Ben and I can show you the sights of the city," she smiled. They had become good friends, she thought.

The weather took on a different character Monday afternoon. The storm front began to pelt them with rain instead of snow. Some thrilled at the weather change, sure it would lead to freedom from their white world. More experienced heads, though, knew that the warming trend would only bring more danger. Rain-sodden snow was heavier and the warmth would loosen the hillsides from their frozen facades.

With a great stamping of his boots, Jennings climbed on board No. 25 in the late afternoon and the passengers welcomed him. He had decided the train needed him more than Scenic and because of the tough journey toward Windy Point, he had concluded he might not make it back if he continued. Instead, he gave his list to one of the other men and turned back toward Wellington. The rain-covered snow created impossible footing. His eyes scanned the mountainside for indications of avalanches.

Angry passengers demanded again that the train be moved into the tunnel and Jennings parried their demands with the news he had no authority to do that. Exhausted, he went into one of the sleepers to rest before moving through the cars to reassure his passengers.

Another protest meeting convened in the smoking car and the passengers agreed to demand that someone representing Lindsay hear their complaints.

When Eddington came back from the rotary at Windy Point, he climbed into Lindsay's private car. Lindsay's stenographer told him a protest committee wanted to talk to him. The man, exhausted from his labors of the last week, told the stenographer to talk to the committee.

The secretary repeated what Jennings had told them, "I do not have the authority to move the train or take the passengers out to Scenic."

They insisted on seeing Eddington who expressed anger at being assailed by them. He roared, "I am in authority, and what you ask is crazy! You have nothing to fear. You're hysterical and I'll tell you what you've no doubt been told before, there has never been a slide down across here and there never will be!"

He calmed down and lowered his voice to a tolerable level, "Even if I thought the tunnel was a safer place, which it isn't, I couldn't put the train in there. The coal tender is almost empty, and if we used what little fuel there is getting up the grade, there'd be none left to heat the coaches. Besides, that tunnel is a miserable, dangerous hole. It's entirely out of the question."

In his reply to the query about taking the passengers to Scenic he erupted, "Are you completely insane? You surely wouldn't take the women, children and sick people from the warmth of the train along that horrible trail to Windy Point where slides are apt to come down any minute, would you?"

When some of the men said they were going to take the rest of the passengers out without Eddington's permission, he railed at them, "You will not take the weaker passengers from the train. I will use force to keep them where they're safe."

In spite of what Eddington had to say, some decided to trudge out to Scenic. Maggie declared she'd go with them but Laurie said she had better not try it, her decision based on the baby she carried. No one on the train knew she was to become a mother.

"Be sure to wait for me in Everett, Maggie. Call Mr. Hunt at the newspaper and he'll take care of you until I get there." She sighed and added, "When this is all over, we'll laugh and cry about our experiences on this train."

The determination of the small group to leave the train led to a lighthearted community sing this last night they would all be together.

Laurie was reluctant to let go of the conviviality in the coach. While the rest settled down to a better sleep than they'd had for some time, at nearly one o'clock she picked up her journal and made her way back to see if Harry were awake.

CHAPTER 28

Ben slept fitfully Sunday night at the Scenic Hot Springs Inn. He had worked well into the night as he composed his story. He felt constant frustration at his failure to get to Wellington and Laurie. The trainmen assured him he'd make it on Monday with Lindsay.

He waited for news of the rotary moving into the mountains. He haunted the little train station after he filed his story, anxious to get to Laurie. As the day dragged into the afternoon, he felt the warmth of the wind, a Chinook, he thought. Elated by the snow's end, he gloried in the realization he'd have Laurie in his arms soon.

As it began to rain in earnest late in the afternoon, he expressed his excitement to the station agent who cautiously refrained from sharing his knowledge of rain, snow, and the mountains' vagaries. The agent turned to a trainman and said quietly, "I know that young man's wife is up on the hill so I don't want to tell him warm wind and rain pose far worse dangers than digging through snow drifts." The trainman nodded solemnly.

Ben finally went back to the inn after he extracted a promise from the station agent that should Lindsay start out on the rotary, he'd let Ben know, a promise the agent didn't honor.

Exhausted from worry, anxiety, interviewing, writing, Ben fell into an uneasy sleep where his white nightmare engulfed him again.

Laurie, with her coat pulled closely around her, shoved her journal inside next to her chest, and held both of Harry's hands trying to soothe him. They each needed the comfort the other could give. The pelting rain thundered on the roof of the car.

A great flash of light filled the sleeper followed closely by a monstrous clap of thunder. Maybe thunder and lightning were always worse in the mountains, thought Laurie with little consolation.

The Similkameen started to tremble and a horrendous roar grew in volume until it enveloped the sleeper where everyone was now awake. Grinding and loud snapping noises swelled the roar. Laurie got onto Harry's berth on her knees and looked out the window toward Windy Mountain just in time to see the white wall sweeping toward the train. She turned to speak to Harry but no words came. They looked at each other with horror and then they were enfolded in the white torrent.

Ben heard shouts outside his window at the inn early Tuesday morning. He hastily donned his clothes and hurried to the depot. An hysterical section hand, moaned nearly incoherent, "They're gone, all gone; tracks, trains." Bruised and scratched from his Windy Point slide, he continued to rave. Lindsay took the man into his makeshift office at the station. The superintendent had been on the rotary during the night but they had come back to Scenic for fuel and water.

Word by word, he extracted the story from the distraught section hand. The story he pieced together, and later told Ben, filled him with dread. Shortly after one o'clock, the south face of Windy Mountain sheared off and swept the two trains, his private car, and various pieces of equipment over the lip of the ravine into the chasm below. From what he could learn, there were survivors, how many, he didn't know. The man told of shrieks, moans, frantic digging by rescuers. It had taken the man six hours to reach Scenic and the exertion, along with the horror he had seen, pushed him into unconsciousness.

Lindsay called the station agent to help the inert man then sent a coded message to his superiors and ordered a relief train. Later Tuesday, the world heard of the disaster.

Ben demanded that Lindsay tell him what had happened. "It's not because I'm a reporter," he said, "but because my wife's up there."

As gently as he could, Lindsay told him of the disaster. "The section hand said there were survivors so don't lose heart." He brushed his hand across his eyes wearily and his dark mustache stood out starkly against his ashen face. He added. "When the relief train gets here, I'll send you up with the first party. A male nurse from the inn is on his way. A couple of railroad workers are carrying in his medical supplies."

"I'm going to catch up with them," Ben said as he started out the door.

"No, I can't let you do that. A distraught husband is something they don't need to deal with yet. You'll only be a couple of hours behind," Lindsay said as he clutched his hands into fists in an attempt to control their shaking. It had been a very long ten days since this series of terrible storms had begun. Now an avalanche had wiped out the trains he had ordered onto the passing tracks at Wellington. He had assured the passengers they were safe but now some of them were gone.

Ben couldn't stifle the terrible thoughts of Laurie in pain with a broken body, or even worse, dead under a pile of debris. His nightmare had come true except he hadn't been with her. He tramped up and down the tracks, around the depot, in and out of the inn until the relief workers arrived at Scenic from the train which had reached within three miles of the town. Ben saw one of the doctors marshalling his supplies with the two bearers who would escort him up to Windy Point and along the track to Wellington.

"I'm Ben Davis from the *Everett Daily Herald*," he explained. The doctor, Gerald Stassen, had hurried to board the train in Monroe where he practiced. He had brought all the supplies he could muster from Stephens Hospital there.

Although of medium stature, his commanding manner made him seem much taller. The intense man focused on the task ahead of him. He knew not what awaited him at the disaster scene but time was important. He pushed Ben away by his manner without touching him.

"Let me come with you, doctor," pleaded the young reporter.

"I'm sorry, Mr. Davis, we have a job to do and you'd only get in the way. When the rest of the reporters are allowed in, you come with them."

"For God's sake, man, my wife's up there! I don't know if she's alive or dead. Take me with you!" he begged.

Dr. Stassen, really a compassionate man, said, "All right, come along, but you'll have to carry your share of the medical supplies and you'll have to watch out for yourself. We must get there as soon as we can."

The cavalcade started out from Scenic with determination. No one believed it would be an easy trip. With a packer behind and one ahead, Dr. Stassen and Ben scrambled up the eight-hundred-foot bluff to Windy Point. The rain on the snow slickened the hillside and they frequently lost their footing. They finally reached the railroad grade.

As they trudged along the track filled with slides from ten to seventy feet deep, they slithered, slid, crawled, crept, and skidded through and over the slippery snow.

Dozens of other relief workers including two registered nurses who had donned boots and pants for the trek up the hill followed them. The path up to Windy Point soon resembled the Chilkoot Trail during Alaska's gold rush days, except supplies were not abandoned alongside; they were far too precious to the Wellington disaster survivors.

As darkness closed in, lanterns lit the way. In one place along the track, the fierce wind blew down Windy Mountain and extinguished what little light the lanterns gave. It took precious time to relight them so the trek could continue.

At ten o'clock, Dr. Stassen's group stumbled into Wellington. Little could be seen in the darkness except winking lanterns bobbing along the ledge and down in the ravine. They made their way toward the lights of the hotel where Mrs. Bailets directed them to the makeshift hospital in the motormen's bunkhouse. The freight shed had become the morgue.

Ben brushed the thought aside that Laurie could be in the freight shed and went with Dr. Stassen to the bunkhouse.

I'm so cold, thought Laurie, and tried to pull her coat around her. She heard someone calling her name. She raised her head and felt such an excruciating pain in her chest she sank back into unconsciousness. Again, someone called her name and she answered weakly, "Yes."

"Laurie, Laurie, wake up," Harry shouted. "Don't pass out again, stay awake. Are you all right?"

Waves of nausea and pain coursed through her body. "I think I have a broken bone somewhere. It's very painful when I lift my head. Where are you?"

"I'm just above you on the hill and I seem to be undamaged, just a little worse for wear," he said with a touch of humor. "These pajamas aren't very warm."

The men who piled out of the bunkhouse heard them talking and rushed to their sides with lanterns that pierced the black night.

Still dazed, Laurie asked them, "What happened?"

"An avalanche came down off Windy Mountain and pushed the trains and everything else over the edge of the ravine," they said in a rush as they loaded the two survivors onto makeshift sleds to pull back to the bunkhouse.

"But where are the rest of the passengers?" Laurie asked plaintively.

"We don't know yet, ma'am," one of them told her, "We've just begun to search."

Laurie now heard the shrieks and groans coming from the abyss. She drifted into shock and began to whimper. Intent on their rescue efforts, the men pulled their sleds away from the devastation to the hastily created hospital.

Ben went from cot to cot in the bunkhouse as he looked for his wife. The more he looked, the more distraught he became. Each cot he passed without recognizing Laurie filled him with pain. He clung to the hope that she might be here among the injured. The room had been divided by makeshift curtains into two sections, one for men and the other for women and children.

Glimmering blonde hair triggered an instant response in him. She's alive, my beautiful Laurie. The male nurse told him she drifted in and out of consciousness. "Is she hurt?" Ben asked with alarm.

The nurse told him, "I think she has some broken ribs but the doctor will look at her as soon as he tends to the more severely injured."

Ben sat by Laurie's cot for a while and waited for some sign she roused from her stupor. He started to pull the blanket closer to her chin to keep her warm and discovered she still clutched her journal.

For nearly an hour Ben listened to the moans of others who had been injured in the horrible accident. He told himself, how lucky I am that Laurie still lives. Tears coursed down his cheeks.

He bowed his head and was startled when Laurie's hand brushed away the drops flowing down his face. He grabbed her hand and covered it with kisses. "Oh, sweetheart, you're with me. Don't ever run away again."

With a groan, she tried to move but Ben pressed her into the blankets on the cot again. He told her to breathe shallowly because some of her ribs were broken.

"Is Harry all right?" she asked.

"Who's Harry, sweetheart?" Ben asked.

"He's the one who kept calling to me to keep me awake," she said. "His whole leg was in a cast and I was trying to comfort him in the sleeper when the avalanche hit us."

"I'll find out, sweetheart, and now that I know you'll be fine, I'm going out to help the searchers."

With a slight shudder, Laurie fainted again. It's better that way so she couldn't feel the pain, thought Ben and didn't worry about her drifting off.

He found Harry in the men's section of the bunkhouse. It wasn't hard to determine who he was with the cast partially shattered around his leg. Ben went over to him and introduced himself.

Harry asked if Laurie were going to be all right, and Ben said, "Yes, thanks to you. She told me you kept calling to her to keep her alive."

"She was so nice to me on the train and I was glad I had a chance to repay some of that," Harry said keeping his feelings carefully hidden.

"Are you hurt anywhere?" Ben asked.

Harry replied, "They'll have to recast my leg. Miraculously, the rest of my bumps and bruises aren't serious."

"I'll tell the nurse so he can tell Laurie that when she wakens again. I'm going to help the train crews," Ben said with a grateful clasp of Harry's hand.

Harry called after him, "I wish I could help, too."

Ben worked side by side with the train crew as they sought bodies of the victims. It was now nearly twenty-four hours since the avalanche. The last living survivor had been rescued about noon, a mother with an infant she had held in her arms when the avalanche hit.

For a few hours, she knew the baby lived, the rescuers told Ben. She'd held her breath to feel the baby breathe. The weight of the debris on top of her made it impossible for her to move and as her ordeal continued, the baby suffocated under her. She was rescued and was the most severely injured survivor. Her voice had been so weak the searchers almost passed her by.

The train crewmen had worked all through the day first rescuing survivors then bringing out the bodies of those who had died in the disaster.

They told Ben how they had heard moans coming from beneath the snow and then had frantically dug down to find the source of the cries.

As daylight dawned, he saw that the snow bank above had been cleaved cleanly where the slide had broken away on its mad rush toward the trains. The tracks had been swept clear of all railroad equipment.

To one side lay the remains of the Similkameen sleeper where Harry and Laurie had been. It had been shunted aside and popped open like a baked potato with some of its occupants thrown into the snow.

Ben heard stories of heroism as he worked. He filed them away to use in his account of the disaster. One of the stories concerned a trainman who had been hurt as he responded to a cry from under an overturned locomotive. As he rushed to dig away the snow he fell into a cauldron of seething water where the steam from the engine had melted the snow around it. Other crewmen pulled him out, his leg very badly burned.

The searchers told Ben they had heard a plea for help and started to dig toward the sound. A hand reached through the snow toward them like someone reaching out from a grave. They grasped the man's arm and pulled him to safety. A number of trainmen burrowed out of their snowy caves by themselves.

When hope for finding more survivors was almost gone, the diggers had heard some faint tapping noises down in the ravine many hours after the avalanche had roared over the ledge. As they frantically dug the snow away, the workmen recognized the end of the mail car which had split open under the impact of snow and debris. They carried out several railroad employees, all injured but none seriously. Ben made a mental note to include this story in his news reports.

In the daylight, little could be seen of the trains flung into the ravine. Snow, tree trunks and boulders covered most of them. Ben saw that the trees with trunks as big as a man had been snapped like toothpicks by the force of the avalanche.

As the rescuers worked, they were joined by more helpers who had come up the steep incline at Windy Point with Lindsay. He had arrived to take charge of the rescue effort. Along with them came reporters, photographers, undertakers and some distraught relatives. Already twenty-seven bodies reposed in the morgue.

With the added shovels and manpower, bodies were exhumed from the wreckage, some mangled by shattered tree trunks, others impaled by railroad rods, and several merely suffocated by the snow's weight. The rain turned to snow again and veiled some of the horror.

Ben, close to exhaustion with the arduous trek and emotional strain, became nauseated at the gruesome sights he saw. He joined others who vomited into the snow before shoveling some more.

Mrs. Bailets had sent some whiskey out to the shovelers and Ben drank some to steady himself. I'm sure Laurie won't mind, Ben thought with wry humor. There's no fancy lady with me.

As the ranks of the diggers grew to one hundred and fifty, Ben made his way back to the hospital to see Laurie. Dr. Stassen had just examined her and confirmed the nurse's diagnosis of broken ribs. The compassionate doctor said Laurie would be fine but it would take time for her to recover. "We don't know how soon we'll be able to get these patients evacuated," he added with a sigh.

After he told Ben of broken bones, cuts, bruises, contusions, sprains, crushed feet, internal injuries, and the trainman's scalded leg, he added, "Oh, and your baby's going to be fine."

CHAPTER 29

Ben's jaw dropped at the doctor's remark about a baby and asked himself, what baby?

Laurie, with her heart in her eyes, held out her hands to him. He took them gently still in a daze and waited for her to speak.

"Dearest Ben, I wanted to tell you myself," she began quietly. He had to lean over to hear her words. "On the day I left, I had gone to the doctor. He told me I was going to have a baby. I could hardly wait to tell you and that's when I found you in the saloon with that woman and screamed like a banshee."

Ben started to interrupt her with his explanation.

She put a finger across his lips and continued in the same quiet voice, "I couldn't bear the thought of you in a saloon with another woman, no matter who she was, and the wonderful news I had to tell you stuck in my throat. I was furious! I'm embarrassed to remember the scene I made. On the train headed to Spokane I decided to come back to hear your explanation and I vowed it had better be a good one, but now it doesn't matter. Yes, sweetheart, you are going to be a father, that is if you still want me and our baby."

Coming out of his shock, Ben started to hug Laurie but then realized how painful it would be for her. He kissed her on the brow instead. It dawned on him they were starting a family of their own. Dim memories of his parents made him wonder if they had felt as he did when they were expecting him.

Laurie asked, "How's Maggie?" She explained to Ben about Maggie and how close they had become during the ordeal. "I invited her to stay with us in Everett for a few days so she could really learn about the west. I told her you would be a perfect guide."

The woman in the next bed motioned Ben over. "Maggie was killed in the avalanche," she said, and Ben held Laurie's hands tightly as he repeated what the woman had told him.

"I can't bear to hear what happened to the others right now," Laurie said with a catch in her throat. "I want to sleep."

Ben assured her he would be back soon and went out into the swirling snow. He was aghast to see scavengers and thieves taking jewelry and clothing that had spewed from the railroad cars as they were dashed into the ravine. Railroad workers drove them out of Wellington at gun point. How can people be so vile, Ben asked himself?

Diggers still searched through the snow to find victims' bodies. The work continued into the night and the next day. Lindsay descended into the abyss to see the carnage for himself. His railroad employees had told him of the thunder which had echoed through the canyons and the dreadful roar of the avalanche.

As he came up out of the crevasse, Ben strode toward him. "Did you find your wife, Ben?" Lindsay asked cautiously.

"She's got some broken ribs and is in shock but she'll be fine," Ben assured him. "And I'm going to be a father!"

A half-smile split the grim face under the black mustache. "That's great, Ben," Lindsay said. "Amidst death, there's life," he added.

"How many of the passengers survived?" Ben asked gravely now assuming the role of a reporter.

"We're not sure yet, but so far, eight of them are in the bunkhouse," Lindsay said.

As Ben went back to the hospital, he thought about what an emotional load this man carried and wondered how it would affect him for the rest of his life.

Laurie grew stronger and Ben roamed about the Wellington disaster site as he gathered facts for his newspaper stories. When bodies were found, they were bound to one of the fifteen Yukon sleds hauled into Wellington on Thursday and taken to Scenic.

With each sled went six men to pull it along the track and to lower it by ropes down the cliff at Windy Point. Eventually they called it "Dead Man's Slide" which graphically explained its grim use.

Relief trains continued to arrive in Scenic and on their return trips to Everett and Seattle, they carried the bodies of avalanche victims wrapped in tarps and blankets.

Ben helped where he could. As Laurie got stronger, the question about how to evacuate the injured, some still in shock, became of prime importance. With the westward track still clogged with slides, Lindsay pursued the easier route for a train from Leavenworth.

He told Ben the rotaries were clearing the track on the east side of the tunnel and that a train would be brought in from there as soon as possible.

As long as Laurie improved, Ben wasn't really impatient. He filed his stories by sending them with train crews who accompanied the bodies down the mountain.

Turmoil erupted around Wellington, some instances due to the frightful contemplation of the accident. The conflict that surfaced between undertakers about who had the authority to take charge of the bodies appalled Ben. How could these people be so ghoulish and so insensitive in such a disaster? Arguing about who got the bodies was obscene.

Finally, on Monday, March 7, the first train to make it into Wellington after the avalanche came from the east and prepared to evacuate those who had been injured, a few hours short of seven days after the disaster.

Ben personally supervised the movement of his wife and his unborn child. She was put aboard the train on a stretcher and carefully transferred into a berth.

As the train chugged slowly toward Leavenworth, Laurie mused about how she had fled in anger from Everett just two weeks ago. So much had happened, so many people killed, and so many feelings to sort through. She had lived through a calamity just like the San Francisco earthquake she had helped report. She recalled dear Mrs. Kirby who had brought about her change of heart and was grateful even though it had led Laurie into what she learned later was the worst railroad disaster in United States history.

She and Ben shared their feelings on the eastward trip. "I've done a lot of growing up during this ordeal," she said. "Maybe I've gained some wisdom at Wellington." Tears flowed down her cheeks when she thought of Maggie. "I'm going to follow Maggie's quest for the essence of the west. I will write the story she would have written." As she looked at Ben, so concerned for her, she offered a prayer of thanksgiving for her deliverance and his forgiveness.

Laurie grimaced in pain as Leavenworth hospital workers moved her from her berth to a stretcher for the trip into the hospital. Right behind her came Harry Davis chatting with his stretcher bearers.

Once in the clean white bed, she relaxed as she tried to blot out the tragedy at Wellington.

Ben continued to file news stories but he also spent a great deal of time in Laurie's room. They spoke about the future.

Laurie asked, "Do you think it's time to get a home of our own?"

"In one way it would be so special to have our baby in our own home but then I think of Aunt Maud and how she'd delight in having a baby in the house. We'll talk to her and think about it before we make a decision."

"I think I've finally discovered why I fly into those jealous rages," Laurie said pensively.

"I don't care, sweetheart," Ben said as if to dismiss her revelation.

"But I need to tell you. I think it's because I lost my brother and my mother and almost lost my father. When I see you with another woman I think I'm going to lose you, too, and I just can't stand that thought. Now that I know the reason, I should be able to recognize the signs and control myself." She sighed as if a great burden had been lifted from her.

"I'll do my best to avoid any behavior that might cause you to worry, Laurie."

Just then, a bumping at the door announced the arrival of Harry in his wheelchair. "How's our princess doing, Ben?"

After Laurie explained the nickname, Ben answered, "She's doing just fine, Harry. It'll just take time for the ribs to heal." He bent over, kissed Laurie's cheek, and hurried off to wire his story to the paper.

"Harry, I've never really thanked you for saving my life. If you had let me lie there, two lives would have been lost."

"Two lives?"

"Ben and I are going to have a baby."

"With parents like you, the kid will be born with a pencil in his hand," Harry laughed.

Ben dashed into the room. "They've cleared the track and we'll be going home tomorrow, sweetheart," he beamed.

Neither Laurie nor Harry said a word.

CHAPTER 30

Enthusiasm filled Ben to the point he didn't notice the look Laurie and Harry exchanged. He ran from the room to make arrangements for the following day.

"Harry, I don't know if I can ride through Wellington without going into hysterics," Laurie said slowly.

"I understand, princess. I know I seem happy-go-lucky but the thought of going through that place chills me," Harry said solemnly. "I guess we have to realize it's the only way we're going to get home. If we concentrate on that, we'll make it."

"It helps so much to have you here. When two people go through a tragedy like that, it forms a bond, doesn't it?"

"You bet, princess. Someone who hasn't experienced it would find it hard to understand." Harry clumsily maneuvered his wheelchair closer to Laurie's bed, grasped her hand. "We'll make it through together." He abruptly wheeled out and down the hall.

Sun brightened the sky as orderlies loaded both Laurie and Harry onto stretchers for their trip to the train which would take them through Wellington and on to Everett.

Ben hovered like a mother hen over his wife and made sure no one jostled her. He knew broken ribs were painful and also realized a broken bone could puncture a lung if she were moved too much.

The westbound survivors of the disaster exchanged looks of compassion with each other. Harry gave a cavalier salute to Laurie as he was placed in the berth across from her.

In a few hours, we'll be in Everett, Laurie kept telling herself; just a few more hours. As the train slowly wound up the mountainside, she gripped the sides of her berth and tried to quell the panic that rose in her throat.

"What's wrong, sweetheart? Aren't you glad to be going home?" Ben asked when he saw his wife's wild eyes.

"Of course, Ben. It's just very hard to forget what happened at Wellington. We'll be going right past it all and I don't know if I can stand it." She shook and then winced with the pain.

"I'll be right here, Laurie. I'll give you strength." Ben grasped her hands. "It'll be tough for me, too. I didn't tell you, but I had a recurring nightmare about you, the train, and the avalanche. I was with you but I couldn't reach you when the snow hit. It turned out to be a premonition."

"Maggie had a premonition, too, although she didn't talk about it," Laurie said quietly. "I was just so anxious to get back to you I guess I let my selfish optimism cover other people's anxiety, and my own."

Harry chimed in, "Don't let her fool you, Ben. She did so much to cheer everyone up. We'd have all been in the dumps if it hadn't been for her."

Ben asked him, "Do you feel the same way about passing through Wellington?"

"Sure do, Ben. It's so hard for a railroad gandy dancer to put into words but I'm scared, too," Harry said as he continually smoothed the blanket covering his cast.

The sun glared off the snow as the train reached Cascade. "This is where an avalanche wiped out the cook shack where we ate before going to Wellington," Laurie told Ben. "Those men were so nice to us and to think they were swept away just a day after we left makes me…" She couldn't finish her thought as she cried for them.

Electricity had been restored at Cascade so the engineer throttled down as the cables were attached so the power would pull them through the tunnel.

In the blackness, panic made Laurie physically ill. Ben held her as she retched into a pan, the pain of her broken ribs nearly intolerable.

"Hold me, Ben, I think I'm going to faint," she cried.

When the train emerged from the tunnel, Laurie put her hand across her eyes at first then found the courage to look at the scene of the disaster. She expected to see broken rail cars, bodies, workers digging furiously, but a white blanket covered it all. As the train paused to take on coal and water, Mrs. Bailets came aboard with hot coffee and homemade rolls.

When she came to Laurie's berth, she leaned down and kissed her cheek. "You'll be just fine, Mrs. Davis. Your husband said you were going to have a baby and I'm so glad for you. You probably won't believe it now, but the pain of losing your friends will pass and you'll remember the good fellowship."

"Maggie had so much to live for," Laurie said with a sob.

"So she did, but so do you. You helped everyone on that train and there was absolutely nothing you could have done to save anyone else. It was fate." Mrs. Bailets left the train.

"She's right, sweetheart," Ben told her. "I know survivors feel guilty because they're alive and others are dead but the choice wasn't yours."

Harry added, "And that goes for me, too, princess."

Laurie breathed easier as the train wound around Windy Point and through the tunnel at Horseshoe Mountain. The closer they got to Everett, the more eager she became.

Ben described the waterfront to her as the train made its way to the station. "The depot has been a starting and ending point for our most memorable times, hasn't it, sweetheart," he said.

"Yes, Ben, it has. It's so good to come home."

Hospital workers came from Providence Hospital to prepare the patients for their trip from the train up the hill to the hospital before anyone else could debark or board.

"I'm still very grateful for your help, Harry," Laurie said as the litterbearers started down the aisle. "Please keep in touch with us."

"You can bet on that, princess," Harry said with a catch in his throat.

When Laurie's litter reached the platform, dozens of people cheered. She was astounded that so many people she knew were there to greet her. Mr. Hunt's hair stood on end, Aunt Maud looked impeccable but with a tear in her eye, and there stood her father.

"Oh, Father, I'm so glad you're here, too." Tears filled her eyes. "You're going to be a grandfather," she blurted.

Tears washed the faces of Laurie's inner circle.

Epilogue

The Wellington disaster was the worst railroad accident in United States history until 1918. Of the forty-three passengers aboard the No.25 train, only eight survived. Thirty-five passengers along with sixty-one trainmen and postal employees perished, a total of ninety-six. Some lives were saved through the courage and perseverance of volunteers at the scene.

The majority of the eight passengers who survived the disaster were in the Similkameen sleeper when the avalanche struck.

There were many heroes, even those who buoyed the spirits of the passengers until the wall of snow, trees and boulders plunged the trains into an eerie grave. James O'Neill, division superintendent, was a hero with all of the responsibility resting on his shoulders.

A lawsuit filed by a victim's family was heard all the way to the State of Washington Supreme Court which ruled the disaster an act of God exonerating the Great Northern Railway employees.

Some newspaper and historical accounts differ about the number of passengers, the timing of events, and even the cast of characters involved in the tragedy. This story is a consensus of those accounts although it is not intended to be a history book.

The spirit of those killed at Wellington still inhabits the site. The area is mostly covered with brush and trees now, but one feels reverence standing on the brink of the ledge over the Tye River where the trains plunged.

In 1976, Congress designated several thousand acres of land surrounding the Wellington area as part of the National Register of Historic Places. The action preserves the historic properties of railroad expansion and protects the site of the disaster from souvenir hunters.

A new eight-mile tunnel, completed in 1929, now bypasses the Wellington site and the old tunnel so steeped in tragedy. The new tunnel was touted as the best investment the Great Northern Railway ever made at twenty-five million dollars.

The characters in this book are fictional although some of them are based on actual persons on the ill-fated trains. The only name of an actual person used is Mrs. Bailets which is needed to preserve the historical integrity of Bailets Hotel. Every effort was made to follow the factual events of the Wellington disaster even though written accounts differ.

Nellie E. Robertson
nelleva@msn.com
2004

Bibliography

Riverside Remembers I, II, III—1987—Committee of Everett

The Last Wilderness—1955—Murray Morgan

Newspapering in the Old West—1965—Robert F. Karolevitz

Mill Town—1970—Norman H. Clark

Everett Daily Herald newspaper

Northwest Disaster: Avalanche and Fire—1960—Ruby El Hult

America West Magazine—1983—Oliver Chappel

Where Mountains Meet the Sea—1986—James R. Warren

Women Win the Vote—1989—Betsy Covington Smith

World Book Encyclopedia—1991

Monroe Monitor newspaper

Monroe Monitor-Transcript newspaper

Everett and Snohomish County—1984—Robert M. Humphrey

History of Snohomish County—1926—William Whitfield

Memory Lanes of Old Everett and Its East Riverside—1986—Helmer Malstrom

River Reflections, Part II—1981—Snohomish Historical Society

Journal of Everett and Snohomish County, No. 5—1983—Everett Public Library

River Reflections—1975—Snohomish Historical Society

Typhoid Fever, Its Causation, Transmission and Prevention—1908—George C. Whipple

(from the University of Washington Library)

Sources and Consultants

David Dilgard, Everett Public Library Northwest Room librarian

Marilyn Virta, former Monroe Public Library librarian

Monroe Historical Society

University of Washington Library

State of Washington Secretary of State's office

Greg Hovander, pharmacist

Tony Lukin, former narcotics officer

Esther Rust, former linotype operator

Marguerite Graden Ellwanger, nonagenarian

Virginia Fyke, consultant

0-595-31083-4

Printed in the United States
17681LVS00002B/283